A LOVELY LIE

A LOVELY LIE

JAIME LYNN HENDRICKS

SCARLET
NEW YORK

For the rest of my family:
Victoria, Jim, and James Overpeck;
Nicole, Mike, and Mia Slininger;
Angela and Paul Sala; Susan and Gary Claypool;
Kristin Homrighausen, and Bethany Walter.

∞

A LOVELY LIE

Scarlet
An Imprint of Penzler Publishers
58 Warren Street
New York, N.Y. 10007

First Scarlet Press edition

Interior design by Maria Fernandez

Library of Congress Control Number: 2023922785

cloth ISBN: 978-1-61316-518-8
eBook ISBN: 978-1-61316-519-5

10 9 8 7 6 5 4 3 2 1

Printed in the United States of America
Distributed by W. W. Norton & Company

PROLOGUE

Pepper
Senior Picnic
June 1999

The silence is deafening on the ride home. Scarlett hasn't said a word to me for the last ten minutes. She's pissed. I pass the time with chain-smoking, exaggerating as I inhale and exhale out of the passenger side window and she stares straight ahead, the muscle memory directing her to my house. She'll give in eventually. She always does.

"Hey." I try again. "You know why we left them there."

"Enough, Pepper." She says it while facing the road, but she shoves her palm in my direction. "I can't believe you didn't let me call the cops."

I turn left to face her and give her my explanation, *again*, speaking in a soothing tone. A delicate whisper that almost gets lost in the noise of the world passing us by through my open window.

"Look, I can't be stuck in a jail in Florida. It was for the best. It was an accident." I throw my cigarette out the window before closing it and wince—my arm is killing me.

Despite her own injury, her head is wildly shaking back and forth, unable to come to terms with the last half hour, but she doesn't say anything else. My eyes are drawn to the flatness of the surrounding roads, the way the moon highlights a path through the darkness, steering Scarlett's car toward my house. It all looks so different now. Just a few short hours ago, we were going in the opposite direction for the last night of senior year debauchery, with the sun setting a dark red line for us to follow instead.

Now, the only red lines I remember are bloody ones, flowing out of two dead classmates in Rockland Park.

PART 1

SCARLETT

1

My pen taps against the desk as I watch the clock at the end of the day—fifteen more minutes of dealing with tourists before I can go home. At this time of the year in Florida, the hotel is full of snowbirds escaping the cold or dining in our fine eateries. They all live up north, usually hailing from New Jersey and New York in places like West Palm Beach and Delray, but here on the west coast of the state, they come from mostly Michigan and Illinois. They're all retired and over seventy so now, at 4:45, it's prime dinnertime. And yes, some wear socks with their sandals.

I promised my son, Luke, his favorite meal tonight—chicken parm—and I still have to stop and get groceries before I go home. He's probably already back from swimming practice, skimming the pool like any good seventeen-year-old. My husband, Vince, owns the pool service company with his best friend of thirty years, Chris Parker, and Luke is the star employee.

Adjusting my necktie—yes, the hotel makes all of us wear neckties like we're carrying briefcases and walking onto the trade floor in the eighties, like Charlie Sheen in *Wall Street*—I dip my head from side to side, cracking my neck. I'm almost free for the evening when a young woman approaches my desk.

"Hi," she says. Her eyes are hazel, her face is pale, and she's tall and thin. She's wearing a green sundress with a multicolored wrap around her shoulders, black combat-style boots that lace up the front, and her sunglasses are on top of her shiny, dark hair, pushing it back and exposing her huge eyes. She looks familiar in a way I can't place.

As the concierge manager, I have to be welcoming, even on days when all I want to do is leave. "Welcome to Gulf Sands and Suites. Can I help you?" I ask with an obligatory smile.

Her eyes squint at the name tag attached to my blazer, which I'm also required to wear. Even during the summer when it tops a hundred degrees daily. "You're Scarlett."

She says it just like that, a two-word statement, and looks at me expectantly, like I'm supposed to know who she is. She *does* look familiar. Is she one of Luke's friends?

I raise my eyebrows. "Yes. Do I know you?"

She laughs. Nervous. Eyes darting. "No. No, but you're Scarlett Kane, right?"

Everyone has known me as Scarlett Russo since I was twenty-three. Who is this girl?

"Well, yes, formerly Kane."

Her shoulders drop, not in a defeated way, but in a relieved way. "Oh, good, I found you. I was hoping you could help me with something."

I narrow my eyes, trying to place her. "And you are?"

"Oh, sorry. I'm Zoey Wilson." Her voice dips higher at the end, almost like she's asking a question. Her eyes quirk up, hopeful, like I should immediately come from around the desk and fling my arms around her and reminisce. "Zoey Wilson." A firm statement this time.

She repeats it like that clears it up. Is she a guest at the hotel? Did I screw up her windsurfing reservation? Is she here for Tampa Lightning tickets? Restaurant recommendations? Probably not, if she knows my maiden name. I have no idea who Zoey Wilson is. My blank stare causes her to go on.

"Of course she never told you," she says, eyes rolling. "You knew my mother."

I tilt my head like a puppy begging for a treat. Did a Wilson check in recently? "When was this? Who's your mother?" As soon as the words escape, I know exactly who she's talking about.

Her face clouds. "Pepper Wilson."

My entire body goes stiff, and my lips press to a straight line. My deer-in-headlights eyes stare right through her. That's why she looked familiar. She's the child of my former best friend.

My body goes cold at the memory of Pepper and the feelings I had for her back then. Adoration. Worship. And unfortunately, guilt.

I clear my throat. "Oh my, I haven't heard that name in quite some time. How is she?" I look down and shuffle papers around on the counter for no reason, wondering when the phrase *oh my* entered my vocabulary. I want to look busy. I haven't seen Pepper since the day after the senior picnic when the accident happened.

Zoey's face drops as she continues. "How is she? Dead. Hit by a drunk driver when she was out on one of her runs. Complications from internal injuries. It happened about a month and a half ago."

An involuntary tear threatens to fall. Pepper is dead?

The news does nothing to wash away the shame I've been carrying for her—for both of us—since that night. Pepper Wilson, the one I would do anything for once upon a time, is dead, hit by a car. An accident. It's all too familiar, and for a hot second, I feel guilty when I think *You deserved that*, because no one does. My head feels like it's being filled with molten lava and I'm going to fall over from the weight of my mistakes.

The car lurching forward. Classmates. Blood. Pepper, leaving a scant couple days later like nothing ever happened. Leaving me with the mess. At the same time, I mentally calculate Zoey's age based on her looks. There's no way that she's—I gulp.

Oh my God. This isn't happening.

"I'm so sorry." I clear my throat again, my smoking-when-I-drink habit getting the best of my voice today. No, that's not it. My teenage insecurities rush back, the ones that led Pepper to railroad me into anything and everything, including lying to the cops. "I haven't seen Pepper in a long time. Since right after senior year. That was over twenty years ago. We were close back then, but as you probably know, we lost touch. What can I do for you?" Don't say it. Don't say it. Don't say it.

She shifts her glance from side to side, looking for no one. "I was hoping you could help me with something."

My fears are all but confirmed as Zoey reaches into her cross-body bag, retrieves a letter-sized envelope, and places it on the counter in front of me. It's opened jaggedly from the top, and I recognize Pepper's loopy handwriting on the front, the metallic pink marker pen that she loved. It's addressed to me, to my old surname, and my old address, when I lived with my parents in high school.

"What's this?" I ask nervously. A confession?

"I found it in her stuff when I was packing it up."

We stare at each other for a couple of beats, me not wanting to touch it and her likely willing me to pick it up and read it. She has the same gaze Pepper had, the one that made me do anything she said.

I don't want to read it. I don't want it all resurfacing.

"Whatever is in there is old. That was my address in high school. I'm not sure how I can help. I doubt whatever she was going to say to me over twenty years ago would matter now."

"Oh, it matters." Her eyes tear and then she pushes the emotion down, her assertiveness dominating. "Read it. I need to know the truth about something."

Oh shit.

She's insistent in the way that Pepper was back then—you don't get to be the head cheerleader all through high school otherwise. Zoey has clearly inherited her mother's determination.

With shaky hands, I pick up the letter. What does she want to know the truth about? That Pepper murdered someone and made it look like an accident as I stood silently by? And I even helped her lie about it? The paper inside the envelope is trifolded like an accordion. I unfold it and read the short paragraph.

> *Dear Scarlett,*
>
> *I may never mail this letter, but I feel like I need to get this out. After surviving the accident and not losing the baby, I feel like it's a sign. I know I said I was going to get an abortion as soon as I got to New York, but I couldn't do it. Everything else that happened that night at the senior picnic—you know why we had to leave. I had to. I have a lot of regrets from that night. With them.*
>
> *I hope you are okay.*
>
> *Pepper*

Tears sting my eyes, and I don't know why. I reconciled that night long ago, when the choice I had was college or prison for being an accessory to murder.

No one else knows that. Sure, the letter is vague enough, but now my buried past is staring me in the face, asking questions. I do my best to look confused even as I know it's not going to land.

"Okay, I read it," I say with forced nonchalance. "We did a lot of stupid things. It was over two decades ago. We were stupid teenagers. But I don't know what she's talking about here."

I know what she's talking about. *We'll never mention this again. Deal?* It's a promise I have to keep. I haven't uttered a word of it. Not even to my husband, and he was—well, let's just say he knew everyone involved. Me. Pepper. The dead kids.

"She was going to get an abortion," Zoey says, her eyes downtrodden. "She didn't want me."

I swallow heavily. That has to be a gut punch to see it in writing like that. "But she had you." In my peripheral vision, I see my manager, Frank, staring at me intently. "Look, I'm sorry I couldn't be of more help. I have to get back to work. My manager is watching me."

"Don't worry, I'm a customer. I'm staying until Monday night." She pauses. "I haven't even told you what I need help with yet."

My gaze darts to Frank, then back to Zoey. "Okay, great. Can I set you up with some reservations or activities while you're here?"

She looks at me like I'm an ant she wants to stomp. "No. I need something more personal. Mom never told me who my father was. And I'm pretty sure you know who it is, judging from this letter."

My face falls. Of course I know who her father is. Pepper's exboyfriend of four years.

My husband, Vince.

INTERVIEW THE DAY AFTER
THE SENIOR PICNIC

Detective Logan: Scarlett Kane. I understand you knew the victim. I'm sorry. *Victims.*

Scarlett: Of course I knew them. Chloe and Julian were in my class.

Detective Logan: Did you see them last night?

Scarlett: The senior picnic is a big fair. We saw lots of people.

Detective Logan: We?

Scarlett: Yes, we. I was with my best friend, Pepper Wilson, all night. We were with a lot of classmates. Everyone was there.

Detective Logan: So, you did see them, then?

Scarlett: Yes.

Detective Logan: And what condition were they in?

Scarlett: Chloe was drinking. A lot. She had vodka in a water bottle.

Detective Logan: And Julian Ackers?

Scarlett: I didn't see him.

Detective Logan: You just said you did. Which is it? You did or didn't?

Scarlett: I saw him walking in. I didn't see him again the rest of the night.

2

I get Lila vibes all over again. Lila, Vince's decade-old affair, which almost produced a child. Well, it *did* produce a child, one that never went full term, but that's yesterday's news. I forgave Vince because I didn't want to tear apart my family, even though everyone else told me I should leave. My sisters. My neighbor who had become my close friend. Even Vince's best friend, Chris, said I was stupid for staying, but at least Chris understood my wanting to stay for Luke's benefit. Divorced and childless, Chris thought of Luke as the son he never had. Sometimes, I think Luke loves Chris more than Vince. However, this child, this kid, this *young woman* is here . . . I have to get control of this, and fast.

"I'm sorry, I really can't help you. She wasn't seeing anyone at the end of senior year," I say. "She hid a lot of stuff from me back then. We hadn't been as close as we used to be."

It's a half-truth. Pepper had dumped Vince a few times senior year, but they always got back together. She'd be coy about other guys whenever I asked if she was seeing anyone else. I know I'm trying to talk myself out of the very real possibility that my husband is her father.

Yes, I knew Pepper was pregnant at the end of senior year. Yes, I knew she planned to have an abortion. Yes, I knew she was traumatized, more than once, the night of the senior picnic. I didn't blame her for running as far away from Florida as possible, but even twenty-plus years later, it bothered me how she completely forgot about what she did. What she made me do.

I peer at Zoey's face, and there's another layer of familiarity under the Pepper resemblance. Not exactly Vince, but more than Pepper.

"What accident was she talking about?" Zoey asks.

Not meeting her eyes, I throw random papers into a folder, probably mixing up someone's reservations for the sunset tour and the one for the microbrewery. I place the manila folder standing upright and bang it down twice on the counter to get all the papers in line. Even if they're all wrong. My eyes go up, in fake thought. Trying to keep consistent with the lies I told the detective when he questioned my injury the next morning.

"She tripped that night. Fell down the hill. We were drinking, and she hurt her arm. I hurt my neck. But she thought—well, she was afraid the spill would cause her to have a miscarriage, and then she'd have to go to the doctor, and then everyone would find out about her pregnancy, which she wanted to keep a secret for obvious reasons. It was a long time ago and people weren't as—forgiving. So, I took care of her. That must be what she meant." Divert. "Really, Zoey, it's been so long. I haven't spoken to her in decades. Where did you guys live? Still in New York? I know she was planning on NYU."

Take. The. Focus. Off. Me. Off that night.

Obviously upset that I'm giving her nothing, she frowns. "Yeah. In the city when I was really young, but I don't remember that. She was an actress. Had a few bit parts. Mostly 'Girl Number Two'–type stuff. A small stint on a soap opera, which she made way more of a big deal about than she should've. We moved to Brooklyn after 9/11 happened. That's where we—I—live now."

I flash backward to Pepper always telling people she was going to run off to New York City, take acting classes, and win an Oscar. She actually got some parts—good for her. "Wow. That's great. It was her dream." I glance at the clock. Halle-fucking-lujah. Five after five. "Look, it's time for me to go home. I wish I could've been more help."

She eyes me suspiciously, like she knows I'm lying through my teeth. Like I've been doing for decades. Not that this has come up. At all. *We'll never mention this again. Deal?*

"Right," she says. "Well, I'll be here, so I guess I'll see you tomorrow."

Yay. Can't wait. "What are your plans while you're here?" I ask, against my better judgment.

Her eyebrows raise. "Well, you haven't given me a lot to go on. I guess I'll go to the high school, research other friends—see if anyone can give me any details about her senior year. I just want to know who my father is."

Damn it. If she's going to snoop, she'll find out there *was* an accident that night—a bad one. She'll dig. She might uncover something the cops never did. Like the truth.

No. Impossible. Pepper made sure all the bases were covered. It's been decades, and no one has asked any additional questions. It looked like an accident.

"I really wish I could've been more help, but I have to go home. I suppose I'll see you around?"

Her lips purse. All Pepper. "Count on it." She turns on her heels and sashays away.

My breath lets out with a *whoosh*. I wait another minute or so, letting my heartbeat return to normal. How am I supposed to explain this to Vince? *Hey, you'll never believe it, but you might have yet another ooopsie-baby! And get this, it's Pepper's daughter and she's here in Florida!* It'll bring up too much. Sure, Vince doesn't know anything—*anything*—about what really happened at the senior picnic. No one does, because to be honest, what happened earlier in the night to Pepper wasn't my story to tell. As her best friend, my lips were zipped. After a thorough police investigation, it was deemed an accident. When the cops interviewed all the friends the next day, they were just going through the motions.

The case was cut and dry. A drunk driving accident. They all thought there was no one else there.

They were wrong.

In our early twenties, when Vince and I got together, we never talked about senior year. We hadn't even been properly dating, just seeing each other casually for a few months. To be honest, the first time I ran into him, he was with Chris, and I thought maybe Chris and I would rekindle that onetime hookup we had in high school—my first time—but he was engaged to Jennifer. After that, Vince and I always ran into each other at the bars in town, and well, after too much vodka, one thing always led to another. Then I got pregnant with Luke. He did the right thing when I told him—right for his family, anyway, before I'd even decided what I was going to do. After all, his father was the deputy mayor. No babies out of wedlock for the Russos.

Vince told me the truth about Lila when she got pregnant ten years ago, hoping to keep our marriage together once the whole thing came out in the open. Lila had a miscarriage, his affair ended, and our marriage never really recovered. We deal with it for Luke. I wonder how he'll feel about this now.

INTERVIEW THE DAY AFTER
THE SENIOR PICNIC

Detective Logan: Vincent Russo. Correct?

Vince: Yeah. Call me Vince. Vincent is my dad.

Detective Logan: Captain of the football team?

Vince: You've heard of me, then.

Detective Logan: Can you tell us what happened last night?

Vince: What, with that asshole, Julian? Sorry. I know I shouldn't speak ill of the dead, but I'd be lying if I said we were friends. We weren't. Fuck him.

Detective Logan: Right. I heard there was an altercation earlier in the night.

Vince: There was. That was at the fair. I wasn't driving the car that hit him in the park.

Detective Logan: And Chloe Michaels?

Vince: What about her?

Detective Logan: What was her state of mind?

Vince: Fuck if I know. She was dating a buddy of mine. Chris Parker. They got into a fight that night—everyone saw it. There were some rumors going around. She was ripping through vodka in her water bottle. I won't lie, Detective, we were all getting hammered. We just graduated. I saw her all fucked up. And if I'm not mistaken, she drove the car that killed the guy, right? No one else was even with her. Why are you questioning everyone? We were drunk. No one is going to remember shit.

3

I give a tense smile and a terse wave to Frank as I grab my bag from the bottom left drawer and hightail it the hell out of the hotel. Smoke only when I drink, my ass—the first thing I do is grab a menthol, go around to the side of the building, and light it. I can feel the nicotine, and all the other yummy killers, coursing through my body. On my second drag, I realize my hand is shaking.

I've been kidding myself for the last twenty-two years. How could this be happening now, a month before my fortieth birthday? I made it this long, keeping that secret with no one being the wiser. Why did Pepper have to write it out like that? What was she thinking?

Pepper had a baby. Alone. In New York. God, how hard that must've been on her—and she never even called me or let me know. But I don't feel any sympathy. Pepper deserved to have her life turn into hell after what she did. I'm a distant second—I really wasn't involved—but still, I should've said something. I tried to convince her to call the cops when it happened, and she refused. Gave me all the lines I needed to hear. *"We'll go to jail, Scarlett. Jail!"* But the truth is, back then, I worshipped her and did whatever she said.

That's not her fault, that's mine. I knew right from wrong and should've gone to the cops.

Then maybe I wouldn't have to deal with my current problem: Zoey.

I stamp out the cigarette on the ground, then feel bad about littering and pick it up, toss it into a garbage can, and walk to my almost four-year-old Honda CRV. My soccer-mom car, but hey, we bought it when Luke *was* playing soccer. The lease has a few more months, and a couple months after that, Luke will graduate high school, and then Vince and I can be empty nesters and get another impractical car, like the sporty roadster he bought for himself. If we're still married by then.

I remove my necktie and blazer and throw them in the back seat, all willy-nilly and not giving a shit if they get wrinkled, then pull out of the parking lot. We don't live far from the hotel—less than ten miles—and I'm usually home in fifteen to twenty minutes. Today, though, my right foot doesn't have the wherewithal to press any harder than necessary. It doesn't want to take me home, to Vince. To dump all this history out like I'm serving it for dinner.

I turn my twenty-minute commute into thirty. The traffic isn't so bad today on the lone roadway that leads up St. Pete Beach, with the gulf on the right and Boca Ciega Bay on the left. I pass all the other touristy hotels and motels, staying in the right lane, even when cars drive at a glacial pace like they all do in snow-bird season. I pass the big pink hotel on the right, one I'm still waiting for a second interview with (fingers crossed), and head into Pass-a-Grille.

It's an adorable section of St. Pete beach. The whole area has had a massive renovation over the last decade, and while most properties now run into the millions, we were lucky to get this place when Luke was five, at what now would be considered a bargain-basement price. Back then, the mortgage almost killed us. That was before the explosion of development. Our home is a small three-bedroom, but it does have a dock in the back on the inlet where we keep a fishing boat. It's not a huge thing, just a little nineteen-footer with a canopy. No cabin, no bathroom. It's great to have three out of four seasons. Now, in January, I think it's too cold to take out, but Vince and Luke love to go fishing with Chris tagging along, the wind blowing in their hair. The west coast of Florida in winter is a fickle thermometer and can be forty degrees or eighty degrees on any given day.

When I pull into the driveway, Luke's car is there, but not Vince's. Taking a deep breath, I namaste the hell out of my inner self before I open the door. Luke's head is buried in the refrigerator like a typical growing boy. Not that he's growing taller anymore. He's over six feet tall and is the spitting image of his father—blond haired, blue eyed, and athletic. Luke has the same deep-set eyes and high cheekbones, the same muscle mass as his father did in high school. However, Luke isn't meaty like Vince was at that age. Vince played football and Luke is a swimmer. They're both the opposite of short, dark-eyed, strawberry-blonde me.

Luke hears me and turns around. "Hey," he says.

"Hey." My boy. I put my bag on the counter and then—"Shit!"

Luke's eyes go wide. "What, what? Are you okay?" A curse word will get him to glance up from the refrigerator. Not much else, though.

"I forgot to go grocery shopping." *Sigh.* Zoey has my mind everywhere other than where it should be. "Do you mind if we just order the chicken parm from Mama Leoni's tonight?"

He smirks. "It's fine. You don't love me. I'll eat the stuff with the chemicals."

Jokester. I reach up and lightly tap the back of his head—a love tap. "I'm sorry." I *try* to make sure we eat all organic. But such is life.

He was an easy kid to raise, thank God, since Vince and I were still kind of new to each other in *that* way. Sure, I'd known him for ten years, all through middle school and high school, but he was Pepper's boyfriend. Not mine. Luke is a dream—no real temper tantrums as a child, he never gets into trouble, and he's a solid B student. We introduced him to a variety of sports and instruments when he was younger, then let him decide what he liked. He chose soccer and swimming. Since this past fall, though, he's been golfing with Chris every other Sunday. A new hobby they're learning together.

After placing the order for delivery, Luke and I make small talk about school until the squeak of the garage door sounds and I hear the *vroom-vroom* of Vince's sports car. A present to himself a few years ago when their business had its tenth consecutive year of growth. That's what he'd claimed, anyway. More likely, he got the little convertible to attract women again. *Stop it.* I close my eyes.

"Hey, are you seeing Beth tonight?" I ask Luke.

His girlfriend goes to a neighboring high school. They've been dating around seven months, having met right at the beginning of last summer when Luke tried his hand at being a lifeguard for the first time, since he was such a strong swimmer. My little dolphin. I don't want him here when I talk to Vince about Zoey and Pepper.

"Yeah, we're going over to her friend Lynne's house. Going to play Cards Against Humanity."

Thankfully, Luke isn't into video games like most of his generation. And mine, for that matter. My Super Nintendo practically babysat me, but Luke belongs to a book club. Mr. Smarty Pants.

The door near the laundry room opens, the one attached to the garage, and my stomach knots. I don't turn around, and his steps are behind me, the chlorine scent wafting into the house already. Vince pecks me on the head from behind, something he does out of husband-shaped obligation rather than affection. Then he raps the back of Luke's head—it's a sign of endearment for both of us. Luke does it to us too. Then Vince dramatically sniffs the air.

"Smells good. I thought you were making chicken parm?" he asks.

Luke sticks his tongue out at me, and I give a pathetic chuckle. "Sorry. I got distracted after work. I had to stay late and I just—I'm scatterbrained. I ordered from Mama Leoni's."

"Oh. We could've gone out. Had a family night."

Family night, my ass.

"Can't," Luke says. "I'm leaving right after dinner for a few hours. Beth's friend." He blushes, then grabs his phone and heads upstairs to his room. "I'll be down in fifteen."

Vince disappears to shower the chemicals off and change into comfortable clothes. By the time he's done, dinner has arrived and is plated on the table. Luke wolfs his down in record time, then complains while holding his stomach.

"It's the high-fructose corn syrup in the food. I'm dying," he says, still smirking.

"Hilarious. Don't you have someplace to be?" I ask while clearing the table.

"Yeah, yeah." He stands and helps me clear the table and load the dishwasher before his exit, things Vince has never helped with. Luke grabs his keys. "I won't be late."

I know he won't. He never is. My boy.

Vince leans back in his chair. "Should we open that Cabernet that Chris and Kelly brought us last week?"

Kelly is Chris's recent girlfriend. His marriage to Jennifer barely made it five years—they were too young, just like Vince and me—but they didn't have a kid to cement them together like we did. Last week was the first time we met Kelly. She's at least a dozen years younger than Chris. Men and their midlife crises.

"Yes. Open the wine," I say. I need to be nice and liquored up.

We bring our glasses to the back deck so we can stare out onto the inlet. I prefer Florida falls. Winter is a challenge for me, especially once the sun goes down, like now. As it is, I'm wearing a hoodie, which I pull tightly against my chest, while Vince is in short sleeves like it's June.

"How was work?" Vince asks once we settle into our respective chairs. "Why'd you have to stay late?"

I clear my throat and light a cigarette—something Vince hates, but I only do it when I drink. I swear.

"Difficult customer," I say, and clear my throat again, like I'm forcing the words out. "A girl is staying in the hotel who might cause a bit of a—a problem." That's putting it mildly.

"What problem? Who is she?"

"Her name is Zoey Wilson."

"And?"

"And . . . and she's Pepper Wilson's daughter."

INTERIEW THE DAY AFTER
THE SENIOR PICNIC

Detective Logan: Mr. Parker, first let me say, I'm sorry for your loss. How long were you dating Chloe Michaels?

Chris: Thank you. Almost a year and a half.

Detective Logan: I know this is a difficult time, but I have to ask you some questions. About what went on last night.

Chris: I don't know what good I'll be. I was drunk as a skunk, and I wasn't even with her at the end of the night.

Detective Logan: Why not?

Chris: (shrugs)

Detective Logan: People say you were fighting.

Chris: So what? We fight all the time. We're in high school. It's not like we're getting married. *Were* getting married.

Detective Logan: That's rather callous. Your girlfriend just died.

Chris: Sorry. I still can't believe she died. I'm still trying to process that, and the other stuff.

Detective Logan: Other stuff?

Chris: Yeah, other stuff. I heard from like five people last night that she was cheating on me.

Detective: I'm sorry to hear that. Did you find out with whom? We'd like to talk to him.

Chris: You can't. I heard it was the dead guy.

4

Vince nearly spits his wine out. "Pepper Wilson. Wow." I know he's reminiscing because I've seen that look on his face—the face of true love. One I haven't seen him wear since he was with her all those years ago. I'm no fool. "I haven't heard that name in a long time." He takes another sip. I'm sorry, a gulp. "Were you in touch with her?"

It's a tough ask. *Hey, wifey, were you still speaking to the girl I was obsessed with for four years?*

"Were *you*?" It comes out before I have a chance to shove it back in.

"No."

He doesn't say anything else, which means he hasn't connected it, that Zoey is his daughter. But why would he? I never said her age—the girl could be twelve, which would mean he's certainly not the father. And he didn't know Pepper was pregnant back then. All secrets. He startles me with his next question, and I can't believe I haven't told him.

"So, how is Pepper doing?"

Maybe I should've started with that tidbit.

"Pepper, she . . . she died."

He sits up in his chair and faces me. I see the heartbreak, and it kills me. He never loved me the way he loved her. He never would've, either. Now she's going to be immortalized. Not like she wasn't before. "Holy shit, are you serious? What happened?"

Seventeen years of togetherness, no matter how distant, tells me he's holding back a tidal wave of tears.

I take a deep breath. Namaste. "She was hit by a car. Complications from internal bleeding. A couple of months ago."

"Ah, man." Vince shakes his head lightly back and forth, his mouth turning downward into a frown. Then he collects himself and speaks nonchalantly, likely trying to prove that she's a thing of the past. "That's a shame. Was she still in New York? We didn't keep in touch," he says again, trying to prove to me that he's over her when I know he never was.

Well, of course you didn't keep in touch, dear husband. What was he supposed to say to her, that he married *me*? The less fantastic best friend? The one he slept with for a few months while we were partying after college, and *oops*?

"We weren't in touch either," I say. "She wasn't on Facebook or Instagram, as far as I could tell. When she left for NYU, she just . . . left."

When she left nearly two months early. When she left both of us. She left him heartbroken and devastated, and she left me overwhelmed and guilt ridden.

"Well. That's a shame," he repeats. "How's the kid doing? What's her name, Zoey? How's her husband dealing with it?"

I'm unsure how to approach this conversation, especially after he got Lila pregnant too. He'd confessed the affair when he missed Luke winning his junior swimming championship because he was at the doctor with Lila after her miscarriage. Asshole. Every time I think I'm over it, my blood pressure reminds me I'm not.

I could give him facts and let him put it together. Then again, Vince wasn't the brightest in school. The football jock stereotype was well worn on him—he used to start fights and shove kids into lockers and throw paper airplanes at the backs of people's heads in class back then. Assuming he'll do the math is . . . a lot.

"She wasn't married."

"Wow. That sucks." He's looking into the distance, watching the water, and he's stiff as a board except for when his arm curls, lifting his glass of wine to his mouth. The torch is still there. Suppressed, sure, but this brought it out and threw gasoline on it. He's probably thinking that she could never marry anyone else but him. He shakes his head. "Poor kid. Is anyone taking care of her until she can be on her own?"

I find myself vibrating, so I finish my cigarette in three long, silent drags before I mash it out in the ashtray, a little ceramic thing Luke made at summer camp after fourth grade. Then I take a deep breath, ready to get it out.

"Zoey came back here because Pepper never told her who her father was, and she wants to find him."

He looks confused. Not connecting. "Huh. Why would she come to Florida looking? Her father was probably some—" He stops. Maybe co-owning a business forced him to improve his math skills. "What are you saying, Scarlett? I haven't seen Pepper since the end of senior year. That night at senior picnic. The night that—well, you remember what happened with everyone. The accident."

My chest tightens and a lump forms in my throat, as it always does right before I almost say it. Instead, tears fall. I can't help it. I cover my face with my hands, because yes, Vince, I know what really happened, and no, Vince, you don't know the truth. I cry for their deaths again—Chloe's and Julian's—and I cry because my life has irrevocably changed for the third time. The accident, the affair, and now Zoey.

"I remember, Vince. I only saw Pepper as I was coming out of the police station after my interview, and she was going in. She called me later that night and told me she was leaving early the next day for New York and . . ." I have to word vomit before it kills me. ". . . and that she was going to get an abortion once she was there."

His eyes burn a hole through me. "What do you mean, an abortion? She wasn't pregnant at the end of senior year." The realization hits him, hard. I see it. "She was pregnant? And you knew?" Vince places his glass on the table between us and stands, puts his hands in his pockets, and walks to the end of the dock.

I stay exactly where I am, glued to my seat. I zip the hoodie and cross my arms. It seems to have gotten colder suddenly. Our marriage won't survive this—it's been beaten to a pulp. This time, Zoey's holding the bat.

The sky behind him is burnt orange, the sun a fiery dot in the distance, making everything else into silhouettes like—

"You fucking knew about this!" Vince shouts. Loudly. Breaking my scenery serenity. "You knew she was pregnant with my kid! How could you never tell me after all this time?"

We don't have much acreage—such is Florida on the bay—so our neighbors are within shouting distance. Thank God I don't see any outside. Standing on wobbly legs, I move toward him and he takes a couple of steps back, making sure not to fall into the water. Then again, in his state of mind, he's probably hoping it's a plank and I'm the one-eyed pirate about to spear him off with my sword. Which, I kind of just did.

"No, Vince, I didn't know she kept the baby. Like I said, I haven't seen her since that night either. She said she was getting an abortion. I believed her. Why would I assume anything else? She was going to NYU. I figured she didn't want to be eighteen and pregnant her freshman year."

He shakes his head. "And you never thought to tell me that I knocked her up in high school? After we got *married*?"

"You didn't think to tell me you knocked someone else up while we *were* married?" Low. And deserved. But that was a whole other story. "Pepper swore me to secrecy. Plus, why would I tell you? It wasn't my business."

"Right. I guess it wasn't mine either." He winces as if he's been slapped across the face.

"Vince, she wasn't even a thought by the time you and I did this." Lie. I got pregnant by her boyfriend when I was twenty-two, and we got married before our son entered the world. Of course I thought about Pepper. "She disappeared into thin air. She wasn't part of my life anymore. Yours either. I tend to think if she was, this—" I wave my hand between him and I, "—this never would've happened, which means Luke wouldn't be here."

Luke, my boy, the only thing in my life I ever did right, even if everything surrounding it was wrong.

He scoffs. "What am I supposed to do now?"

I shrug. "I'm not sure. She just told me she was here looking for her father. She found an unsent letter addressed to me, one that Pepper wrote a hundred years ago. So, she came and found me, told me she had a feeling I know who her father is. What was I supposed to say, that I'm married to him? That she has a brother?" I pause, letting that sink in. "I didn't say anything. But she's going to be here until Monday night. She's going to start poking around. Asking questions. I wonder if it's better to get ahead of it and just tell her."

"Jesus, Scarlett. What are we supposed to tell Luke?"

"Nothing, right now. He didn't know about Lila either," I say, my words dripping with snark. The look on Vince's face stabs me in the heart when he thinks about hurting Luke. I turn his head to face me. "Vince, we'll deal with this, however we have to. It's not the worst we've faced."

He sighs, letting his shoulders sink. "I just wish I knew about this back then."

"Why? Would it have made a difference?"

"No. I don't know. I don't—look, this is just a mess. I certainly would've kept in better touch. Even if she kept the kid in New York and I was still here in Florida. I could've helped. I would've—"

He doesn't finish that sentence, and he won't. Because he knows as well as I do what he's going to say, and it's going to hurt me, and while he's not Mr. Softie Romantic Guy, he doesn't want to do that purposely. *Again.* I know he wants to say he would've dropped out of college and married her. I know this because when I told him I was pregnant, he proposed to me as soon as the shock wore off; before I'd even *really* decided what to do with my unplanned pregnancy, there was a tiny ring from a mall jewelry store and Vince on one knee before he'd even said *I love you.* He would've done the same for her back then, but with the love behind it. And then Luke wouldn't be here, and Vince imagining a life without him is hurtful.

"I guess the real question is, why didn't *you* keep in better touch with her?" Vince asks. "You guys were like the fucking Bobbsey Twins in high school. BFF to the core. Going away to college doesn't just change that, you know."

I did try, once social media became a thing. She was a ghost. I shrug. "She never looked back. What was I supposed to do, chase her? She just wanted to get away from here and start her life. I have no idea why she wanted out so badly."

And here I am, lying to him again.

INTERVIEW THE DAY AFTER
THE SENIOR PICNIC

Detective Logan: You said you were with Pepper Wilson all night?

Scarlett: Yes.

Detective Logan: And you were also with her boyfriend, Vince Russo, and his best friend, Chris Parker?

Scarlett: Ex-boyfriend. I already said, most of the senior class was there.

Detective Logan: And you had no ill will toward Chris's girlfriend, Chloe Michaels?

Scarlett: Why would you even ask that? Me and Chloe are friends. Sorry. *Were* friends.

Detective Logan: Some people have told me you have a history with Chris Parker.

Scarlett: Oh God, that barely even counts.

Detective Logan: Was it a long relationship?

Scarlett: No, it wasn't even a relationship. We hooked up at a party, I think it was sophomore year. Forever ago.

Detective Logan: How did you feel when you saw him and Chloe fighting that night?

Scarlett: I didn't see them fighting.

Detective Logan: Did you know the other victim, Julian Ackers, well?

Scarlett: Only stuff you hear in school. We never hung out. I didn't really know anything about him.

5

Luke comes home just after nine, even though his curfew on school nights is ten. I'm watching sitcom reruns in bed when the garage door squeaks open, and then his typical teenage boy sounds after that. Sneakers skid across the hardwood, keys drop on the front table, refrigerator door opens and closes. His footsteps ascend and then stop in front of my bedroom. He lightly knocks on the half-open door.

"Hey," he says. "Everything okay?"

I clear my throat and do my best to sound reassuring. "Yes, of course. Why do you ask?"

He nods his head toward the stairs. "Dad—he's curled up in a ball on the couch. Pillow and blanket and everything."

We can't stand to be near each other right now, but I save Luke from that knowledge. I rub my throat. "Yeah, I feel like I'm coming down with something. He doesn't want to catch it."

"Oh. Are you still going to work tomorrow?"

That's what's really making me sick. "Yeah, I'll be okay. I just didn't want to thrash around tonight and keep him awake. You know I have nightmares when I have a fever. Just like you."

"Okay. Hope you feel better."

He throws me a kiss and walks to his room. My boy.

As I toss and turn, I realize I was only half lying about the nightmares. Pepper was my best friend, and I know why she ran. It pains me that she died. Fine, we haven't spoken in over two decades, but we shared everything from sixth to twelfth grade. We joined dance club together (Pepper was captain), we were both cheerleaders (Pepper was the head), and we were both on student council senior year (Pepper was president, I was her VP). She was there to pick up the pieces after I hooked up with Chris Parker in that bedroom at that party sophomore year—my first time. I liked him, I thought he liked me, and I thought it was the start of something when it clearly was not. He started dating Chloe a few months later.

As much as I put it all from my mind after Pepper left, it all comes crashing back.

Crashing back is a horrible description. Especially since we *were* in the car with Chloe Michaels when she hit and killed Julian Ackers. No one knows. Just me and Pepper.

Actually, just me. The others who knew—Pepper, Chloe, and Julian—are all dead.

My short, labored sleep is interrupted by Vince in the morning, getting ready for work. I lift my sleep mask from my eyes and glance at the green lights on my alarm clock—it's only seven a.m. He usually doesn't shower and leave for another forty-five minutes. I sit up straight and lean against the pillows.

"Morning," I say. "Why so early?"

He hesitates for ten grueling seconds before answering, taking the time to sit at the edge of the bed and put his sneakers on. "I have to catch up on my paperwork early. I was going to have lunch with Mark next week, but I'm going to see if he can see me today. I should find out if there's anything I should know. Legally."

"Jesus, Vince. I should go with you. I'll take a half day."

Mark Grenning is a guy Vince met in undergrad at Tampa University. Mark isn't too far from here either, just a few miles away in Pinellas Park. And he's a lawyer now.

"What's the point of seeing him, anyway?" I ask.

He stiffens. "I need to know what my options are. What I'm legally obligated to do."

"The girl is twenty-one—an adult. You're not *obligated* to do anything."

He shrugs. "I need to know what can happen to my life." His voice raises when he says it. That pisses me off.

"*Your* life?" I tear the covers off and stand in front of him. "I'm your *wife*. You didn't care so much last time this happened. I'm in this too, or did you forget?"

"Guys! Enough." Luke is at our door, upset, and likely figuring out that Vince didn't sleep on the couch because I said I had a cold. "I can hear the shouting from my room. I'm leaving for school. I'll grab a bagel in the cafeteria." He slams the door shut.

We both soften. We don't like to fight in front of Luke, and we have no explanation for our behavior right now. At least nothing we can tell him.

Vince finishes getting ready in silence. I don't know what to say to him.

"I'll call you later," Vince says as he leaves.

It's Friday, usually a busy day at the hotel, so I decide to get up myself. I know why I want to get there early—I haven't had morning sickness like this in almost eighteen years, and I know it's not because I'm pregnant. It's nerves. If I don't stay busy, I'll think, and thinking will only make me feel worse.

When I pull into the hotel parking lot, my insides fizz like I just downed two liters of soda. I check my watch, twenty after eight. I don't start until nine. I give a curt smile to my coworkers as I pass and settle into my desk, deciding to immediately hit the telephone with my catalog of clients on waiting lists for certain activities.

And I do that, with success, until nine. On the dot.

"Hi, Scarlett."

Zoey again. This time her bikini straps show underneath a linen strapless jumper with long, wide legs. She has a hoodie tied around her waist, and wears a fedora, one with a wider brim. A straw tote is tucked under her arm and one of our pool towels—seafoam-green with a white shell trim—is sticking out the top. She takes a seat without me offering, not that I really have to offer. She's a hotel guest and this is my job.

I smile. "Hi, Ms. Wilson. Isn't it a little chilly for a day at the beach?"

"It's Zoey. And this is heaven when you just came from two solid months of below-freezing temperatures."

I fold my hands in front of me on the desk. "What can I do for you today? We have a neighboring beach club. I can get you a cabana." The further away I can be from more questions, the better.

"No, not that." She reaches into her tote and pulls out a small notepad, something that looks like what a detective uses in all those cop shows on TV. She flips a few pages, and as she's doing it, my heart stabs. She looks *so* much like Pepper. "I started doing some digging yesterday and came across someone named Juliet Duncan. We spoke last night." My eyebrows knot, and then she says, "Sorry. That's her married name. Her maiden name is Juliet Ackers."

Right. Juliet Ackers. Julian's twin sister. I graduated with her. Well, with both of them.

It's easiest not to act shocked and pretend I didn't know about the accident, even though Zoey is going to go right back to that damn letter Pepper wrote. I make my solemn face. "Right. Her brother died, if I'm not mistaken?" Okay, I'll lie a little.

"Mmhmm. The night after graduation. At something called senior picnic. He was killed in a car accident. An *accident*. My mother mentioned an accident in the letter. Also said something about *regrets with them*. Curious, no?"

I nod. "Yes, the cops questioned almost everyone the next day. Tragic, really. I'm sure you know how stupid kids are when everyone is drinking. No one should've been driving." I pause, trying to collect how much she knows. "Did Juliet tell you how Julian was killed?"

Zoey shrugs, nonchalant. "Some girl, Chloe, drove drunk and rammed her car right into him at the opening of a park in the middle of the night. She hit her head or something and died too." She looks away. "It was from either brain damage or internal injuries. Just like my mother."

I push the coincidence, the justice, out of my head. But my heart squeezes. I had my opinions of Pepper and that night, but she was still a mom to Zoey. And now Zoey is a young girl without a mother.

"Juliet didn't think much of my mother," Zoey continues. "Or of you. Or of that girl Chloe."

My stomach flip-flops, and I don't know why—it was true. Juliet had no reason to like us. We didn't run in the same crowds. "Well, I'm sure cliques still exist. Juliet and Julian were what was known as 'goths' back then. They wore a lot of black and chains and dark makeup. Julian even wore black eyeliner."

"So what? That's not so strange."

Right. "It was two decades ago." Men wearing makeup is normal now, and suddenly I feel old as shit. "Juliet and Julian used to smoke pot in the back lot every morning before school with their friends. Our paths didn't exactly cross at parties. Why does any of this matter on your quest to find your dad?" I debate what's worse—her finding out more than she should about the accident, or her finding out who her father is.

"Juliet also told me my mother was dating some football guy all through high school and that they were madly in love."

My stomach grips—that didn't take her long, to find out about the long-term boyfriend. For one split second, I'm about to tell her the truth and get it out there, consequences be damned. But then she presses on about her conversation with Juliet.

"She also said her brother was seeing that girl Chloe. In secret."

Lots of things were said that night—it's not the first time I've heard that information. I nod. "I heard that rumor too. But I was friends with Chloe. She never mentioned it to me."

Of course, there'd been rumors about them. No one believed it. Okay, maybe Chris did. Chris and Vince—and the rest of the football team—used to pick on Julian constantly. In any case, I was thankful that Zoey's train of thought was bouncing around, away from her mother and my husband. I relaxed slightly.

"It wasn't a rumor. Juliet told me she saw Julian and Chloe together a few times. But everything had to be secrets. Fucking high school hypocrites."

She was right. In high school, there were secrets around every locker. Still—that was *true*? Chloe, a frenemy cheerleader, and Julian, a vampire? If only that was the worst thing about him.

There's no reason to reveal his other sins now.

"Anyway," Zoey continues, "you know my mother wrote something in that letter about surviving an accident that night. Awfully coincidental, that there *was* an accident. One that killed people."

And we're back to that. I gulp. "I told you. She fell. She probably felt guilty that we left the fair early because we were drunk. Who knows what would've happened if we had stayed? Maybe we could've stopped Chloe from driving."

"Right. That's what you told me. I'm going to see what I can dig up at the police station about the accident." She attempts to stand when I grab her forearm, then quickly release it when I realize how desperate it makes me look. I switch tactics and soften.

"What was your mom like when you were growing up?" I honestly don't know who Pepper turned into as an adult.

Her eyes consider whether or not to tell me anything about her late mother. Then she half smiles, likely wanting to reminisce and keep her memory alive. "Busy. She worked a lot. She loved acting, but it paid shit, so she did rando temp jobs during the day, and sometimes waitressing at night. My grandparents moved to Brooklyn to help when I was really young, so I got to grow up with them too. They watched me most of the time because my mother—" She pauses and catches her breath. "Well, not for nothing, but she was young. She partied a lot. My grandfather is still alive, but he has a nurse living with him up there. Grandma died about ten years ago."

I'd heard Pepper's parents moved north. I obviously didn't know it was to take care of their grandchild.

"Did she ever go to college?" I ask.

"I'm sure you knew about NYU. She dropped out after the first semester. I came on February 22. I guess she knew she wouldn't be able to balance both."

My heart tugs, and I wonder why Pepper didn't even attempt to get in touch with me when her daughter was born on my birthday. She didn't forget. Pepper's birthday is—was—January 11, and she always loved to say that she was "one-one-one" and I'd always be "two-two-two." She was always first, I was always second. I recognize the gaslighting now that I'm old enough. Back then, she got the cookie and I got the crumbs.

"Well," Zoey finishes, "I'm off to the beach and the police station. Maybe by the time I get back, you'll remember who my father is."

She stands and unties her hoodie.

"Zoey," I say softly. "She was weird at the end of senior year. She might have been dating other guys. She might not have known who your father was. I swear, she never told me." That part is true. When Pepper told me she was pregnant, I naturally assumed Vince was the father. She never said anything different.

My eyes narrow but with compassion, praying she believes me, and she walks out without answering. Now I *do* feel sick and wish I'd just stayed home in bed. I wonder if Vince has called Mark Grenning yet. If Zoey digs any further, I'm the one who might need a lawyer.

I wonder what the statute of limitations is for lying to the police and being an accessory to murder.

INTERVIEW THE DAY AFTER
THE SENIOR PICNIC

Detective Logan: So, you said earlier you didn't know much about Julian Ackers.

Scarlett: That's right.

Detective Logan: I heard from another student that Chloe Michaels was seeing Julian Ackers.

Scarlett: That doesn't make sense. At all.

Detective Logan: Why not?

Scarlett: Julian wasn't a good guy. Chloe wouldn't cheat on Chris with him. Plus, I didn't even think they knew each other.

Detective Logan: Ms. Kane, you're going to have to pick a story and stick to it. First you said you saw Julian last night, then you said it was only on his way in. Then you said you don't know him, but now you seem convinced he's not a good guy. Did you or did you not know him?

Scarlett: I didn't. I swear. You can ask anyone.

Detective Logan: (stares her down)

Scarlett: I didn't know him, but I've heard things. It's just rumors. Some people think he got too aggressive with girls. But you're right, I wouldn't know for sure.

6

haven't heard from Vince all day, and I don't know if he saw Mark today or not. He's avoiding me on purpose.

Obviously, Vince and I didn't have a traditional boy-meets-girl-and-they-fall-in-love-and-start-a-family story. We weren't "in love" in the sense that love moves mountains. We enjoyed each other, we both loved Luke, but that's about it. He started the pool business with Chris when they were twenty-five, and Lila worked for them as a receptionist. Vince said the affair didn't start until years later and only lasted four months. I don't know why I didn't take Luke and leave. Maybe because life was easy. Comfortable. Chris and Jennifer got divorced at thirty without having kids, but somehow, beyond all expectations, Vince and I are still together.

At least for now. This Zoey business might be the final straw.

I find it hard to concentrate on my job the rest of the day, having to ask customers to repeat things because I'm zoned out half the time, always looking behind their shoulders, waiting to see Zoey standing there, tapping her foot, judging. I only have an hour left on the day before I can leave the hotel, and Zoey, for the weekend. Hopefully, she'll decide this whole thing is a dead end and just leave. Although now that she knows her mother dated "some football dude" all through high school, her showing up at our door feels inevitable.

I just hope that's all she finds out, and that she doesn't tear open the Pandora's box about the accident. The scene really was cut-and-dried when we left it—I don't think the cops had much reason to look further. Unless she gives them one. Like that damn letter.

Zoey waltzes in, slightly tan, a few minutes before I'm due to leave. She looks like the cat that ate the canary as she walks over.

"Hi, Scarlett."

I smile and nod. "Zoey. Did you enjoy the day?"

"I did. I really did." She doesn't take her eyes off me. She sits down in the empty chair in front of the desk and settles her tote and straw hat in the chair next to her, camping. She's prepared to stay a while. Which means she has something to say.

"You got some color," I say.

"Yeah, my friends back home are going to be totes jeal," she says while admiring her outstretched arms. "I'm going back Monday night. School starts up again on Wednesday." I nod, inviting her to say more, like we're old friends having tea. "It's just community college. I'm in my third year of the two-year plan, but I graduate in May, finally. I had to pay for it myself, and I couldn't afford it without working a lot, which interfered with a full school schedule. I'm sure you know what it's like. Or maybe not. I bet your parents sent you to college."

They did, even though they had to put off their retirement. I was a "surprise," as they put it, when they were done having children. I'm the youngest of three—eight years younger than the middle child, Hannah, a fitness instructor in Miami, who is only a year younger than the oldest, Crystal, a fashion marketing genius who lives in Paris. I'm relatively close to Hannah, but I only see Crystal once every few years, and she's "too busy" to email me back. Ever.

"I went to the University of Florida. In-state tuition is pretty cheap," I say, trying to seem like I'm relating to her. "What's your major?"

"Investigative journalism."

Terrific.

"I'm naturally inquisitive," she says.

No shit. Which means she knows exactly how to dig. This whole thing is a big project for her. I decide to save myself the trouble of anxiety.

"So, what did you find out, then?" I ask.

"Lots of stuff. More about my mom's boyfriend in high school." She raises her eyebrows and smirks while nodding to the name tag on my blazer. "I found out his last name is Russo."

INTERVIEW THE DAY AFTER
THE SENIOR PICNIC

Detective Logan: Your girlfriend was friends with Chloe, correct?

Vince: If you're talking about Pepper, she's my ex-girlfriend.

Detective Logan: Oh, so you aren't dating anymore? I was told you guys were prom king and queen.

Vince: We were. That was weeks ago.

Detective Logan: So, you weren't with Pepper Wilson last night?

Vince: *With*, how? Of course I saw her there. I already told you everyone was there, and everyone was fucked up.

Detective Logan: What about the after-party? At Chris Parker's house?

Vince: I don't remember. Maybe she was there. Maybe she wasn't. But I don't remember a lot of things from last night, and I don't know what she even has to do with this anyway. I'm sorry, I'm afraid I'm the worst person to be interviewing right now. Do you have any aspirin?

7

Zoey knows Vince's last name. She knows my last name is Russo.

January in Florida has always made me shiver. Now, however, my armpits are stuck closed and my back is sticking to my chair. Perspiration springs from every pore on my body.

"You're married to Vince Russo, aren't you?" Zoey asks. "My mother's boyfriend."

I gulp.

She throws back her head and laughs. A sarcastic laugh. "Now you're going to tell me that you weren't my mom's little lapdog and followed everything she did. I bet you couldn't wait for her to leave and get your claws into her boyfriend. Man, she's rolling over in her grave right now."

I panic, but I try to sound sure of myself. "That's not what happened. After high school, I didn't see Vince again until we both finished college."

"Still—you don't think this is weird? Like, at all? I swear, these small towns. So incestuous. Why don't you people ever meet anyone new?"

St. Petersburg isn't exactly Podunk, Mississippi, with one general store and the annual church bake sale. "Come on, Zoey. It's not like that."

I have no idea why I'm letting a child intimidate me. The way she's staring me down and ripping insults reminds me of—well, of Pepper. Zoey looks exactly like her. I feel like a middle school student all over again, with Pepper pointing a finger in my face and demanding that I do this or do that . . . or else.

Zoey doesn't miss a beat in her tactics, just like her mother. "So, like, should I come to your house tonight, or do you want to call him now and tell him to come here, or . . ." Zoey lets the sentence trail off, and I decide I hate her. I fucking hate her.

My voice shakes when I answer. "Actually, I'm waiting for Vince to call me back. I told him about this yesterday. That Pepper has a daughter." I clear my throat and straighten up. I speak more confidently. "That she was pregnant when she left Florida. He knows." I won't let her intimidate me.

"Oh. Great! Family dinner, then?"

She's taking such casual joy in upending my life.

"We already have a family." One that you will not screw with, little one.

"I have brothers and sisters?" Her eyes look hopeful for a second, before she remembers why she's here: to terrorize me. "Of course you had kids. With my mother's boyfriend."

She can have all the fun she wants with me, but I will *not* let her terrorize Luke. "Just one. He's seventeen."

She stands and straps her tote around her shoulder. "Tell him I'm looking forward to meeting him. I'm going to shower and change, and I'll be over a little after six, I guess." She pats her bag. "I have your address. Don't worry, I don't plan to stay long."

What the— "We're not going to be home. We have dinner plans," I lie.

"I'll just wait at your house until you get home. Let's rip off this Band-Aid."

"Zoey," I say threateningly. "Don't."

She scoffs. "Or what? I'll see you later. Plan on six."

That's only an hour. She's barely across the lobby by the time I skid out of there like I'm on fire. I feel like I am, anyway. My mission is to get Luke out of the house. My screeching car sounds like it's in a Hollywood blockbuster as I peel out of the parking lot. For some reason, every damn light is red, and I'm about to cause an accident ramming into everyone. At (yet another) red light, I grab my phone and text in all caps *I NEED YOU TO CALL ME BACK ITS AN EMERGENCY* to Vince. Enough of the games.

A minute later, I see his name pop up on my Bluetooth screen, and I accept the call.

"Where the hell have you been all day? Why have you been avoiding me?" I don't mean to start with a confrontation. Hell, maybe I do. I barely know my name at this point.

"What's the emergency?" he asks, cool as a cucumber.

"Get home. Now. That girl, that Zoey . . ." I can't. I can't call her his daughter. "She's coming over in an hour."

"What? What did you say to her?"

"Nothing. She found out your last name. She knows we're married. She's asking questions about everything. She went to—look, I'll tell you everything, just get home. Now."

I disconnect the call because it shows the urgency. Get home *now*.

I tear into the driveway, and Luke's car isn't there. Thank God. He's probably with Beth or hanging out with his friends somewhere. It's Friday night, after all. I grab my purse and go inside, punching in the alarm code by the garage door and heading straight for the refrigerator. A nice cold glass of Sauvignon Blanc is needed. But instead, with my heart beating at twice its usual rate, I just unscrew the top and take a nice long swig right from the bottle. Then another. I lean my head on my forearm next to the open door, contemplating my options, before I take one more swig and then cap it and put it back. That should dull the anxiety. At least temporarily.

I change into jeans and a sweatshirt and sit at the kitchen table. Waiting. My stomach is a ball of nerves at the shitstorm I'm afraid Zoey will bring into my home.

Ten minutes later, the garage opens, and I hear the roar of Vince's car pulling in. Thank God it's not Luke. I don't want him coming home in the middle of whatever is about to happen. I quickly text him, asking where he is. Not abnormal. He writes back that he's at his best friend Kevin's house with Beth and some other people, and they're going to barbecue and swim in Kevin's indoor pool, and then get a movie on pay-per-view. I send a smiley face back and tell him to take his time.

The kid is trustworthy. So are his friends. And I know their parents. I don't think he's at a raging house party, getting hammered and then driving around and murdering people who may or may not have deserved it.

That's the only thing that's kept me sane for twenty years. Remembering that Julian deserved what Pepper did to him. I was a bystander; Pepper was judge, jury, and one-hundred-percent executioner.

Vince comes in, sees me at the table, stoic, and just says, "Okay. What now?"

He's so flat. Zero emotion. I can't tell if it's toward me or the situation. Probably me. To some degree, it's always been that way.

"*What now?* Zoey is a journalism major, and she did some digging about Pepper. About who she was back then."

Vince rolls his eyes.

"That's not all," I say. "She spoke to Juliet Ackers. Juliet Duncan, now, but—"

"Juliet Ackers? That fucking asshole's sister?"

Now it's my turn to roll my eyes. "Come on, Vince, have some respect. Stop being a jerk-off. You didn't get along with Julian in high school. Who cares? You're a big boy—let it go. It was over twenty years ago. And he's dead for God's sake."

"Good."

Good? His words shock me. Who is this man I married? Like I should talk—I've held the secret about Julian's death without once having enough respect for the truth to tell it. By the time Vince and I got together, we barely spoke of the night at the senior picnic. It didn't involve him, he didn't think it involved me, and with Chloe being Chris's girlfriend at the time, the whole thing was kind of off limits. Now Zoey wants to stir it back up.

"Why would she talk to Juliet anyway?" he asks.

"There's something I didn't tell you. About the letter that Pepper wrote. The one that was addressed to me. She said something in there about surviving an accident and that's why she decided to keep the baby." He scoffs at the mention of the baby—*his daughter*—and turns away from me, but I continue. "She fell that night when we were walking home. But of course, Zoey found out there was an actual accident and now she's digging up all this old shit, and honestly it's all just so stupid."

I lie because that's what I'm good at when it comes to the accident. *We'll never mention this again. Deal?*

Still, Vince looks . . . nervous? It's the same glassy look he had in his eyes when we said our vows over my seventh month old baby bump. Nerves. Fear. Regret. "She can dig all she wants," he says. "I don't remember anything, anyway. I was drunk, and then I went to Chris's house for the after-party. I slept there. I don't remember anything. Only that my mom called the next morning when all the parents found out about Chloe driving drunk and killing herself and Julian. My mom freaked out because I never made it home."

That morning, I woke up snug in my bed, like nothing had changed, but everything had. My mother came into my room and "broke the news." Told me the police wanted to talk to everyone. I complied, with the story that was fed to me on a platter by Pepper. Our new truth. The lovely lie.

Still, Vince's demeanor is off. He's talking too fast. He's brushing it all under the rug.

"Why are you acting weird?" I ask. He's acted like this once before, and my instincts kick in, ones I will never second-guess again.

Are you having an affair?

Don't be ridiculous.

He lied then. He's lying now. "What are you hiding from me?" I ask.

His mouth opens, then quickly closes. He doesn't have time to answer. The doorbell rings, and I see her face through the window.

It's Zoey.

INTERVIEW THE DAY AFTER
THE SENIOR PICNIC

Detective Logan: Were you at Chris Parker's after-party?

Scarlett: No, I didn't go.

Detective Logan: Why not? It was the popular place to be. All your friends were there.

Scarlett: I was too drunk to drive. Pepper and I started to walk home from the fair. It was late and dark.

Detective Logan: You walked home last night?

Scarlett: No. Well, we started to, but we couldn't find a ride.

Detective Logan: Be specific, Scarlett. Were you walking or looking for a ride?

Scarlett: We started to walk, figured we'd see if we could catch a ride. We didn't. One car passed us, but they just beeped the horn and yelled out the window, probably on their way to the party. Some guys from the team. I saw Jordan Kessler, I think John Nelson, and Kurt Hyatt was probably driving. I know his car. You can ask them.

Detective Logan: I will. If they were friends of yours, why didn't they stop?

Scarlett: You'll have to ask them. They were probably drunk.

Detective Logan: But you *did* drive home last night, correct?

Scarlett: Yeah. After a while when we couldn't find a ride, we turned around and walked back to my car. I was sobered up by then. It was late, and I was so tired. I dropped Pepper off at her house and then went home.

Detective Logan: I see. What road were you walking on when you decided to turn around?

Scarlett: That long, dark road. Three Bridges Road.

Detective Logan: The road that leads to the park where we found Chloe and Julian. You never saw her car go by?

Scarlett: No. We only saw that one car with the guys in it.

8

Vince and I look at each other. *You get the door. No,* you *get the door!* He sits at the table and crosses his arms.

Decision made.

I look at him with disgust—really, when did he become spiteful? I stomp over and pull open the door. There she is, mini Pepper. She's even dressed the same as her mother would be right now, with red-framed sunglasses pushing back her shiny dark hair, revealing her hazel eyes. A black tank top emblazoned with silver writing that—what does that say? *Call My Agent.* The cracked, faded letters on the ribbing tell me it was indeed Pepper's. She used to wear that all the time. Is this a psychological experiment to break me?

"Hey there," she says, casually, smiling, not a care in the world. Not like she's about to meet her father for the first time. Again, I wonder which she wants more—to meet him or terrorize me. Or if she's simply punishing me for not telling her I was married to Vince the second I met her.

"Hi, Zoey. Come on in." I widen the door and scoot to the side, her heels click-clacking on the tile as she enters. I mean to close the door normally, but there's a little bit of slam as I quickly move to pass her before she walks around like she owns the place. "Follow me."

We go through the short hallway that leads to the kitchen, and Vince stands. I see it on his face when he looks at her: memories of Pepper. He opens his arms, then sheepishly pulls back and offers a hand to Zoey, and they shake.

"Hi. I'm Vincent Russo."

Ugh, he uses *Vincent*. He always joked he'd never use that because *I'm Vince. Vincent is my dad*. Hardy har har.

"Hi, Vincent," she says.

"Bad joke. It's—" He stutters. "Call me Vince."

They awkwardly stare at each other, both looking for recognition in the other.

"Have a seat, Zoey," I say. "Can I get you a drink? Water? Juice?" Bleach?

Ugh, what a horrible thing to think. She's just a kid.

She shoots me a look as she pulls back a chair. "Wine, if you've got it. I'm sure you do, don't you? I'm not a kid, you know. I'll be twenty-two next month."

Yes, remind us of your age, which means that Pepper became pregnant right about when—yep. Right about *when*.

Zoey sits next to Vince at the table and lays right into him.

"So, you're the guy that my mother dated for four years," she says.

"Yes," Vince says. "Wow, you look exactly like her."

"I've heard that before. Were you together at the end of senior year?"

Zoey is all business. She's on a fact-finding mission.

"No. Well, yes, but no, not at the very end. We hung out a few times while we were broken up and, you know . . . But yes, we broke up a few times. She started acting weird after the holidays and kept breaking up with me. I always tried to get her back. Young love and all that. Man, your mother meant the world to me."

I really try not to slam the wine glasses, the bottle, the opener, the cabinets, the refrigerator . . . but it's getting harder.

Vince continues. "She was going away to college, but originally we planned to do the long-distance thing and then to get married after. She left early and then just disappeared into thin air. You have to believe me—I swear I didn't know she was pregnant."

Well, this is news to me. I'm here, married to Vince, because Pepper decided to keep his child hidden from him and be a single mother. If she'd come back after college, they'd be a happy family, and I wouldn't have Luke. I wonder if that's why Vince even started up with me in the first place. Was he trying to be close to Pepper, or hoping she'd hear about it and get jealous?

Slam. Oops. "Sorry," I say as I gently take down another wine glass. "Red or white? We have both."

"Red," they both say at the same time, then look at each other and laugh. *How adorable.*

Then Zoey takes over. "I believe you, Vince. She talked about you, the one that got away. Never mentioned your name, though. And she clammed up when I asked if you were my father. I think she was super embarrassed. She always maintained that she never told my father. So, I know you didn't know."

He nods. "I looked her up a few times with all the social media stuff," he says.

More news to me. We've been married for seventeen years. I'm talking flip phones and PalmPilots and printed telephone books. Cameras were a separate piece of equipment you had to bring to parties. The phrase "dot-com" was becoming mainstream. Our whole marriage, Vince had been looking up, apparently, the love of his life.

"She didn't have social media," Zoey says. "She never got into it, which is shocking considering how much attention she always wanted. You wouldn't have been able to find her anyway. She legally changed her last name for acting—Pepper Zarra, with two Rs. So silly, right? She acted like she was some in-demand award winner, which she clearly wasn't. Total delusions of grandeur. She actually used to say *Don't you know who I am* if she wanted to cut a line at Starbucks. The answer is no, no one knew who she was." She curls a lip and shrugs. "My grandparents mostly raised me. My mother was kind of selfish. She'd rather party in the city than deal with me."

The more things change, the more they stay the same.

Zoey continues. "I don't know where she thought she was going with the whole acting thing, being the 'tah-dah' girl for the new car model at the local dealership. Though she had an arc on *All My Children* once upon a time. A decade ago." She turns to me. "I'm surprised you didn't recognize her, Scarlett."

"I don't watch soaps. I have a job." Bitch!

"Did she ever get married?" Vince interrupts. Of course he wants to know if he was replaced.

Another shrug. "No. She had a ton of boyfriends, though. Dated a few costars, and I use the term *dated* lightly. I mean, I wasn't stupid. My mother would leave in skintight clothing and red lipstick and the highest heels you ever saw. My grandparents used to yell at her for not being responsible. She met some guy, Alex, when I was about ten, I guess. They were together for a while, but again, she liked to party too much, and I guess it didn't work." This time, she laughs. "But no, no marriage. I don't think she ever got over you, to be honest."

Pride beams off Vince's face as he likely relives every sexual and romantic moment with Pepper and what the last twenty years of his life could've been like. As fast as it appears, it leaves, and then

Vince's face is downtrodden. "I'm sorry, Zoey. I'm sorry I wasn't there. I really didn't know."

I carry a glass of red for each of them over to the table, fighting the urge to dump it on both of their heads, then go back for my white and sit at the table with them. I fake sympathy because I feel my marriage crumbling and getting worse by the second.

"Zoey, I swear," I say, and even touch her forearm, "I had no idea she had you either. She told me she was getting an abortion."

"I'm sure," she says. "Actually, I wanted to talk to you a little more about that accident my mother referenced in her letter. That line that said *you know why we had to leave.* Leave what? I mean, it all seems so specific, but you say it was about her falling. Then I find out that there was a horrible car accident and people died. It's just weird, you know?"

I shake my head. Not because I'm saying no, but because I'm getting scared. "I don't remember. Maybe it was about her being pregnant."

She looks at Vince. "Do you remember anything?"

Vince stiffens and his jaw locks, and I see the tension seep down his neck muscles. "Yeah, it was my friend's girlfriend who was driving—"

"Chloe Michaels?" Zoey interrupts. Little twit *did* do her research.

"Yeah, Chloe, and apparently she hit the kid she was cheating on him with. His name was Julian Ackers." His neck muscles haven't released. "What an asshole that guy was."

Zoey's first face is *Huh?* Her second is sly. Narrow, inquisitive eyes. Just the facts, ma'am. Damn wannabe reporter.

"I was really drunk that whole night," Vince says. "I stayed at my friend's house. Woke up on the floor in the basement. Not my proudest moment. High school, you know?"

"Yeah, I hear you." She sips her wine, first slowly, then in gulps. "I drank a lot my senior year too. Managed not to get knocked up at eighteen, though." She finishes the wine. "Wait. Is my brother here?"

That sentence knocks the wind out of me. "No," I say quickly. "You understand, we haven't said anything to him yet."

"Yet? Like, you're going to? That would be cool. I leave in three days. It would be fun to meet him."

Vince and I lock eyes, and for the first time, he's on my side. "Zoey, you have to give us some time to figure this out," he says.

She smiles. "I said I will. Three days. In the meantime"—she stands, looks at her watch, checks her phone, and brushes herself off—"it was nice to finally meet you. I said I wouldn't take up too much of your time. You guys have fun at dinner. If you want to know what I find out tomorrow, I can let you know."

"Tomorrow? What's tomorrow?" I ask.

"Today, I found this retired detective, and I told him about the letter I found. Detective Logan. He's meeting me at the station tomorrow morning at eleven. I want to know if there's more to that accident, and now, so does he. He said he always thought something was fishy. After all, a fall down a hill doesn't usually get you to reevaluate your life and keep your baby, you know?"

That's the game she wants to play? I'm a Jedi master at this game. Before she ruins my life, I need a little bit of truth too.

"Good. Maybe I'll meet you there. I'd like to see if we can get a speedy paternity test," I say.

INTERVIEW THE DAY AFTER
THE SENIOR PICNIC

Detective Logan: How many people came to your party?

Chris: I have no idea. I was hammered.

Detective Logan: What time did people start arriving?

Chris: I don't know. There were already people there when I got there. Everyone knows my house is the party house.

Detective Logan: Okay. What time did you get there?

Chris: I don't know. Ten? Ish?

Detective Logan: Did you arrive alone?

Chris: No, I was with my buddy, Vince.

Detective Logan: Right. He stayed over.

Chris: Yeah, I guess. I thought he went home at one point because he was passed out on the basement floor, and then next time I went down there, he was gone. Must've been hooking up with some chick, though, because he was there in the morning.

9

Vince walks Zoey to the door, and when she leaves, he and I are alone. The range of emotions in my chest are suffocating me, and I stand and pour another glass of the white. Well, okay, half the bottle, right to the tippy-top of the glass so I have to lean down and suck some out before I pick it up and spill it everywhere.

"Classy," Vince says.

He's pissed. Good. I'm terrified—that letter is going to be the end of me. "You'll have to excuse me. It's hard finding out you're seeding yourself all over half of Florida. And you know what? We shouldn't just take Zoey's word for it. Let's be honest here, your perfect little Pepper was probably screwing other people every time she dumped you."

I want to hurt him, emotionally. We've never really talked about Pepper, the unspoken bond we both had, the one girl we both loved two decades ago. My love for her may have been lost that night at the senior picnic, but it's become painfully obvious in the past twenty-four hours that he still carries a torch. Well, she's dead, and I don't have to keep her secrets anymore. It was over twenty years ago.

"Whatever," he retorts. "At least she didn't screw my best friend."

My fist knots so tightly over the glass I'm afraid I'm going to bust it into a million pieces. "What did you say to me?" Another thing we didn't talk about when we got together—the fact that I lost my virginity to Chris Parker when I was a sophomore. It was one time, at a party, and that was that. "Actually, you don't know that she didn't screw Chris, do you? Everyone had secrets back then. But this isn't about me. This is about you and the fact that you have another fucking kid!" This time, I do slam the glass, and it breaks.

"Terrific." He grabs my forearm to pull me out of the way so I don't walk on the pieces. "Don't move."

He goes down the hall to the utility closet and takes out the broom and the dustpan and sweeps up around me. The bigger chunks go in the pan, but since the wine is everywhere now, the smaller shards get stuck to the bristles. I don't move, as told, but I can't move anyway. I'm beyond stunned at what's happened to my marriage in the last day—it feels just like a decade ago, but worse. I suppose Zoey is forcing us to confront things that we should've talked about before. Apparently, we were both holding a lot in.

Maybe I should've told him about what really happened that night. Maybe he'd see his precious Pepper differently. Is this my fault?

No, it's not. But there's still a huge lie between us. One that I have to at least partially tell him.

"Vince, we need to talk about something."

"Mmhmm."

He's still wiping up wine glass shards, and I'm still standing like a statue as he runs back to the closet and comes out with the smaller broom, a brush really, to get the smaller pieces. Then he wets a sponge and taps it on the floor to pick up the slivers we can't see. When it's finally safe to move, I don't miss a beat and grab another wine glass and pour.

"I'm sorry about what I said about Pepper screwing other people. I never should've said that."

"Mmhmm."

"And you're sorry about what you said about me and Chris?" My tone changes.

He sighs. "Yes. I was just trying to hurt you back."

"Well, there's more. Can we go outside?" I need a cigarette to tell him what I'm about to tell him.

Vince grabs a beer, and we go to the back. I take his hand in mine in some sort of show of solidarity and lead him down the dock, but it doesn't feel right. Neither of us clasp our fingers, we kind of just hang our palms next to each other from muscle memory. The sunset on the west coast is beautiful, even over the bay, and the boats in the distance have been painted black by the sun fading behind the horizon. I sit down at the edge of the dock and dangle my feet over—they don't reach the water, and Vince's won't either, so he does the same.

We're both stiff, no longer touching, and I feel it next to me. The tension is in the air around us. There's something he has to know.

"Hey," I start. "Look, you don't know everything that happened the night of senior picnic."

He blows out a puff of air. "Whatever. It was a long time ago. I barely remember it."

"Well, I do. It's impossible for me to forget." I can't tell him the whole truth, so I have to tell him Pepper's truth. She's dead, and it doesn't matter anymore. I close my eyes and silently apologize to her. "Something happened to Pepper."

"What do you mean?" He's still staring straight ahead. His words have no shock, no emotion, which is a direct contrast to just minutes ago.

"I've kept this secret for a long time, and I'm only breaking it now because I want you to understand her frame of mind that night. Why she left a day later. Probably why she kept all of this from you."

"Okay. I'm listening." Same. Flat, unemotional words. He's still staring straight ahead.

"Pepper—she and I got separated at the fair at some point. You remember, everyone was around, and everyone was drunk. I wasn't exactly looking for her. And I feel terrible about that."

"Why?"

"Because when I found her, it was late, and she was by the edge of the woods." I take a deep breath. "Pepper was assaulted that night." I have to get it out. He needs to know. "Sexually. By Julian Ackers."

Complete silence. Until he speaks.

"I know. Why do you think I'm glad he's dead?"

INTERVIEW THE DAY AFTER
THE SENIOR PICNIC

Detective Logan: You've had your aspirin. Feeling any better?

Vince: Not really.

Detective Logan: Did you stay at Chris Parker's all night?

Vince: Of course. I was in no condition to drive.

Detective Logan: People who saw you said you disappeared. And then reappeared.

Vince: So? I was probably taking a leak.

Detective Logan: How did you get here today?

Vince: My mother picked me up at Chris's house.

Detective Logan: Why are you rolling your eyes? She was concerned.

Vince: It was stupid. Everyone started to hear about Chloe and Julian being killed, and all the parents whose kids didn't come home started overreacting. My mom is the one who called me and told me, but she was already like three minutes away from Chris's house when I got the call. She came running in, all screaming and hugging me. Like I'm a baby or something.

Detective Logan: And then what happened?

Vince: She said the cops wanted to talk to everyone. So here I am. She brought me straight here.

Detective Logan: Then I have to ask—why are your sneakers so filthy?

10

"What do you mean you knew about Pepper's assault?" I ask. He won't meet my eye, but there's no way Vince knew about Julian almost raping Pepper. It's impossible.

After the accident, I took her home. I saw her the next day at the police station. And then she was gone. She wrote me that letter that she never mailed. Did she write Vince a letter that made it to his mailbox?

"How did you know, Vince?" Now I'm furious. At him. Mostly at Pepper. *We'll never mention this again. Deal?* If she wasn't already dead, I'd kill her.

His gaze hasn't met mine, and he's still staring at the water. "She called me and told me."

"When?"

"After it happened."

What? She called Vince before I found her that night? Before the accident? Why did she call him, anyway?

"Well, not right after, if that's what you're thinking." Vince reads me like a book. "It was in the middle of the night. I don't even know what time. She was already home, and I was at Chris's.

I was drunk. I just remember she said you ditched her, then he found her, and . . ."

He says that with an edge, as if he's blaming me. That it's my fault that something happened to his beloved Pepper.

"I didn't ditch her. We got separated. I found her, and I drove her home. What did you say to her?"

He shrugs. "Don't really remember. I remember being pissed off, obviously. She wasn't making sense. Rambling. And then the next day, the kid was dead anyway. Excuse me for not lighting a candle in his memory. Fucking asshole," he says, repeating his earlier sentiment.

Vince knew, this whole time, about Pepper's assault, and that Julian did it. For twenty-two years. I wonder if this is why he never mentioned Pepper the entire time we've been together—he was as beholden to her secret as I was. But while Vince may have known about the assault, I'm pretty damn certain he never would've married me if he knew my part in the accident—Luke or no Luke.

"You never stopped loving Pepper, did you?"

He pauses for too long before he answers, and it tells me all I need to know. "It doesn't matter. She's dead."

"That wasn't my question."

"Come on, Scarlett. It's not like she's going to come between us."

"She already has. You have Zoey now." I put my head in my hands. "I didn't know you were looking for Pepper all this time. What if you found her? What would've happened then? My God, what are we going to tell Luke?"

For me, it's all about Luke. My priority, my number one.

Vince doesn't try to comfort me like when my grandfather died, or when I was passed over for manager a few years ago, or when my parents' dog had to be put down. A simple arm around the shoulder would suffice. But he does nothing.

Pepper is in his thoughts. I can already see him turning to stone, a shell of himself, knowing he never got to tell her how he felt all these years, all the "what if" possibilities, and now she's gone. Add Zoey, with her declaration that Pepper always talked about him and never stopped loving him. I have no doubt that if Pepper was alive and showed up on my doorstep, he wouldn't even pack a bag. He'd just go. Leave. Follow her. Be a family of three. She always said he'd drop everything for her. He would—even me. Especially me.

"I'm going to grab a slice of pizza," Vince says. "I didn't have dinner."

"Neither did I." Not that I have an appetite.

"Well, I've got to get out of here for a little while. I'm going to text Chris and see if he's around."

With that, he gets up and leaves.

Of course, beers with Chris on a Friday night is going to turn into shots and coming home after midnight after God knows what else. We all got married too young. But if we survived the affair, and almost ten years of Chris being single and asking Vince to come out and play with him all the time, we can get through this.

Do I want to?

I try to put myself in his shoes, to feel what he's feeling, but I can't. I never stepped out on our marriage. I don't have a secret kid. I'm not in love with someone else.

Not even a dead person.

INTERVIEW THE DAY AFTER
THE SENIOR PICNIC

Detective Logan: I've heard a lot about you already. State your name for the record.

Pepper: The incredible Pepper Wilson, and I want it on record just like that. I actually want to trademark it, you know.

Detective Logan: Thanks for that info. I'm sure you know why you're here?

Pepper: Why don't you tell me why I'm here?

Detective Logan: Did you see Julian Ackers or Chloe Michaels last night?

Pepper: I saw Julian at the beginning of the night, but I didn't talk to him. We aren't friends. I saw him with his sister and some other creepy goth kids.

Detective Logan: And your boyfriend had words with him, I hear?

Pepper: I don't have a boyfriend. I'm single. Very single. Legal age, too.

Detective Logan: Did you witness Vince Russo having a fight with Julian?

Pepper: They always fought. I mean, not really like physically, but Vince didn't like Julian. Vince doesn't like many people. Half the kids you interviewed probably told you what a bully he is.

Detective Logan: I'm not asking the rest of your class questions about Vince Russo. I asked you. So, you saw Julian at the beginning of the night when he fought with Vince, and that was it?

Pepper: That's what I said. Although his name came up a lot. There was a rumor that Chloe was cheating on her boyfriend, Chris, with him.

Detective Logan: Yes, I've heard that from several people. Did you see Chloe last night?

Pepper: Of course. She's a good friend of mine. I was hanging out with her on and off all night. Until—well, until she started getting completely hammered. She was chugging vodka from a Poland Spring bottle.

Detective Logan: Are you sure it was vodka?

Pepper: Of course it was. I had some. Are you going to arrest me, Detective?

Detective Logan: Is there any reason you should be arrested?

Pepper: Nothing besides the underage drinking. But I feel like you've got bigger fish to fry right now. Is it true that Chloe hit Julian with her car? That's honestly tragic. But I guess the rumors were true, then. My mother heard from her mother that there were calls on their phones to each other a little before it happened.

Detective Logan: We don't know exactly when it happened. We're trying to figure out the timeline, which is why we want to know when people saw each of them. Some say you disappeared for a while during the fair.

Pepper: You're going to trust what a bunch of drunk people said? That's classic detective work right there.

Detective Logan: Did you leave the fair at any point?

Pepper: Who cares? I thought the accident happened after the fair was over.

Detective Logan: Why are you holding your arm like that?

Pepper: I fell last night. And it still hurts.

11

"Where's Dad?"

I look up from the book I'm reading in bed—a domestic thriller about a lying, cheating, douchebag husband, and I'm eating it up, laughing about how life imitates art—and see Luke at the door. I glance at the clock. It's a little after eleven. Losing track of time has been a blessing.

"He went out with Uncle Chris. Boys' night."

Luke's glare tells me he doesn't believe a thing I'm saying. Between Vince sleeping on the couch last night, Luke hearing us fight this morning, and now Vince being just—gone. He knows better.

"Everything okay?" he asks. "I heard you guys fighting."

I force a smile, and I know it's a weak one that doesn't show any teeth. But I try, because I'll do anything for him. "Everything's fine, honey." I hold my book up. "This just got really good. I'm about to find out who's lying. We'll talk in the morning. I promise."

He looks sad, his blond hair swooped down over the front of his face, and I hope we're not damaging the kid beyond repair. "Okay. Love you."

"Love you too." I throw a kiss as he closes the door. My boy.

Although the book *is* getting good, I'm mentally exhausted, and now Luke knows something is up. I dog-ear the page because I can't find my bookmark, and I don't feel like getting up to see if it fell under the bed. After placing the book on my nightstand, I turn off the light and lay on my right side so the bedroom door and Vince's side of the bed are behind me. Counting sheep isn't even necessary because I feel myself drifting off within minutes.

I'm startled out of my sleep by a tug on my shoulder—I know what that means. My eyes open and the clock reads two a.m. Did Vince just get home? I grunt out a noise, one I hope he interprets as *no*.

Vince was probably trying to impress everyone and doing shots all night like he's not pushing middle age. I cringe at the way he acts sometimes, like he's still in high school at a kegger. I'm cringing at a lot of things about him now, things that had bothered me before, but I was more interested then in keeping the peace. In keeping Luke's life idyllic. No longer.

The tug on my shoulder becomes rougher, and he kisses my neck. I smell him before I feel him and think I must've been right about the shots. He probably spilled some tequila on his shirt, which now he's removing. Too little, too late. I don't turn around and instead nudge him gently with my elbow.

"I'm sleeping," I say.

"Come on," he says. Not like desire, like a whine.

If he thinks I'm going to turn over and have sex with him right now while he thinks of Pepper, well, he better guess again. His hands roam for another minute until he gets zero response, then he sighs loudly—actually, it's more like a groan—and grabs his pillow and leaves.

Good.

I set an alarm for eight a.m. and fall right back to sleep.

When I wake from the blare, I quickly shut it off, get out of bed, and go downstairs. Vince is splayed on his back on the couch, mouth open, dead to the world. I don't realize how disgusted I am with him until I try to wake him and he doesn't move. I push him over and over, and he just rolls with each one, never even closing his mouth. He's probably still drunk. Finally, I shake him and yell.

"Vince! Get up."

His eyes flutter open as he tries to focus. "What? What happened?"

My repulsion sits in second place to Luke's emotional well-being, and I won't let him see Vince on the couch a second time. "Get upstairs and get in bed before Luke gets up. I don't want him to see you down here again."

Vince begrudgingly stands, wobbles, and grabs his pillow. Stops in the kitchen for a bottle of water, pops some Advil, and then goes up the stairs and falls into bed like a drunk teenager. At forty.

These things never used to bother me like they do now. What a difference a day makes.

I crawl in bed next to him, but I stay awake, playing mindless games on my phone. I don't have the brainpower to read the news or my book or do anything productive. I'm thinking about Zoey, going to the police station, and if there's anything we should say to Luke.

Luke wakes around nine, and the shower turns on. Right. He works all day most Saturdays. Thank God. He won't be around when we leave together and subsequently come back together. Still, we'll have to prepare him for a hefty talk tonight if we're able to speed through those paternity results, which I'm willing to pay for no matter what the cost.

Vince rolls over. "I'm hungry."

I bet. "Long night, huh?"

"Yeah. Me and Chris got talking. I told him what's going on."

Great. Half of me knew he was going to tell him, but it doesn't make it any easier knowing our dirty laundry is out in the world. Especially because Chris obviously knew about Lila too. Boy, there's a sucker born every minute, and with Chris knowing how Vince constantly humiliates me, well, that sucker is me, because Chris has told me to leave him several times. It must be hard for Chris, knowing that his best friend is an awful husband.

"And? What did he have to say?"

Vince shrugs and gets up. His blond hair is sticking out everywhere, like he's Bart Simpson. He catches a glimpse of himself in the mirror and pats his hair down. "He thinks everything is fucked up too. Look, I'm sorry for being an asshole about this. I know nothing is your fault. I just—I don't know. It's hard."

I soften, but only like one percent. "This is hard for me too. It brought up a lot of unresolved stuff. About Lila, and what happened ten years ago."

"Well, it brought up a lot of unresolved shit for me too, about Pepper. And then last night, about Chloe, for Chris. He never really dealt with Chloe's death. He was too pissed off about the rumors going around about her and Julian that night, then she was found with him. He kind of blocked it all out. And when I brought this all up to him and told him you knew Pepper was pregnant—I'm sorry, we just spun out." He sits at the edge of my side of the bed. "I don't want to fight about this forever."

I grit my teeth. "Well, it's also been hard finding out you've pretty much been in love with Pepper our whole marriage. I just wonder if you would've walked out on me and Luke if you knew about Zoey. If you found Pepper on social media when you were looking for her."

"Luke is my son, and he's the most important thing in my life."

"That didn't seem to matter a decade ago, did it?"

My legs swing over the side of the bed, and I grab my robe from the chair near the window and put it on. "Let's try to have breakfast as a family. United front, even if it's just for Luke. We have to leave for the police station in a couple of hours."

"We don't have to go. I'll get a paternity test somewhere else if it'll make you feel better."

"No, I want to find out about this today. They've got to have some high-tech forensics team, or they'll know someone who will jump through hoops for them today. I don't care about the cost. I want it done. And I want to find out why she's stirring shit up with that detective who questioned everyone, all because of some vague line Pepper put in a letter over twenty years ago."

"Yeah, I know what you mean. That guy was a real prick to me."

"The detective? Why?"

"I don't know. He just kept trying to get me to say something, backing me into a corner. Thought I did something secretive because my sneakers were filthy. Sure, Detective, I killed them both, then rolled around in mud like a pig in a pen. There was no mud at the scene. I don't know why he was being such a jerk."

I glare at him. "How do you know there was no mud at the scene?"

He shrugs. "We've all been to Rockland Park. The opening by that big boulder where they found them is asphalt. It's best whatever happened that night stays closed. No one else knows about Julian attacking Pepper. Having that come out will just open a can of worms."

Whatever happened that night. Vince knows more than he's let on, for all these years. Did Pepper tell him anything else? Did she tell him we were there?

Why does Vince look scared?

INTERVIEW THE DAY AFTER
THE SENIOR PICNIC

Vince: My sneakers? I'm an all-star athlete. I go through sneakers like a hooker goes through condoms. I ruin a pair every couple of weeks.

Detective Logan: I like to pay attention to details. Comes with the job. No one else's shoes are caked up like yours are.

Vince: Did they all come straight here like I did?

Detective Logan: You're getting awfully defensive, Mr. Russo.

Vince: What do you expect? We were at a fair. Half of it was in the field beyond the parking lot. The ground is made of dirt, if you didn't know. It's June in Florida. You may have heard it rains sometimes. I was drunk, and I wasn't paying attention to where I was walking. Why don't you call my father?

Detective Logan: Ah, yes, the Deputy Mayor. Vincent Russo Senior. Why should we call him? Is there something you're trying to protect yourself from?

Vince: For the love of God, dirt on the quarterback's shoes. Let's alert the media.

Detective Logan: Just saying. It's not football season, and that's an awful lot of mud. Do you mind if we test your shoes? (Pause.) What's so funny, Mr. Russo?

Vince: Test them for what?

Detective Logan: Blood.

12

"Is there something you're not telling me?"

I have to ask Vince, because ever since I brought up Pepper's letter and the detective's renewed interest in the accident, he's looked like he's about to shit his pants.

"No, nothing. The detective was just a real asshole. The whole sneaker thing."

"What sneaker thing?"

He rolls his eyes. "You didn't hear about this? God, I thought everyone did." He rubs his hand over his hair again. "My sneakers were caked with dirt, and that gave the detective a hard-on. He tried to make me turn them in. To test them for blood."

My heart stops but restarts just a second later. Vince is innocent. He wasn't there when they died; I was. "Blood? I don't understand."

"I didn't either, and my parents weren't happy about it. When I refused to hand them over—"

"Why would you refuse? You weren't there."

"That's not the point. I knew my rights. When they told my parents, my father started up a shitstorm about my rights and whatever. Then my mother got involved and told me since I didn't do anything wrong to shut them up and let them do the stupid tests."

"Wow." I swallow hard. "What happened?"

"Nothing. I never had to hand them in. The accident was open and shut, which is why you never heard anything about it. They wouldn't have found anything—my father said a sample of the dirt in Rockland Park would be comparable with the dirt in the field where the fair was held. That detective hoped something else was going on. He couldn't get it through his head that Chloe drove drunk, went to meet her secret boyfriend, and probably hit the gas instead of the brake because she was a hot mess."

He paces the room, his hand on his head. Nervous.

"The thing is, I don't want Pepper's assault coming out. She's not alive to explain to anyone what really happened. Neither of us knows the whole story, and honestly, Zoey doesn't need to know about that."

I hate to admit that he's right. The last thing I want is to bend over backward to make sure that everything in Zoey's life is peaceful and warm and fuzzy—especially since mine is falling apart—but she doesn't need to know what happened to Pepper. Julian paid for what he did. Pepper's words from that night reverberate in my brain.

"Fuck him. He got what he deserved."

Still, I need more details, so I don't slip. I'm not a hundred percent sure that Vince doesn't know more than he's telling me.

"After Pepper told you about . . . the assault . . . you let it go? Just like that?"

Doesn't sound like the behavior of the Vince I knew in high school, the one who let Pepper treat him like garbage, yet still ran back to her every time she curled a manicured finger in his direction. He always took her bullshit on the chin, with a smile.

"What do you want from me? I don't remember. Jesus, this shit was almost twenty-two years ago. I barely remember last month."

Maybe I'm pushing too hard. Pepper is the guilty one, and I'm the guilty one by association. Thank God Luke pokes his head into our bedroom. He's dressed, his wet hair brushed off his face.

"Hey, I'm leaving. I'll be back a little after five." He looks at his dad. "I'm doing rounds with Uncle Chris today."

"Okay," Vince says. "Do you have plans tonight? I want us all to go out to dinner."

Luke makes that sad-sack teenage face that they all make when their parents want to spend a Saturday night with them. "Can we go early? Beth's friend's older brother is having a birthday party on a boat."

"Excuse me, how old and what boat and who's driving?" I ask.

"No one's going anywhere. God," he whines. "Her best friend's brother just turned twenty-one and their parents have some big boat, and we're not leaving the dock, we'll just be on the boat instead of in the house. It's just music and a bunch of kids."

"Why does a twenty-one-year-old want a bunch of high school kids around?" I ask.

"It's his sister and a few of her friends. It's not like we're all strangers. I've met the guy before. He plays for Florida State."

"Well, that's an automatic *no* from me," I say.

I'm a Gator, and fraternizing with a Seminole is a no-no. Luke is on UF's wait list. He must know I'm half kidding. He's doing that thing. Making that face again. I must be such an embarrassment to him.

I narrow my eyes because I know what kids do nowadays. Smoke pot, drink their faces off, and find bedrooms to hook up in. So, not much different than when I was his age. I'm also pretty sure I looked at my parents the same way before:

embarrassed. At least he has Beth to keep him out of trouble. Seven months together, and he truly seems to care for her. That's the type of kid he is. I just hope they're being careful—I'm sure he's not a virgin—but I have to trust him. He's not me. Thank God.

"I want to know the address where the boat is docked. And yes, we'll go to dinner as soon as you come home from work," I say. "You can go to the party after. Same curfew."

"Fine. Gotta go. See you guys later."

He turns to leave, done being grilled like a baby. His feet rumble down the steps, the door opens and closes, and his car starts up and pulls out.

"Well," I say. "I guess we should shower up and grab breakfast on the way."

Vince lets out a deep breath. "Yep," he says as he heads into the bathroom.

While he's in the shower, I look up rapid paternity testing in case the station wants to give us a runaround about wait times. Apparently, there's new technology now that can do facial recognition as a way of identifying a child and a father, but I don't trust it. I click through the results until I find a place that offers same-day cheek swabs for a staggering $795, but I don't care. The facility is only twenty minutes from the police station, and I'll drag Zoey there by her fucking ponytail if I have to. I plug in my American Express number and make an online appointment for noon, the last available time slot for same-day results. Zoey is meeting the detective at eleven, so at the very least, it'll be an excuse to stop the questioning.

When we're both showered and dressed, we stop at a breakfast café on the beach that's open five days a week until early afternoon. Vince gets a sausage, egg, and cheese on an English muffin with a black coffee, and I get the same, diverting from my normal fruit cup and lemon water. I need sustenance and grease and caffeine to plow through the next few hours.

We're mostly silent. Vince doesn't want to face Detective Logan again. I'm trying to put together scenarios in my head for when the detective asks about what Pepper meant in the letter. And Vince probably thinks that in a few hours, he'll have confirmation that he has a daughter with Pepper.

Pulling into the police station, I get the same feeling in the pit of my stomach that I had when I rode in the car with my parents the day after the senior picnic: dread. How to divert. How to lie. How to preserve Pepper's appearance of innocence, because my freedom hung in the balance as well.

The station looks the same, pretty much. Still brick on the outside, but it looks as if it's been refaced recently. There are two uniformed cops standing outside the entryway, one smoking a cigarette and the other slurping coffee. They stare Vince and I down as we pass, and we both tip our heads and smile with some generic "Hey how are ya" greeting.

Vince opens the door and ushers me inside, and Zoey is already sitting on a metal bench to the right. She smiles at us; actually, it's more of a smug face, her eyebrows moving with her lips, and she stands.

"Hi, guys. I told that woman I was meeting the detective." She points to the curly-haired cop manning the desk. "He's not here yet."

Zoey and Vince look at each other and do the awkward *should we hug or shake hands* dance before he just pats her on the shoulder. I'm all business this time.

"I made an appointment for us at the paternity clinic today at noon. It's twenty minutes from here. They give same-day results. I just think we should nip this in the bud, the sooner, the better."

She squints and tilts her head. "Well, the detective wanted to come here because he still knows people in the department. He's retired, but he wants to see if we can get access to some of the files. And he said my mother's letter should be enough to at least take another look."

I nod, still wondering what her endgame is. "I'm unclear why you want a detective to look this up. I thought you came here for your father." I nod at Vince. "Well, here he is."

She shrugs. "If my mother was involved in something that got people killed, I honestly want to know."

"I don't know what purpose that will serve. I mean, have some respect for her memory."

"Jeez. You sound guilty as hell." She blinks rapidly. Innocently. Bitchy. "Plus, it's good practice for me. Digging for the real story. I told you I'm majoring in investigative journalism, right?"

Yes, you did. I stop myself from lunging at her and squeezing her tiny little neck. I have no comeback and am saved by the bell. Literally. It rings through the speaker, indicating a visitor, and there he is: Detective Logan. He was in his late forties the last time I saw him. Now, he's two inches shorter and frail looking, with a beer belly. He's gone bald except for a few tufts of gray above each ear. He's dressed in worn jeans and a Hawaiian-patterned button-down shirt. White shoes. Old Florida man to the core. Before I can address him, he looks at my husband.

"Vince Russo. Not entirely surprised to see you again."

INTERVIEW THE DAY AFTER
THE SENIOR PICNIC

Vince: You're lucky my father hasn't had you fired yet. Good luck with that.

Detective Logan: Well, at least your mother was trying to be cooperative.

Vince: That's because she believes me.

Detective Logan: Tell me about your relationship with Julian Ackers. Why didn't you get along?

Vince: Because he's a puny little freak.

Detective Logan: And you're captain of the football team, making him beneath you. Is that right?

Vince: What's the matter, Detective? You didn't have cliques in your high school? Don't act like I'm the only person alive who never got along with someone based on their looks and their taste in music and how they dress.

Detective Logan: Certainly not, Mr. Russo. What happened with him last night?

Vince: He's just a smug son of a bitch. Always staring down my girlfriend.

Detective: I thought she was your ex-girlfriend?

Vince: Shit, don't start with semantics. Come on, man. Haven't you ever been in love? No matter what, Pepper will always be the most important woman in my life. And I didn't like the way that asshole was staring at her. Again. So, I pushed him. He's lucky that when I threw the bottle at his head, I missed.

Detective Logan: I heard that. So much for being the star quarterback. Anyway, the reason why we're concerned is that you're the only one last night who said you were going to kill him. So, you understand the issue we're facing, no?

13

"**G**ood to see you, Detective Logan," Vince says.

Between what he told me this morning about them wanting to have his sneakers tested and the detective's smug attitude right now, Vince is anything but happy to see him.

They shake hands, and Detective Logan looks at Zoey. "You're the one who called, I presume? Zoey Wilson? Pepper Wilson's daughter?"

"Yes, hi," she says to him and offers a hand as well. Then she nods toward me while still addressing him. "Do you remember Scarlett Kane? She was my mother's best friend back then. She's married to my mother's ex now. Vince. He's my father. Convoluted, right?"

I don't understand what Zoey's problem is and has been since the second she laid eyes on me. "Hi. Scarlett Russo," I say and extend my hand, which he takes while still staring at Zoey. "Yes, what she said is true. Vince and I got together after college. Crazy, huh?"

"Small-ish town. I've seen crazier," he says, finally looking at me. "I understand you all want to see some files? There may be new evidence on that accident?"

We don't want to see anything; Zoey does. She pulls the letter from her bag and starts to take it out of the envelope, then shoves it back in and points to me.

"It's addressed to her, but it was never sent. I assume my mother wrote it after she got to New York. Can we sit somewhere?"

"Sure," Detective Logan says. We follow him to the front desk, where he mutters, "Hi, Lisa," and she presses a button that releases the door to the right. Down a long hallway, he opens a windowed blue door on the left, and inside, it's a plain room with a wooden table and four chairs. No two-way mirror, no cameras, and it smells faintly like antiseptic or some other hard-core cleaning chemical. "Have a seat. I'm going to grab Detective Watson. He's in charge now. I put in a call to him yesterday regarding the files."

The door closes behind him. Zoey, still clutching the letter, places it on the table and takes the seat in front of it. Vince sits next to her, and I next to him. The only sounds in the room are all three of us fidgeting—our clothes rustling, the chairs scraping the floor, breathing. Screw it.

"How's the hotel treating you?" I ask.

"It's fine. I went out to some bar off the beaten path last night. Met a cute boy, too. Bruno. He's a wide receiver at Florida State. It's his last weekend at home before he goes back. I may meet up with him and his friends later; I haven't decided yet."

I check Vince's face to see if he flushes, to see if he's going to go all *Dad* on her.

"Just be careful," he says. "You don't even know this guy."

"Okay, *Dad*," she says with exaggeration. "It's not like I'm a virgin."

Vince's face goes red and the door opens, another quick save. Detective Logan walks in with a tall Black gentleman who's carrying a file box, wearing khaki slacks and a navy polo, a police shield hanging from a chain around his neck. His chiseled features look like they were cut with a saw. He's around my age, maybe a couple years older, and I wonder if he's from around here and if he remembers any of this. We all stand, and he raises a hand as if to say *no, sit,* then places the box on the table. He gestures to the last empty chair for Detective Logan to take, which the old man does. The new detective looks at Zoey.

"Zoey Wilson?" he asks.

"Yes," she says.

"Right. I'm Detective Benjamin Watson. So, this is an old case, pretty open and shut, but you think you have new evidence?"

She glares at me, then turns back to Detective Watson. "Well, I found this letter when I was packing up my mom's things," Zoey says and pushes it toward him. "I mean, I came here looking for answers about my father, but something about this just isn't sitting right with me. Especially since I found out there was an actual accident."

Her hands are now folded in her lap, and she looks like she could be on a convent interview. Meek expression, face turned down, all prim and proper. She must've picked up *something* from Pepper in the acting department.

Detective Watson pulls the letter out and reads it. His brows furrow. No lines on his smooth skin. "Okay. I'm not following."

Thank God.

Zoey shoots him a *how dare you doubt me* look and points to a specific spot on the page. "See what my mother said? About surviving the accident, and why she had to leave? It was addressed to this one." She refers to me with a hitchhiker's thumb and doesn't look at me. "My mom never mailed it, though. I found it a few weeks ago. What does it all mean?"

Watson reads the short letter again and then looks at me. "Anything to add?"

I shake my head. "I honestly don't remember. I mean, Pepper fell down a hill that night when we were walking. She hurt her arm. I hurt my neck trying to lift her up. We were drinking. I can only assume that's what she was referring to."

"She said she decided to keep the baby," Zoey finishes. "*Me*. And something about leaving *them*? I doubt she's referring to falling down a hill. Please. Imagine my surprise when I talked to Juliet Duncan—formerly Ackers—and found out that people were killed that night. In an *accident*."

Watson pats the box in front of him and trains his gaze on Zoey. "I looked through this when Detective Logan called me yesterday. I'm not sure what you're looking for. Chloe Michaels was drunk. There were phone calls between her and Julian. It was an unfortunate accident."

"I told you, I never believed what they said about those blood spatters," Detective Logan chimes in. "They were too far away from the car."

Detective Watson gives Detective Logan a look, a *this is my department now, old man* look. "It was an impact splatter. The only one who was ever considered for foul play was Vince Russo, and he was cleared."

Zoey looks at Vince. "Excuse me?"

Vince shifts in his chair, shoots a quick look to Detective Logan, then back to Zoey. "My sneakers were filthy that night, and they had some ludicrous notion that somehow I was involved."

"Yes, until Daddy had a talk with my boss and told me to back off," Detective Logan says.

"Oh, come on," Vince continues. He looks at Zoey. "This was all based solely on the fact that I love your mother and didn't appreciate that the guy who died was staring at her the way he was." He shifts again. "Julian was predatory with her, and I got defensive and said some stupid shit every teenage boy in love says, you know, that I would kill him. It was a coincidence he ended up dead. But not by me—that was on Chloe. And it was an accident."

The room is silent. Well, not the thoughts in my head. Those are going a mile a minute and at ten decibels. Go ahead, Vince. Say it again. *"Solely on the fact that I love your mother."* Love. Not *loved*.

Detective Watson looks at Zoey. "I'm not sure I need to reopen a decades-old case because of that letter."

Good.

"I knew Pepper was pregnant at the end of senior year," I say. "She told me she was getting an abortion once she got to New York. I assumed it was Vince's and that she went through with it. Yes, it's a bit of a wrench that she never did. She didn't tell Vince about it at all, and she didn't tell me she kept the baby. We stopped speaking when she left for New York." I make a show of checking my watch. "Look, I have an appointment scheduled for us at that facility in Pinellas Park at noon. A same-day paternity test. We'll find out for sure."

"And then?" Watson asks.

"And then? And then what? Then we'll have to welcome Zoey into our lives. Have her meet our son. We'll figure it out, Detective." I point to the clock on the wall, another desperate move to let them know we're out of time. "We should get going soon."

"You said it's twenty minutes away," Zoey snaps. "We have five more minutes. And if my mother was involved in something illegal, where kids ended up dead, I want to know." She looks at the retired Detective Logan and motions toward Watson. "You said he'd help me!"

Detective Logan raises his eyebrows. "Never could put my finger on what bothered me about it. But it's his bag now. If he doesn't want to reopen it, there's nothing I can do anymore."

"Wow. This sucks. What a waste of time." She holds up the letter. "Well, *I'm* not done."

I almost tell everyone in the room everything, just to get her to shut up. About Pepper's assault and Julian's guilt. But I'm not that stupid. It only gives Pepper more of a clear motive. And I'm already on record with my lie—saying we never saw Chloe after we left. Never saw Julian. Even though we were in the car with her. I remember Pepper mocking the entire situation when she coached me what to say.

We tried to grab a ride on Three Bridges Road. When we couldn't get a ride, we sobered up and went back for the car. We didn't see Chloe after we left the fair. She was drinking and driving. It's a shame, really. She probably hit the gas by accident. Alcohol dulls your senses, you know.

I look at Vince and stand. "It's time to go."

INTERVIEW THE DAY AFTER
THE SENIOR PICNIC

Detective Logan: Do you know any reason Vince Russo would be involved in this?

Scarlett: Pepper's boyfriend? I mean, ex-boyfriend? How would that even be possible? He wasn't really friends with Chloe. They'd spend time together, but only because she was dating his best friend. And wasn't he at the after-party?

Detective Logan: What's wrong with your neck? You keep making faces every time your head moves.

Scarlett: Nothing. Well, Pepper fell, and I guess maybe I pulled something helping her up. Then I probably slept on it wrong.

Detective Logan: I see. Did you hear Vince threaten Julian Ackers?

Scarlett: Yes.

Detective Logan: And you didn't think to tell me?

Scarlett: Why? I hear people say they're going to kill people every day in school. It's not like anyone actually does it.

14

Zoey follows us in her rental car, some little bright blue thing in the shape of an egg that probably doesn't even have power steering. She likely got it for ten bucks a day. I'm speeding, and she's zig-zagging all over the place to keep up, weaving in and out of cars.

"Slow down," Vince says. "We're going to be on time."

That's hardly the point. I want to be early, I want this over with, and I want to know what we're going to say to Luke at dinner tonight. He always asked for a baby sister or a puppy, and we never gave him either. How are we going to explain this? I can't exactly put a bow on Zoey's neck and say *Surprise!*

I ease into the brakes at the last turn and pull left into the parking lot. It's a typical strip mall. I drive past the dollar store, dry cleaners, pizzeria, liquor store, post office, pharmacy, and all the way at the end, there's a two-story structure with a red hospital sign, so I know that's the medical building. I park in front, and Zoey parks a few spaces away.

We don't speak as we approach the building. Vince holds the door open, first for Zoey and then for me, and follows us in. There are two people waiting in blue fabric chairs in front of the desk: a mother and a toddler with the sniffles. A young woman with dark-framed glasses sits behind the counter, and she looks to be about Zoey's age. Her name tag says *Wendy*, and her blonde hair has blue and purple streaks and is pulled into a tight bun. She smiles, but it's crooked and doesn't show teeth.

"Hi. Can I help you?"

"Hi. Yes. I'm Scarlett Russo. We have an appointment at noon." I don't want to say for what out loud. I still can't believe this is my life.

She taps into the computer and then says, "Yes, for a rapid paternity test." Her voice reverberates and I cringe at what the young mother behind me must be thinking. She probably thinks it's *me* who's Zoey's mother, and that *I* don't have a clue who her father is, and that this is my only alternative besides Maury Povich. "Fill out these forms and we can get st rted."

She places two clipboards on the counter, each with an attached pen and three pages of needed information. Vince and I sit next to each other as he fills out his medical history and insurance information, and Zoey sits a few chairs over doing the same. Wendy asks for their insurance cards and photo IDs to copy for their files. They hand them over before finishing the paperwork, which they both complete in less than ten minutes. Vince stands and holds his hand out to Zoey, and she hands him her clipboard and he places them both on the counter.

"Great. You can come through that door and go into room five." Wendy points to the right.

Vince opens the door and heads right in, leading the way. I let Zoey go in front of me; I don't want her making a run for it now. Vince finds room five and we go in. There's a table with rolled white paper on the top, and Zoey hops up and gives me that smug look. I sit in the metal chair, and Vince stands with his hands in his pockets.

"The moment of truth," Zoey says.

I glance at the blood pressure device on the wall next to Zoey and desperately want to strap it on my arm, just to see the needle break the glass and fly across the room. "Zoey, can I ask you what you want after we get these results? Half of me feels like you've been doing all of this to piss me off."

Her face scrunches. "Well, not for nothing, Scarlett, you could've just told me you were married to my mother's boyfriend and he was probably my father. You had me going on a goose chase instead of enjoying my time in Florida, getting to know him." She looks down, vulnerable for the first time. "Why did you just ditch my mother?"

I look at Vince in disbelief, then back at her. "What are you talking about? She left and disconnected her phone. I had no idea where she was. Her emails started bouncing back after a month of her not answering, and there wasn't any social media. What was I supposed to do? Take a plane to New York and walk around screaming her name?" I swallow. "I wish things turned out differently for her. For you and for her."

"You can say it. You wish you had contact with her before she died. Do you feel guilty about that? For covering for her? I know she did something bad—that letter said it all."

"She didn't. But—" Why was Zoey trying to ruin her mother's legacy? "But what if she did? What are you trying to accomplish? I just don't understand the venom toward her. And me."

"She lied to me all my life. You lied to me the moment you knew who I was. I know there's a reason for that, and I'm going to find out what it is."

"Can you put yourself in my shoes for a second? My dead best friend's kid shows up, and my husband is the father. It's just—it's a lot." Sniffles start, and I feel the sting of the inevitable tears.

Just then, the technician walks in. He's young, probably in his first year of practicing medicine, which is why he's at a facility like this, doing cheek swabs and taking walk-ins for the common cold. He's holding a clipboard and scans it before looking up and eyeing all three of us.

"Hey there. I'm Dr. Daniel Girard. I assume you're Vince Russo, and you, Zoey Wilson," he says as he nods toward them. "This will only take a minute."

He takes two stickers from the clipboard, which he hangs in a plastic folder attached to the back of the door, then yanks a pair of rubber gloves from the box near the small sink. From a drawer, he retrieves two tubes, both with a cotton swab attached to the cap. He peels back one sticker and places it on the outside of the tube, then repeats the move with the other.

"Vince, you're first." One-two-three. Open mouth, swab, capped. Zoey is next and just as fast. "Okay, that'll do it. The call will come from the lab later this afternoon, straight to the cell phone number that was entered when you registered online." He writes something on a pad. "You'll need this PIN when they call."

"I want a call too," Zoey says, then raises her eyebrows. "You know, for the sake of the truth."

Dr. Girard looks at Vince, assuming he set up the appointment, but I interject.

"It's coming to my cell phone, but I don't mind her getting the same call after me." I have to acquiesce. I'm her stepmother.

Dr. Girard grabs the clipboard and hands it to Zoey. "Great. Write your number down over here"—he points to a specific section—"and I'll give the instructions to the lab when I drop these off." He writes down the PIN for her on a separate sheet of paper.

She does it quickly and then hops off the table. "We good?"

"All set. Have a nice day," Dr. Girard says.

Have a nice day. Like we were just handed a kitten and got a prescription for happy pills.

Zoey dashes out of the room and takes off in her blue egg. Vince and I are quiet the entire ride home. Once there, he heads to the yard to balance the pool chemicals. I stay inside and cut cheddar cheese into cubes, and I pour a huge amount of wine into a glass and make all of it disappear in record time.

Like waiting for water to boil, the minutes are excruciating. I swear that a half hour has passed; I look at the clock and it's only been two minutes. That happens over a hundred times as I clutch the paper the doctor handed me, until my cell phone rings just past four.

I look through the window in the kitchen, the one where we can see the dock and the water in the back, and Vince is sitting in the boat drinking a beer, staring blankly, probably dreaming of the future he never had with Pepper.

He'll have to get the news after I do—I'm not going to get him. I answer the phone with a tentative *hello,* and my voice shakes.

"Scarlett Russo?"

"Yes."

"This is regarding your recent medical case. Do you have a PIN number?"

"Six-Nine-Four-Dash-Zero-Zero-Three." I didn't even have to reference the paper.

"Great." Typing. "Okay, we have the results. It's not a match. With a ninety-nine point nine-nine percent chance, the man did not father the child."

Relief bleeds from my skull to my face, and my muscles all go limp. "Thank you."

I disconnect. Vince isn't Zoey's father.

Who is?

INTERVIEW THE DAY AFTER
THE SENIOR PICNIC

Detective Logan: Is your boyfriend always so protective over you? He started a fight tonight because someone looked at you.

Pepper: He's my *ex*-boyfriend, and yes. God, sometimes it's just sad. Sometimes I feel bad about treating him how I do. Only sometimes. But, I suppose it's nice having a little lap dog that will do anything I tell him to do.

Detective Logan: Huh. Anything?

Pepper: Usually.

Detective Logan: Would he lie for you?

Pepper: About what? I meant, like, fetching me a Diet Coke or washing my car. So no, it doesn't surprise me that he got like that last night. It's not the first time, and it won't be the last.

Detective Logan: Were you cheating on him?

Pepper: We were broken up.

Detective Logan: Yes, I heard that you broke up quite a few times this year. Did you see other people when you were broken up? Anything that would give him extra rage?

Pepper: I really don't think who I decide to sleep with has anything to do with Chloe driving drunk and killing Julian.

Detective Logan: It might. Do you think maybe Vince was seeing someone else while you were broken up? Chloe, perhaps?

Pepper: What in the actual fuck are you talking about? Vince hasn't been with anyone but me in four years.

Detective Logan: Does that make you mad? Thinking of him with Chloe?

Pepper: Right. Like he'd see that dumpster trash fucking pig whore behind my back.

Detective Logan: That's an awfully strong response to someone you called a friend just a few minutes ago.

Pepper: Clearly, you don't have teenage daughters. You have no idea about the backstabbing that goes on when people pretend to be friends.

PART 2

———

ZOEY

15

text back my best friend, Anna, who's been inquiring about my test results.

> **Me:** *They said this afternoon, so it should be any minute now.*
> **Anna:** *R U nervous?*

I picture Anna, my neighbor and BFF, whom I've known since my mother and I moved to Brooklyn from the city when I was two. She's probably lying on her stomach, propped up by her elbows, on her twin bed, box-dyed orange hair in pigtails, feet in the air with her legs bent at the knee. Most likely, she's wearing black and white striped leggings under a black skirt and an off-the-shoulder sweatshirt with some obscure band name on it.

Having grown up together, we've gone through it all—first crushes, first periods, first fucks (boys for me, boys and girls for her), first drinks, and all the others in between. Brooklyn isn't cheap, so she still lives with her parents and I still live in my mom's house, but I know I have to leave there soon. It's nice to have her only four blocks away for impromptu White Claw binges in her basement or just to have someone to walk with for a cappuccino.

Me: *Not really nervous. I mean, it'll be weird to meet my brother and have a whole other family. I just can't wait until Scarlett accepts the truth. I don't know how my mother ever dealt with someone like her. Apparently, they were BFFs for like seven or eight years.*

Anna: *I can't believe she married ur father!*

Me neither. The whole thing is so incestual. Since my mother never told me shit, I'm just discovering this information for the first time. And with all this going on, it's no wonder she lied to me about being from here. I wouldn't want to be from here either. I'm a concrete jungle girl to my core.

Still. It doesn't excuse her. What was she trying to hide?

My text notification goes off again, and I'm prepared to answer Anna, but it's not her. The number comes from a 727 area code.

Bruno: *Hey, it's Bruno from last night. Feel like coming to a party tonight?*

I smile because I was hoping he'd get in touch. I need some sort of a story to go back to Anna with. As it is, she thinks me, a twenty-one-year-old, going to Florida for a long weekend alone is like, the stupidest thing she's ever heard. She offered to come with me, but I told her I was just going to be looking for my father, and I made her promise not to tell anyone where I was going—not *anyone*, no matter who comes looking for me. At least this way, I can go out and meet locals and text her pictures so she doesn't think I'm just sitting in my room watching Netflix on my iPad all night.

I can't put any pictures on social media yet. I have my reasons for that.

Plus, I may be spending more time down here. After all, my father and my brother are here. Scarlett is just going to have to deal with it. So, yes, a party with locals tonight is just what the doctor ordered.

Me: *Sure. Let me know the deets.*

He answers immediately.

Bruno: *Cool. It's my friend's twenty-first birthday. His parents are letting him have people on their boat. We're staying docked, but it's usually a good time.*

I'm crafting a witty response when the phone rings right in my hand, startling me. It's a number I don't recognize, and it also has a 727 area code. Omigod, omigod, omigod. It's them. I know it. They say your life flashes before your eyes right before you die, but mine flashes in the next three seconds before I answer the phone. All those birthdays, first-day-of-school outfits, graduating high school—all without a father there, and now I'm getting the validation I need. My finger shakily hovers over the green button to accept the call before I press it.

"Hello?"

"Zoey Wilson?"

"Mmhmm. This is Zoey." Yes, I'm sitting outside by the pool and it's warm today, but I haven't broken a sweat until right now. Thank God it's super windy, the breeze cooling me immediately.

"This is regarding your recent medical test. Do you have a PIN number?"

"Yep, hang on."

I throw the phone down on the towel and open the beach bag that houses my trash gossip rags and that erotic romance novel

Anna says I have to read. Damn it, where's that piece of paper Dr. Girard gave me? I know it was on a yellow Post-it, and I folded it up so the sticky parts stuck together, and now I'm shaking the book upside down and—oh—here it is. I grab it and pull apart the tacky ends so it lies flat on the towel in front of me.

"Six-Nine-Four-Dash-Zero-Zero-Three."

I hear the *tap-tap-tap* into the computer over the outside noise—seagulls, naturally, and the rough surf hitting the sand from the bay. *Tap-tap-tap.* That's it. It's six numbers, lady.

"Okay, we have the results. It's not a match. With a ninety-nine point nine-nine percent chance, the man did not father the child."

I feel faint, and I blink away all the brown spots around me, the ones that suddenly appear without me having looked directly at the sun. She got a number wrong, that's all. Damn wind blowing into the earpiece. That must be it.

"I'm sorry, I need you to check again. Six. Nine. Four. Dash. Zero. Zero. Three." I couldn't have left more space between those numbers if I had a measuring tape.

"Yes. Right. I see that. It's not a match."

I stand, my head spinning. This can't be right. Fine, he's blond haired and blue eyed, but even I remember that stupid logic they taught me in middle school—darker genes are dominant. That's why I have dark hair and hazel eyes. Everyone always said, since I was in kindergarten, that me and my mom were like twins. But I'm only half her.

Who the hell is my other half?

"Okay. Thank you for the call."

I disconnect and stare at the black mirror my iPhone has become. My life has completely changed, again.

I knot a long orange-and-gold sarong around me, and fetch my straw hat out of my bag and put it on, followed by my huge dark sunglasses. For a moment, I feel like I look luxurious, all old-school Sophia Loren on a yacht off the Italian coast, like one of those postcards my mother had, but then I come crashing back down. I'm hiding myself. My tears.

My mother already lied to me, and I'm going to get to the bottom of it. Scarlett knows more than she's telling me about who my father is. And Detective Logan said something about how that accident never sat right with him.

Looks like I'm about to earn that journalism degree.

CONVERSATION BETWEEN PEPPER
AND ZOEY TWO MONTHS AGO

Zoey: Excuse me, but what the fuck is this?

Pepper: How many times do I have to tell you to watch your language?

Zoey: What is it, Mom? Tell me.

Pepper: I don't know. Let me see it.

Oh. That. Where did you find this?

Zoey: Doesn't matter. It has your name on it.

Pepper: I know. It's just—

Zoey: Just what? The whole thing was a lie?

Pepper: It's complicated.

Zoey: You told me you moved from Florida to New York before high school started. You told me you graduated from Lincoln in Brooklyn. So why does this diploma from a high school in Florida have your name on it?

Pepper: What difference does it make?

Zoey: What difference? I've been looking for my father in New York. Not in Florida. You obviously got pregnant there.

Pepper: Zoey, don't stir things up down there.

Zoey: Or what?

Pepper: Or you're going to make trouble that you can't undo.

16

I pack up my stuff and head inside the lobby to the elevator. It's after four anyway, and the sun is no longer doing what I need it to do, although I did get a shade darker during my time out back reading. Anna will be jealous, and the extra glow means I can wear less makeup tonight when I see Bruno.

Stopping in the gift shop, I grab a few extra bottles of water, and some aspirin for the raging tension headache I developed the second I realized I have no fucking clue who my father is. There are two people ahead of me on the line. One is an old woman with tightly curled hair who's buying six "I ♥ St. Petersburg" T-shirts. Probably for the grandkids. I consider getting one for Anna as a joke—she wouldn't be caught dead in something touristy like that. The other guy in front of me has all the essentials—a razor, mouthwash, toothpaste, toothbrush, and condoms. Aww. He probably just met someone at the bar and needs to stock up for later.

Speaking of, I jump off the line and go to the essentials section to the left. I also grab a three-pack of condoms. Better safe than sorry—I don't need a random STD right now.

Back in my room, I text Bruno asking what time I should be at the party. He texts back immediately saying he'll be there at seven, so I assume eight is a good time to show up. By then, he should have a little buzz going, and if he's doing anything shady, I'll be able to notice immediately. My recent ex-boyfriend, Tristan, wasn't so good at hiding his flirting and actually tried to blame the beer—the beer!—when I caught him with his tongue down another girl's throat at a block party.

That threw me for a loop. I've spent the last six months sleeping with anyone who smiles at me. A lot of good that's done me. Le sigh.

With time to kill, I decide on a nap, which seems like a good idea at first, but as I lie here staring at the ceiling, I can't turn my brain off. I keep replaying every damn conversation I've ever had with my mother regarding my father. I'd gone to her supposed high school in Brooklyn and looked up her yearbook (she said was absent on picture day—*sure*) just to see if I could find any candid pictures of her with a boy, someone who I'd immediately recognize myself in. There was nothing. And why would there be? She lied to me about where she graduated from.

When I first found that letter to Scarlett in Mom's stuff, it all made sense. After our confrontation regarding her diploma, my mother clammed up. Told me to leave it alone, that I was better off. But when I saw Scarlett's old address and did research on the high school whose diploma bore my mother's name, it led me here. I need more information about her high school days. And tomorrow I intend on seeing her real yearbook in the library—I called before I flew down here, and the local library keeps copies of all the year-books since 1979. Sounds like a lovely Sunday afternoon—espresso and research.

When I realize sleep will evade me for the immediate future, I get up and shower and get ready for the party. I was correct in my earlier assumption that my newfound glow means less makeup. I don't even need a bronzer. But as usual, I go super heavy on the dark eyeliner and mascara. My eyes are on the lighter side of hazel, so sometimes they look light blue, or even yellow.

I dress casually—dark-wash jeans and a white spaghetti-strapped tank top, with a hoodie tied around my waist. I've noticed January in St. Petersburg is definitely no winter in Brooklyn, but while the days can be somewhat tropical, there's a bite in the air when the sun goes down. I opt for black wedges instead of flip-flops, just in case this is some fancy thing. Having grown up in the concrete jungle, I've never been to a boat party. I don't know if I'm looking at a mini yacht or a bunch of people jammed into a lower cabin crushing White Claws or playing flip cup and spilling out onto the dock to socialize.

At seven-thirty, I call an Uber. Ten minutes later, I crawl into the back seat of the Kia and say hello to my driver, Micah. The place is about fifteen minutes away. Perfect.

Perfect, until I realize that Micah is one of those super-duper chatty drivers who asks me everything about anything as we ride along the beach, then onto the highway for a couple minutes, and then off an exit where the houses are mostly on the bay. Looks like where Scarlett and Vince live, but this seems to be a couple towns over. I try to accommodate Micah's nonstop talk with a smile; I don't want my rating to go down. I'm relieved when we finally pull up to the address I was given by Bruno.

The house is huge, Spanish style, and I can see the water behind it from the back seat of the Uber. There's a stream of cars down the block, balloons attached to the mailbox, and a sign directing people to the back. When I exit the car, Rihanna plays in the background. The music isn't loud enough to have the cops called, but it will be enough to bother the neighbors in a couple hours when people want to go to sleep. I walk down a thin cobblestone path on the side of the house and see about twenty-five people standing on the dock holding red plastic Solo cups.

The boat is docked, and it's big as well—it looks like the boats I've seen in the Hudson or the East River. White, sleek, darkly tinted windows. Not a yacht, but big enough for a party. I don't see Bruno on the dock, so I assume he's on the boat. I smile at the strangers who stare as I walk around, but they ignore me. There's a group of young kids off to the side. I approach them instead—they're easier to get along with, in my experience.

"Hi, I'm looking for Bruno? Tall, Puerto Rican, plays for Florida State?" I say both like questions.

One girl looks me up and down, but then smiles. "Yeah, he's my brother's best friend. I think they went inside for a sec. Let me get them."

She stands and heads toward the back door of the house and I hear her screaming "Thomas! A girl's here for Bruno!" Then she disappears inside.

O-K. Now I'm standing here with three teenagers. I widen my eyes.

"Hi. I'm Zoey."

"William," one guy says, then points to the back door. "That was my girlfriend, Lynne." He points to the couple next to him. "This is Lynne's best friend, Beth, and her boyfriend, Luke."

"Nice to meet you," I say, and then it hits me.

Luke.

Not just the name, but as soon as I connect it, I realize the kid looks exactly like Vince. So, this has to be my would-be brother. He's the right age, and yeah, oh my God, he's a mini Vince the more I stare. *Stop staring.*

Thank God the door rattles behind me and Lynne comes out with two guys, and once they're in the light, I see that one is Bruno. He's in jeans and a Florida State hoodie, and he holds his arms wide as he approaches me, then pulls me in for a hug. Yes, a hug. I just met this dude last night.

"Thomas, this is Zoey, the girl I told you about from last night," Bruno says as his arm casually flings around my shoulders.

Thomas shakes my hand. "Thanks for coming. Let's get you a drink."

I don't really want a drink right now, but Bruno steers me to the boat from my left, and Thomas links my elbow to his on the right. It's time to play with the adults in the room. But there's only one guy I'm interested in talking to right now, and neither of them are by my side.

CONVERSATION BETWEEN PEPPER
AND ZOEY TWO MONTHS AGO

Pepper: Please, Zoey, just drop it.

Zoey: You always say that. I have a right to know who he is.

Pepper: You don't need to know. What difference would it make at this point in your life? I think you had a happy childhood, didn't you? With Grandma and Grandpa helping to raise you, and I've certainly given you your freedom. I've never hovered.

Zoey: Please. You have to be around to hover. Not dating, or drinking, or spending your time at auditions.

Pepper: Watch it, Zoey. And I always trusted you. Now, I'm just asking that you trust me.

Zoey: Tell me something about him. Anything about him.

Pepper: Fine. If it makes you feel any better, just know that I loved him. I thought I did, anyway. I was young. But don't be so keen on putting him on a pedestal.

Zoey: If you were in love, then why did he let you leave to go a thousand miles away?

Pepper: He's the one that left me, and it broke me into a million pieces at the time. It made me so mad that I—I just have a lot of regrets from that time in my life. Like I said, it's complicated.

17

A beer is thrust into my hand when we step onto the boat, and Bruno keeps his arm around me as he introduces me to people. Ann Marie, Gina, and Stacey, then Al, Marcus, Greg, DeAndre—who also plays for Florida State. It's too much, and I feel like I'm being sucked into a vacuum. I keep looking over my shoulder at the dock, and the four kids are still sitting there off to the side, drinking beers and playing some card game. I place my beer on the table after only two sips.

"Zoey is visiting from New York," Bruno tells the crowd of people that I don't know, and then I get a barrage of questions thrown at me.

"Staying with family?" Ha.

"Checking out schools?" No.

"Break from the snow?" No.

"Hashtag Girls Trip!" Hell no, sorority girl.

Ugh. I think of Anna and my ex, Tristan, and my other friends back home from the neighborhood where I go to school, and none of them are like these people. My friends tend to be on the hipster side, independent, and, well, a little poor. There are no girls' weekends in Vegas wearing feather boas and drinking pink shit while holding each other up on the Strip. No one I know is going to a big school with a famous football team, and none of them have Mommy and Daddy paying for it with a college fund set up when they were infants. We're all blue collar, put in an honest day's work—electricians and plumbers, or waitresses and receptionists—and either go to the bar for a bit after work or come straight home and spend time with the family.

"I just needed to get away for a while. I read somewhere that the beaches here are great, and I had a free weekend until school starts back up," I say to my group of admirers, who have all stopped talking to each other and are concentrating on the New Yorker in their midst.

"Is it like *Sex and the City*?" one girl asks.

"No! It's like *Girls*! She's too young to have a *Sex and the City* life," another exclaims, like she knows me. "God, my *mother* watched that show!"

One of the guys whispers something to Bruno, and he chuckles, while my gaze goes back to the teenagers and I nod. "Who invited the kids?"

"Oh," Thomas says. "Lynne is my younger sister, and those are her friends. That guy they're with is our drug connection, so we let them hang out."

What? Luke is a dealer? Jesus, the way Scarlett made him sound, I thought he had a halo and wings.

I duck out from under Bruno. "Do you mind? I could use something to take the edge off."

"Sure. Hurry back," he says and smiles, and his teeth are so bright white against his dark complexion it feels like a spotlight is on them. And he has dimples.

I walk the plank that leads from the inner deck to the dock, and the four kids are still sitting cross-legged, pounding beers, off to the right. They stop what they're doing and look at me when I approach.

"Hey," I say, looking only at Luke. "Bruno tells me you've got something for me?"

He looks me up and down. "Who're you again?"

Shit. I have to relate, so I sit down next to them, my legs stretched out and crossed at the ankles, propping myself up on flat palms behind me.

"I'm Zoey. Bruno's friend. I'm visiting from out of state, and with TSA the way they are now, you can't fly with the good shit. Just a dime bag is fine, or if anyone wants to share a joint, I'll pay."

All four of them look at each other and shrug.

"Yeah, hang on," Luke says. "I've got a few already rolled inside."

"Great. I'll come."

He grabs his beer and rises. I stand and follow him while his girlfriend glares, but I don't care. What does she think is going to happen? I came here with a wide receiver from Florida State and this kid is in high school. And he was my brother until a few hours ago, but of course they don't know that.

We walk down the gray pavers that lead to the sliding door on the back deck.

"So, do you live around here?" I start.

He takes a sip of his beer, then wipes his mouth with his arm. "No. A few towns over. My girlfriend lives five minutes away from here, so I come here a lot."

I chuckle. "I live in a two-family house, separated by a thin wall, in Brooklyn. With my mother. Well, she died a little over a month ago. I'm going to have to leave there soon."

"Oh, shit. Sorry. What happened?"

I shrug. This isn't why I'm talking to him. "Don't really want to talk about it. Do you live with your parents or in a dorm?" I ask, even though I know.

"My parents. I'm a senior in high school. I'm waitlisted for University of Florida. That's where my mom went. Go Gators," he says as he opens the door. We step inside, and I follow him through the kitchen and then to a door that leads into a sunroom. "But, of course, it looks like I'll be at St. Pete Community college in the fall for a year."

There's a navy-blue knapsack on a wicker loveseat with floral cushions, and he unzips the smaller pocket in the front. I crane my neck over his shoulder, and I see small bags of coke, pills, and weed. This kid isn't fucking around. He grabs two rolled joints from a Ziploc and shoves them toward me with an open palm.

"Twenty bucks."

I grab two tens from my purse and smash them into his hand. "Thanks. Come on, I'll share with you guys."

"Hell no. I don't touch the stuff."

"Really?" That's odd.

"I'm an athlete. If my number comes up for UF, half will be on a swimming scholarship. I just need the money."

"Oh. For what?"

His lip curls. "You were seventeen. Didn't you ever just hate your life and want to get out?" He zips the bag back up, stuffs it in the knapsack, and hides it behind the couch. "My mother is a saint, but my father—ugh. I don't know how she puts up with him. I'm closer to his best friend than I am to him. My dad is such a jerk."

Well, well, well. Looks like I'm going to get more insight than I intended.

"At least you have a father. I never knew mine. My mom—well, I recently learned she lied to me about him. About a lot of things."

"Yeah, my parents lie all the time. Like, what, do they think I'm stupid? I hear what they say when they think they're being quiet. So, I just do school, do my sports, stick to curfew, stay out of trouble, and the sooner I'm out, the better. I can't live there another year if I'm stuck going to community college. I have a feeling my mother is just staying with my father for me. I need to get out so she can have her freedom too."

Yikes. "I'm sure it's not that bad." Tell me!

He starts to walk back to the dock, so I follow him through the house, hanging on his every word. "Please. My dad's had I don't even know how many affairs, and God only knows how many kids he has besides me. Yesterday they thought he had another kid from a fucking high school relationship, and they just found out about it. Turns out, it wasn't his. I heard them talk about that, too. Honestly, a big reason I want to go to UF is so my mother can divorce him. She won't do it while I'm in the house. Like I'm a baby or something."

Oh. My. God.

Apparently, Vince doesn't have wings either. Can't fault him for the situation with me, since my mother was the one that left, but there have been others? Now I know why Scarlett had such contempt for me, and I feel bad. But not *too* bad. I still know she helped my mother cover up something. Paybacks are a bitch.

"Well, my mother died without ever telling me who my father was. But I know I'll get to the bottom of it. Eventually."

"That's cool," Luke says as we get back to the group of teenagers.

I got most of what I need, but I did offer to share. I hold up one of the joints. "Anyone have a light?" I don't plan on inhaling. They're all wasted, it's dark—they won't know.

Luke's girlfriend produces one from the pocket of her cutoffs, but Luke waves her hand away. "Nah, you're the customer. I have enough for us. Enjoy."

"Thanks," I say. "Nice to meet you. Maybe I'll see you guys again before I leave Monday night."

I walk back up the dock, onto the plank, and into the boat, where everyone is sitting around pounding beers. Bruno's eyes meet mine and he pats his knee.

"Come have a seat," he says.

Joint in hand, I oblige.

CONVERSATION BETWEEN PEPPER
AND ZOEY SIX WEEKS AGO

Zoey: I'm thinking about going to Florida over my winter break.

Pepper: That's nice. Just you and Anna?

Zoey: No. Just me.

Pepper: Alone? Why are you—Jesus. This again? I thought we put this to bed a few weeks ago. Drop this "Dad" bullshit.

Zoey: *You* put it to bed. Not me. I told you I was going to find him. What if I have brothers or sisters? I deserve to know all of it.

Pepper: Don't count on it.

Zoey: Fine, he left you. He was a fucking teenager. You expected him to take on the responsibility of being a father? You said I was planned, then you said you never told him you were pregnant. Were you trying to trap him to make him take you back? And you say he was the asshole?

Pepper: You don't know anything about him. He was the asshole. Trust me.

Zoey: Trust you? Not likely. I know that's not the only thing you've lied to me about. That box in the attic had a whole bunch of shit besides your diploma, and I'm not even through half of it yet.

18

I don't drink more than a sip or two here and there to be social, but I don't want my new friend—I think this one is Ann Marie—to think I'm a Moe. I dance on the outer deck of the boat with one of the other girls when things start to get a little crazy, and in general, it's been nice to have a night of letting loose. Last night, I was alone at the bar when Bruno came in with his friends. Party for one. Sorta.

Cardi B dies down, and the girl and I get off the furniture. No one around the dock seems to care. There are a few other boats docked that have people drinking on them. An occasional one goes out to the inlet to the bay and honks its horn as it passes us.

Bruno takes my hand, and when I lean into him, he kisses me. Aware of my surroundings, and the people that are staring at his very public hookup with the strange girl from New York, I ask him if there's anywhere more private.

We walk onto the dock and kiss again. He looks at the back of the house. "We can go in there," he says with raised eyebrows.

I look toward the house, then back at him. His dimples. So cute. "I assume the parents aren't home, but isn't that a little . . . disrespectful?"

If I'd ever let random people hook up in our house, my grand-parents would've had my head; it's not like my mother was around, and hell, she'd probably condone it. *I'm not a regular mom, I'm a cool mom!* Then again, the neighbors would've told her first. Cobble Hill, the neighborhood we've lived in most of my life, has been gentrified to the hilt by now, but we've had the same rental forever, and there are laws about how much they can force us to pay, so we got lucky. Half of the people in the surrounding blocks have been there longer than us and have family-rooted pizzerias and bakeries and cafés. Those are the neighbors that would be knocking on our door, the first to tell my mother of any wrongdoings when she wasn't home. The gentrified half commutes to Manhattan for their cushy Wall Street firms or their fashion designer jobs, and they prefer to grab a Starbucks or a ten-dollar hip pastry after they leave their four-thousand-dollar-a-month rental. They don't give a shit about what we do. They don't bother with us at all. We're beneath them.

"No one cares," Bruno says. "My dude has a rager like this every time we're home from school. His parents are probably at some charity function. What's the matter, you don't trust me?"

Trust. Funny word, *trust*. At this point, the word turns me off. Enough that I just want to go back to my hotel and get a good night's sleep before I hit the library tomorrow. I have to stay focused on my real reason for the trip. I need to find my father.

"Hey, actually, how about a rain check? Maybe tomorrow night? I'm not feeling so hot."

"Really? You looked fine dancing up there on the table." His voice has an edge to it, and I don't like it. His hand is on my waist, and I don't like that either.

I take a step back and retrieve my phone from my purse. "I'm gonna just grab an Uber."

I hit my location to pin it on the map, but Bruno smacks the phone out of my hand, and it skids down the dock.

"What the fuck, Bruno?" My eyes are wide and wild, my rage boiling over. I walk to the phone and he grabs my arm.

All I do is look down at his fingers gripping my wrist and forearm, and it's enough to set me off. Anna and I took kickboxing a couple of years ago. I'm rusty, but from the angle he has my left arm right now, I can smash his nose with my right hand and then roundhouse kick this asshole in the face. Turns out, I don't have to.

"Everything okay over here?"

It's Luke, right behind me.

"Everything's fine," I say sharply. "I was just leaving."

Bruno doesn't let go. I don't make a move. Luke stares at us.

The silence is deafening, even though there's a party going on thirty feet away. Bruno releases his grip. "Whore," he mutters.

That's when Luke goes for him, taking Bruno by surprise, and they both fall backward off the dock, into the water.

"Jesus!" I scream. "Help!"

The party stops, but only for a few seconds. Everyone points and laughs, a few hoot and holler, and someone turns the music up louder. Bruno and Luke both pop their heads up above the surface and get their bearings, then drift over to the ladder next to the boat. Bruno climbs first, then Luke. My naivete shows as I didn't know the water is only about four feet deep, and apparently, "it's not a party until someone falls in," as I just heard behind me. When Bruno reaches the top rung of the ladder, he calls Luke a punk and ascends to the dock. Then, he reaches out a hand and helps Luke up. He calls him a punk again, pushes him on the chest in almost a friendly way, then asks someone else for a towel and a beer.

Luke is standing there on the dock, soaked to the bone.

"I'm so sorry," I say as I rush over. "You didn't have to do that."

He shrugs as someone throws a towel, hard—likely Bruno—at Luke's head. "My mother raised a gentleman."

She sure did. Kudos to you, Scarlett. Even I'll give you credit where it's due. "You sure you're okay?"

"I'll live," he says. "I've been in Florida my whole life. I work for my father's pool company. I'm no stranger to water."

"Oh. I never knew what your dad did."

He scrunches up his face when he looks at me. "Why would you?"

"No. I just mean . . ." Shit. "I thought maybe I'd asked when we were talking about your parents before. But it doesn't sound familiar."

He rubs the towel over the top of his head and the back of his neck when the girlfriend, whatever her name is, rushes over.

"Luke! God, I hate him. What a jerkoff," she says and hugs him around his waist.

He puts his arm around her and kisses her head. "Nah, he's not that bad. He just has no respect for women. Football players. Just like my dad."

Wow, this kid lowkey hates his father.

The girl looks over at me. "Luke's really good like that. Such a mama's boy, without the overbearing mama. You know?"

No, I don't. I only know one side of Scarlett Russo, and it's the one who's probably pissing herself with glee that her husband isn't my father. I can almost picture her, clinking her stinking wine glass with Vince. They're probably laughing. At me.

My mother was screwing Vince for four years, but she said she loved my father. It all happened at the same time. She always talked about her nameless long-term boyfriend, who I now know was Vince. I don't get it. Could the test have been wrong? Did she lie to me because of who he really is? Ew, could it be Vince's father, or Vince's best friend? Does he have a brother that Mom messed around with? I know nothing about Vince, and now, I have no reason to. But there has to be a reason it's all such a secret. Family members and BFFs are usually off-limits.

"Well, I'm going to go. Thanks again," I say to Luke. "Shit, where's my phone? I need an Uber." I look around to where Bruno originally had me, and I see it skidded off to the cobblestone path. Thank God it didn't fall in the water.

"Where are you staying?" Luke asks.

"Oh." Gulp. "Gulf Sands and Suites, over near the beach."

His face lights up. "No way. My mom works there. I can give you a ride."

"Get out! Small world!" Getting smaller. I have to get out of here. "Thanks, but it's not necessary. I'm leaving now. Stay and have fun." I look at the girl. "Nice meeting you."

Thankfully, the Uber is only a few minutes out, and I'm settled back in the hotel in just about fifteen minutes.

It's late, I'm tired, and I have a lot to do tomorrow. I take off the jeans and throw them into a pile with everything else in the corner of the room. I hate packing and unpacking, and usually just leave things in piles until I have to ball it all up and leave. In the bathroom, I let the water run super hot and wash my face, then I pull my hair back into a bun.

I got out of the night unscathed. A near miss with Bruno, and then again with Luke. Things are going my way.

I'm about to crawl into bed but see the hotel phone staring at me, ominous, laughing at me. Blinking at me. Blinking *red* at me. There's a message. I'm convinced it's housekeeping, asking me if I want turndown service or more towels or whatever—I *did* have the *Do Not Disturb* sign on the door most of the day. Still, my finger shakes when I hit the button, because deep down, I know. And I hear that voice.

I know where you are, Zoey.

Shit. I might be looking for my father, but I'm also running from something else.

CONVERSATION BETWEEN PEPPER
AND ZOEY SIX WEEKS AGO

Zoey: I want to know why he left you.

Pepper: I—I can't say it. It's too embarrassing.

Zoey: You have to give me something to go on. You want me to think he's an asshole and stop looking? Tell me something.

Pepper: It wasn't just that. I was complicated when I was eighteen. I was pretty and popular, and everyone loved me. I was head cheerleader. I dated the captain of the football team all through high school. He—I really messed things up with him.

Zoey: Yes, you've told me. The one that got away. And ugh, you were one of *those* girls.

Pepper: Yes, I was. And I know how much you despise them. So, imagine one of them being rejected by someone who told them nothing but lies about their future. Marriage. Kids. I was deceived.

Zoey: So what? You were a teenager manipulated by another teenager. It's not that big of a deal.

Pepper: You don't know what you're talking about—it was a big deal to me. Not only that, he left me for someone else. And there's more people involved than you know.

19

Nightmares grip my brain instead of sleep. Around five a.m., I get up and throw on the provided robe that's hanging in the closet and sit on the tiny balcony. I don't have view of the Gulf—not even a sliver. In fact, I'm on a low floor, third floor out of twenty, and facing the parking lot. Thankfully, the hotel is big and tucked off onto its own property, and not on a highway, so there isn't a lot of traffic noise.

The message left for me last night has me on edge. I stare at the daytime churning its way from the darkness, the cool way the sky goes from black to blue, the way the moon fades into oblivion in the distance. I think of my mother.

Mom was right when we had that conversation about finding my father a few months ago—I didn't grow up wanting for anything. Anything except her affection, of course, but those stars in her eyes always came first. Sure, we weren't flush with cash—I didn't get a BMW with a bow on it for my seventeenth birthday. Hell, I still don't even own a car—I walk or take the subway everywhere, the occasional Uber if I get paid from my retail job that week. But I was loved as much as a narcissist like her was able. Selfish and absentee as she was, she cared for me, and I always had clothes and shoes that fit, even if they weren't Gucci. I don't mind a hoodie from the Gap or ripped jeans from American Eagle. I'm more of a sneakers girl anyway. Growing up on asphalt kind of beats into your brain that you need sensible shoes all the time.

As I grew older, when I had my first crushes, I noticed that even when my mother dated someone, she lacked the sparkle that I had, and I didn't know shit about love. There was always something missing in her eyes. Whether that feeling was lost when she left Vince or my father, I still don't know.

Back then, we were like sisters, really, since we weren't so far apart in age—she was still in her early thirties by the time I was in high school. My grandmother had already died, and my grandfather's dementia had just started to rear its ugly head, so she and I hung out when we could. She had less help watching me, but I also didn't need it as much. We did the brunch thing, the mani-pedi thing. I thought she told me everything.

My mother had many secrets, it turns out.

I'm like her in so many ways.

It's barely dawn, but I'm wide awake. There's one of those little single-serve pod coffee machines on the desk, so I go inside and rifle through the choices—regular, dark roast, and vanilla. Gross—the smell of vanilla makes me gag. I fill the machine with tap water, pop in a regular pod, and wait for the Styrofoam cup to fill. My mind drifts back to the nightmares.

One very vivid one had me and my mother and two other faceless people in a screaming fight—I don't remember about what, but I remember it was unsettling. Another had me hitting a tree in a car accident—that one scared me the most. When I shot up out of bed, I had to touch myself on my head, my shoulders, my legs—just to make sure I was still in one piece.

After my coffee and a shower, it's still early—before eight a.m. The library doesn't open until ten. I consider driving to Scarlett's house, but she'll probably take out a restraining order if I show up. Especially if Luke is there and she finds out we were in the same place last night. My story with Scarlett is far from over, though.

I rummage through my purse and find the two cards—one for Detective Watson and another for Detective Logan, although his is more of a calling card since he's retired. It's thinner than Detective Watson's and doesn't have that fancy raised lettering. Screw it. I call him.

He answers immediately and doesn't even have that I-just-woke-up gravelly voice.

"Hello?"

I clear my throat. I haven't spoken yet, despite the coffee, and probably do have that sound to my voice. "Hi, Detective Logan? This is Zoey Wilson."

"Miss Wilson. Surprised to hear from you. What can I do for you?"

I exhale. "I'm not sure. I came here with one intention. Well, two really. I feel like I haven't gotten any answers on who my father is or what happened that night with the accident. You told me something about it never sat right with you, but we never got into details, and I never got answers from my mother. Do you have any time today to see me? I leave tomorrow night, and I just feel like this whole trip has been a waste of time."

"Is that right? I thought—I thought Vince Russo was your father?"

"He's not." My voice cracks as I say it. "The paternity test said no match."

"Oh."

The word hung thick in the air, like glue, sticky and messy.

"Detective?"

"Right. Okay. I have some time around noon if you want to meet for a quick coffee?"

He gives me an address of a café in town, and I'm ecstatic that my day is already picking up. So much so that I decide to go to the library and sit in the parking lot and wait for it to open.

I don't mind the wait. I'm able to pass the time scrolling through gossip on social media, see what my friends have been up to while I've been gone. My Instagram is full of pictures of my friends together—at restaurants, at houses, a few twirling in the flurries that started last night. Thank God I'm in Florida. I comment on everyone's pictures and finally post my own collection I've made in the last couple of days—sunsets, palm trees, sunglasses, the pool. Fuck it, I might as well let the cat out of the bag.

Apparently, everyone knows where I am anyway.

CONVERSATION BETWEEN PEPPER
AND ZOEY SIX WEEKS AGO

Zoey: Who else is involved, Mom?

Pepper: It's better you don't know. There was a big group of us back then. You know how the cliques are.

Zoey: Yeah, I know how *your* cliques were. I don't get involved with that fake-ass bullshit. Let me guess. You hated all your friends.

Pepper: No, not true. I had a best friend. Scarlett Kane. We were inseparable all through middle school and high school. We did everything together.

Zoey: So where is she now?

Pepper: I don't know. We lost touch.

Zoey: How is that even possible? There were cell phones and email twenty years ago.

Pepper: I came here. She stayed there.

Zoey: So what? Anna's mother's best friend lives in Boston, and they see each other all the time.

Pepper: It was a complicated set of circumstances.

Zoey: You keep saying that. What could've happened that made you never speak to her again?

Pepper: She was probably better off without me.

20

When a little white Honda hatchback pulls into the lot, I stir. Yes, it's the librarian, and yes, they have a reputation for a reason—I'd be able to pick her out of a lineup of career choices. Tall, slender, fifties, bun, glasses, *I rescued my cat* magnet stuck to her bumper—all such a cliché, but here we are. I wait until two minutes after she puts the key in the lock and then I practically bum-rush the door. Why, I have no idea. There are no other people, no line, but they're only open until two. If people are going to start showing up in droves, I need to be the first to get help.

I'm accosted by the smell of books. Old books, new books, paper, ink. I approach the desk. The Bun smiles at me and calls me *dear* when she asks what I need. So cliché.

"Hi. I called here last week asking about old yearbooks for Gulf West? I'd like to see the years 1996 through 1999, please."

"Of course! They'll be filed away in our periodical room." The Bun nods to the left. "It's a bear of a room. We're one of only two libraries in the whole state that keeps the hard copies of Sunday edition newspapers too. There's a ladder on wheels if you need to get anything up top. We just ask that you wear the provided gloves while going through all those things. They're pretty rare, you know. There are boxes of gloves throughout the whole room."

I'm already nodding like a bobblehead, not believing my luck. "Thank you, I really appreciate it."

"May I ask what you're looking for? In case you need help with anything?" She asks with a smile, not fishing for anything sinister.

I give her a huge grin back. "Well, I'm visiting from New York, and my mother grew up here, so I want to look over her old things so I can embarrass her about the way she dressed and stuff," I lie. She doesn't need morbid details about her being hit by a car. "Also, I'm a journalism major. Now that I know the old newspapers are in there, I'd like to see the difference in reporting then versus now. The media is so different, and I need to know what I'm in for. Maybe I'll make it my dissertation for graduation." I'm not in graduate school. She doesn't need to know that.

She claps her hands together, and she reminds me of my grandmother, when she was alive. Grammy Helen used to do that all the time. "How wonderful! Smart girl. I hope you find what you're looking for. Oh, and no flash photography. If you want to take pictures of any pages or documents, make sure the flash is turned off."

"Will do." I salute her and wink, then head to the periodicals room.

The door slides open like a barn door, and the room is at least three stories high. There are only two floors, but the first floor is enormous and taller than it should be. Toward the back, I see a wire staircase that leads to the loft. There are skylights, but they're shaded to filter the sun. The lights are on, but they aren't harsh fluorescent lights. Soft, almost baby blue in nature. The room glows.

I don't know where to begin, and for a second, I forget why I'm there—the place has me in such awe. The table in front of me has hand sanitizer, which I use, and a box of gloves, which I put on once my hands are dry. I start on the left and decide I'll make a full lap to familiarize myself with the place. Two-thirds of the way around the first floor, I see yearbooks, so I stop. I scan the old, leather-bound spines—all in perfect condition. I have to climb the ladder to find the ones from the nineties, and there they are. I take all four off the shelf and head straight for a table.

Even though I really, really want to start with her senior year, I begin with her freshman year, flipping right to the Ws. I find her. Lord, she was beautiful. She looked a lot like I do now—dark hair, fair skin, hazel eyes that I can see even though the underclassmen photos are black and white—but she had that something extra. Exotic? Is that the term I'm looking for? Sneaky? Fierce. She looked fierce.

Of course, next I look up Vince, who looks the same except more of a beanpole in this picture. His hair is flopped over his face and he's wearing—is that a turtleneck? Ha. If he was my father and I had a relationship with him, I'd make fun of him. But he's not my father.

Then I look up Scarlett. I almost don't recognize her and have to check her name twice. Braces. Curls. No mastery of a brow brush. I snicker.

I go through all the candid shots at the back to see if I can find out anything, but all I see is my mom and Scarlett on the "pep team," which is what they called the underclassmen. Only juniors and seniors were allowed to be called cheerleaders. Vince was on junior varsity as a freshman. All the full color candid shots seem to be of the seniors. Nothing to see here.

I go through their sophomore and junior years, just to see their age progression. Scarlett started getting pretty, Vince started getting hot, and my mother became jaw-dropping gorgeous. Vince was now on varsity, and my mother and Scarlett were cheerleaders.

Finally, the moment I'm waiting for. Senior year.

I open the book, and on the first page of pictures, I see Julian, the kid Chloe killed, and Juliet Ackers. The Juliet I met a few days ago looks about the same now, minus the goth. Julian was good-looking, like Juliet, but in a not-cookie-cutter way. His dark hair, obviously dyed from a box, hung longer than it should've been. He had light blue eyes, and even holding his cap and wearing his gown, he had a look that screamed goth, with his black nail polish, just like his sister at that age. I go to Chloe Michaels. She had a bright, cheery smile. Her hair was blonde, and her eyes were blue. It's the first time I feel the tragedy of two young lives lost.

"What happened that night, Chloe?" I whisper out loud.

I flip to Scarlett, and there she is, fully transformed. Soft strawberry-blonde waves, big, round brown eyes, and a smile that proved the braces paid for themselves. Her lips were glossed pink, and her cheeks were blushed perfectly over her peaches-and-cream complexion. A high school princess, for sure. I flip to the queen.

There's my mother. The word I think of now is *vixen*. No wonder Vince was wrapped around her finger back then—she was stunning. Her hair was long, dark, and lush, with slight auburn highlights that trailed to—what's that? Hot pink?—at the tips. Her smile is more of a smirk, and her eyes are undressing everyone. Her senior quote? "I'd like to thank the Academy . . ." This isn't the first time I feel like I've ruined her life.

I go to Vince, and he looked the perfect counterpart. All-American, blond, blue eyed, athletic. Clear skin, perfect teeth, and chiseled. This was her boyfriend for the better part of four years. Why did she cheat on him? And with whom?

I immediately flip to the back, where the sports photos are, and my mother is on the top of the pyramid, arms in the air, on Scarlett and Chloe's backs. Vince is holding the football in front of all his teammates. The elite.

The candid pictures tell me a lot more.

I see a ton of pictures of my mother and Vince—homecoming king and queen, of course, and she told me she was the prom queen, but the yearbook was obviously printed before prom and those pictures didn't make it in. There are pictures of people in groups in the hallway, sometimes candid, sometimes smiling for the camera. When my mother was in them, it was usually with the same people. Sometimes Vince had his arm around her, and she leaned into him, comfortable. Sometimes you could count the inches of distance between them, even if his arm was still around her. Body language.

I studied the same people and wrote down their names. Some guy, Chris Parker, was in all the photos with all of them. Sometimes he smiled a toothy grin. Other times, he was in the background staring. Was he looking at Scarlett or my mother? I couldn't tell, so I flipped back to look him up. He was another all-American, dark hair and light eyes, meaty build. His senior quote? "Let the good times roll. Love you, Chloe. BFF, Vince."

Chris was Chloe's boyfriend. He was Vince's best friend.

I need to speak to him.

CONVERSATION BETWEEN PEPPER
AND ZOEY SIX WEEKS AGO

Zoey: Scarlett was better off without you, why? All teenagers lie. It's a badge of honor.

Pepper: Lie, yes. But my lies—anyway. It's part of the reason I don't want you digging this up.

Zoey: What's the big secret? You lied to your boyfriend? It was twenty years ago. It couldn't have been that bad.

Pepper: It was.

21

I check the time on my phone—I still have an hour until I have to meet Detective Logan, so I head to the newspapers section of the room. The papers are filed away in long custom-made drawers, and they hang over a metal rod in date order. I don't know the exact day they all graduated, but it had to be sometime in early June 1999. I head right for that month.

With gloved hands, I carefully lift each newspaper out, reading until I find what I need. It wasn't front-page news, but it got a sidebar, so I look further.

DEADLY CRASH—TWO LOCAL TEENS KILLED

On the evening of June 10, an accident claimed the lives of two local teenagers, Chloe Michaels and Julian Ackers, both 18. Initial reports suggest Michaels was intoxicated and lost control of the car, slamming into an unsuspecting Ackers in Rockland Park. Interviews with other students the next day alleged that Michaels had been drinking heavily at the senior picnic, an annual fair most students go to after graduation.

*Early evidence found in the car indicates that alcohol
was a factor.*

*Michaels was due to start her freshman year studying
design in Savannah. Ackers worked at his father's restaurant, Dockside Grille.*

Anyone with further information should call the tip line.

I think of what my mother said to me a couple months ago, how
there were more people involved with her situation surrounding
the end of senior year. With my father. The only reason my mother
kept me—the reason I'm alive at all—is because of this accident.
It was that big. That meaningful.

I read the article again and again, trying to make sense of it. I
take a picture of it with my cell phone—no flash, of course—and
save it for later. Then I look through the papers for the two weeks
following the accident, to see if I can find anything interesting. Most
related news is about their funeral services. Chloe's toxicology came
back over the legal limit. Slam dunk.

Seems pretty cut-and-dried. But then yesterday morning I
found out that Vince was suspected of—of what? Which means
something was amiss. They wanted his shoes? I check the time
again. It's almost time to leave and have a very frank talk with
Detective Logan. And I also need to research this Chris Parker
character.

In another quick scan I spot an article about the upcoming
Fourth of July fair. It was the first time there was a fair in the
county since the senior picnic. Detective Logan was interviewed.

*"We're going to have patrolmen everywhere for tonight's fair.
Drinking and driving will not be tolerated. Messing with
a crime scene will not be tolerated."*

Asked to elaborate, Logan said, "I cant discuss anything publicly."

No one wants a repeat of last month's fatal accident that claimed the lives of two teenagers after graduation. According to rumors from those close to the situation, the detective was pressured to close the case, despite instinct telling him there was more to the accident.

Well, well, well.

I put everything neatly away, even aligning the bottoms of the newspapers together on the metal bars in their drawers. I throw out my gloves in a nearby trash can, then use hand sanitizer again and salute The Bun when I leave.

As I drive to the café to see Detective Logan, I wonder what he'll tell me. I wonder what he really thinks about the note my mother wrote? Initially, it was enough to get Detective Watson to meet with us. But now—now, I don't know.

The café is on the beach, and I'm about five minutes early. I order a decaf and sit outside. The tables overlook the bay, not the gulf. It's peaceful. Still, I wrap my scarf around my shoulders—definitely not Brooklyn in January, but today a cold snap has come into west Florida. I hear they come in quick and only last a day or so, but that doesn't help me since I'm leaving tomorrow night. Back to the cold. Back to Brooklyn. Back to figuring out what to do and where to live. These past few days have been a nice escape from my head and my feelings about the last few months. If I let myself think about it for too long, I'll cry. Best to keep moving and deal with life-altering decisions when I have the right headspace for them.

Detective Logan spots me from the back door and ambles over, coffee in hand. He's wearing one of those adorable old man caps, and he takes it off and places it on the table, then pulls sunglasses from his shirt and puts them on.

"Zoey," he says with a smile and offers a hand, which I shake. "I'm glad you called."

"Really?"

"Yeah. I wasn't happy with Watson's dismissal of the whole situation. Sure, they were doing me a favor by digging out the box. Respect for me giving that place almost forty years of my life, I guess. But I remember those interviews. There was something off about a few of the kids." He takes a sip of his coffee, then curls his lip as if to say *too hot* and puts it back down. "Your mother being one of them."

"Oh." I gulp. I knew it. What did she do? "Why?"

He shakes his head. "I can't place it. She came off smug. She flirted with me. She was more concerned with me knowing her hopes and her dreams about being an actress than she was about the fact that two of her classmates were just tragically killed. Chloe was her friend, and she didn't seem upset. At all."

I chuckle. "Yeah, that sounds typical of her. I guess she didn't change much, and she never did get that Oscar. But how could she?" I look down in shame. "She had me instead."

He nods. "It was a surprise when you told me your mother was pregnant at the end of senior year. She was injured too, without an explanation. Her, and that friend of hers. I remember her, and all the kids, saying that she and Mr. Russo were on and off the entire time through school. So I was even more surprised when you told me he isn't your father, and she didn't mention another boyfriend. Her best friend, Scarlett, didn't mention another boyfriend either."

"That's what's got my head a mess, Detective. She never told me who my father was before she died. She lied to me and said she graduated high school in New York, but I found her

Florida diploma. When I found that letter, I knew to go right to Scarlett because they were obviously close. And Scarlett lied to me from the start too—failed to mention she was married to Vince. I thought I'd come here and get answers, but now I just have more questions." I sip my decaf. Gross. "I was originally going to come here just to find out who my father was, but now everyone is being weird about that accident. You saw the letter. Detective, I know something else happened. I read an article from the paper about the July Fourth fair. You mentioned the crime scene being tampered with." I close my eyes and rub my temples. "Why did you suspect Vince of anything?"

Detective Logan shrugs. "Same. Smug. Uncaring. His father was the deputy mayor and made a big stink. I tried to press for details, and the people above my head shut it down once Chloe's toxicology came back. They said she was drunk, and that was it. But Julian's blood was found some twenty feet away. I don't know how it got there. Still baffles me."

I gulp. "Wasn't he—pinned? I mean, could it have splattered?"

"Doubtful. The blood was only on his head. He had bad internal injuries, which is probably what got him in the end, but no, the car didn't split him open, if that's what you're thinking." He sips more coffee. "I mean, Chloe was Vince's best friend's girlfriend. And to complicate things, Scarlett also had a history with Chris."

"Really?" Really now. Scarlett used to date her cheating husband's best friend? Oh yes, I'm definitely crashing this guy's house later. "And there was something about Vince's shoes, you said yesterday morning?"

"Yep. He came straight to the station from Chris's house. Chris hosted an after-party, and Vince stayed over. But Chris said he disappeared at some point. And his shoes were caked with mud. I wanted them tested, but no one back then wanted to listen to me. About the scene."

"There was more?"

"Around the car, the scene seemed to have been purposely, I don't know. Combed over? To erase footprints. Fingerprints. The passenger-side door handle was wiped clean. If this was an accident with an irresponsible drunk driver in the middle of the night, accidentally killing another classmate, I don't know why the outside of the car looked like it did. On the ground. Pristine." He sighs and takes another sip. "The tire marks, too. No rubber shedding from the brakes. But no one listened to me. Once Vincent Russo Senior started barking orders, that arrogant little son of his walked out without another question."

This whole thing feels like a cover-up. Something else happened that night. And with only a day left in Florida, I have to find out what it was.

CONVERSATION BETWEEN PEPPER
AND ZOEY SIX WEEKS AGO

Pepper: Look, I'm being dramatic. You know how I get.

Zoey: Yes, I know how you get. Under pressure.

Pepper: There's no pressure.

Zoey: You're lying. You know what, Mom, you're not *that* good of an actress. What did you lie about that was so bad?

Pepper: I lied to make someone do something stupid. I was a scared kid, with an unplanned pregnancy. I did what I had to do.

22

I thank Detective Logan for his candor and decide not to tell him about the conversation I had with my mother, when she told me she lied about something back then. It could be completely unrelated. At this point, how would they even find out if that's true or not? She could've just been waxing poetic. She *was* a bit of a drama queen.

When I get back to the car, I sit inside and research Chris Parker. It's a common name, so I get a whole bunch of hits in Florida. There are three who fit the age I'm looking for—one is near Miami, one on the Panhandle, and one about ten minutes from where I'm sitting. Crossing my fingers, I decide to take a chance and plug the address into the map feature on my phone.

On the ride, I decide how to approach the whole thing. What if his wife or kids answer? I can't be all *Hi, I'm here to talk to your husband to see if his friends from high school were involved in a possible murder.* Imagine that. And what if it's not the right guy anyway? What if the Chris Parker I'm looking for moved to Miami? Or even Chicago, or the West Coast? I'm probably barking up the wrong tree. But if I'm going to be a journalist, I should get used to knocking on random doors and confronting the people who live there with heavy questions.

Of course, I know I made the right choice as soon as I turn down the street. It's a row of two-story townhouses, and parked in the driveway is a van—with lettering on the side that reads *Parker & Russo Pools*. Luke told me that Vince owned a pool company. Chris isn't only his best friend from high school; it seems they're also business partners.

I park the car across the street and walk over, up the asphalt driveway. The outside of the place has a brick façade, beige in color, with black shutters surrounding the windows, and the landscaping is well kept, with shrubs and a couple of colorful flowers. I look up at Chris's condo—there's movement in an upstairs window.

When I get to the door, I take a deep breath before I hit the bell. It chimes throughout, loud enough to make me feel like I'm inside, and feet reverberate down the steps. Then the door opens, and this is definitely the right guy—he looks almost the same as the yearbook photo, although with a little less hair and a little more stomach. He's wearing a flannel shirt and jeans, and his eyes go wide when he looks at me.

"Hi, sorry," he says. "Can I help you?"

Yeah, it's him. I gather up my confidence the best I can.

"Chris Parker?"

"Yes."

"Yes, you can help me, and I believe you knew my mother. My name is Zoey Wilson, and my mother was Pepper Wilson. Can I come in and talk for a minute?"

He stares. "Oh my God. You're Zoey. Vince told me you were here when I was out with him the other night. The resemblance to your mother is uncanny." He holds the door open. "Yes, come on in."

I enter the foyer, and he closes the door behind me. The place is fully furnished but not fully decorated. The couches don't match the chairs, and I don't see any photos or decorative knickknacks anywhere. I follow him to the kitchen, and he gestures toward the table, a long wooden thing with a leather-covered bench on each side and two proper chairs at each end. I climb over the bench and take a seat. Chris is clearly divorced or has never been married. He wears no wedding ring, and nothing about the house is warm and inviting. No woman's touch.

Nothing but a photo on the wall of him and Luke, of all people. They have an arm around each other, each with a golf club in their other hand. The tee flag is behind them on the green. They must be close, having all grown up together. I'm not supposed to know Luke, so I don't ask him about it.

"Can I get you anything?" he asks.

My mouth is as dry as the Sahara. "Yes, I'll just take some water." I look around. "I bet you're wondering why I'm here."

He grabs a bottle of water from the refrigerator and hands it to me, then one for himself and sits down at the head of the table. "A little. I mean . . . I was with Vince Friday night. So, I know what's going on."

"Have you spoken to him since then?"

He nods. "He texted me this morning. Him and Scarlett and their son are coming here for a barbeque."

"Oh. So, you know, then? That he's not my father?"

"Yes, he told me."

I pause, but I have to ask. "Do you know who is?"

He takes a long sip of water—too long, if you ask me—and shakes his head. "I really don't, Zoey. Vince and I talked about this at length on Friday night. We were both convinced it was him. He and your mom . . . man, he was really nuts over her." He pauses, and I know what he's going to say before it comes out of his mouth. "I'm really sorry to hear what happened to her. So was he. Devastated, to tell you the truth. He cried."

My eyes sting, but I move on. Big picture. "She told me that she loved my father."

He caps the water and chuckles. "Then she should've pursued the acting harder. You'd never be able to tell she was seeing anyone so seriously behind Vince's back. They were the perfect couple. Four years. I honestly thought they'd get married. Not . . ."

"Right," I interrupt. "Not him to Scarlett. Not to my mother's best friend." I look pointedly at him. "Not to your ex-girlfriend."

He puts his hands up defensively. "Whoa. Where'd you even hear that?"

"I'm a journalism major. I know how to find the story. Which is what I'm doing here."

"Look, Scarlett and I were never together. I guess she had a bit of a thing for me, and we hooked up once. But that's all that happened. I love Scarlett like a sister now. We've gotten closer over the years because I'm so close with their son, Luke. I never had kids when I was married. Doubt I ever will. I only have Luke. And she and Vince . . ." His voice trails off. "Scarlett is a saint, and Vince is lucky to have her. I was an idiot back then. Just a kid who made stupid mistakes." Another pause, and he's holding something back. "I was dating Chloe for almost a year and a half when everything went down."

"Yeah, can you tell me about that night? I've been hearing so many different things, from Julian's twin, from Scarlett and Vince, my mother, Detective Logan—I think something's missing about Chloe's death."

He looks down, in thought. Then he stands, goes back to the refrigerator, and grabs a beer. He nods at me as if to ask if I want one, and I shake my head and drink my water instead. I need a clear head. He saunters back to the table and sits down, unscrewing the cap and then snapping it across the room, right into the garbage. Athlete.

"It was a long time ago, Zoey. I don't think any of it matters anymore."

"But it does." I produce the letter out of my bag. "I found this going through my mother's things. Read it."

He places his beer directly on the table, even though there's a pile of coasters in the center, and reads the letter. "Huh. That's weird."

Finally. "Isn't it? Was there a different accident that night?"

"No. Not that I know of. I don't know, maybe there was, and since Chloe and Julian's accident got so much attention, maybe it was buried." He spits out Julian's name like it's acid in his mouth. "Chloe was cheating on me with that guy. That was the rumor, anyway. Who knew, right? Man, I felt like an idiot. But she didn't deserve to die. She was a good person."

"This is going to sound like a stupid question, but are you sure she was cheating on you?"

A puff of air comes out of his mouth, and he leans back, his hands behind his head. "I heard a lot of things that night. All my friends were in one section of the lot drinking when Julian came by. Vince got all out of control and pushed him and acted like an asshole, which honestly was par for the course back then. Vince thought Julian was looking at Pepper, and it always made him hotheaded when anyone looked at her. But Julian was obviously there to see Chloe. I can't even remember the first person who told me they heard a rumor about them, but I confronted her about it, and we fought."

"About what, though? Did you break up?"

"I was trying to get her to tell me what was going on." He sips his beer, then wipes his mouth on the back of his flannel. "Then everyone said there were calls to each other on their cell phones that night. They were definitely planning on meeting up. Where there's smoke, there's fire, I guess."

"You and Chloe broke up, then?"

He shrugs. "I don't know what we were. We were screaming at each other. I mean, she kept telling me it was complicated and she'd tell me everything the next day, that we were both too drunk to be rational about it. Basically, I remember telling her to fuck off, and I walked away." Another sip. A bigger one. "Nice, right? Those were my last words to my girlfriend before she died."

It's quiet for a minute. That had to be harsh. I look around. "You were married?"

He nods. "Yeah. Jennifer is my ex-wife. I have a girlfriend, Kelly, who honestly should be here any minute with the food. She's just shopping for the barbecue later."

"I see." He's ushering me out, and yet again, I've gotten nowhere. "You really don't know who my father is?"

"I'm sorry, Zoey. I have no idea. Pepper acted strangely the last few months of high school. One day she's all over Vince, the next she hates him and breaks up with him. It went on forever. And Vince . . . well, he was just too far gone." He lowers his voice. "He would've done anything for your mother. Between you and me right now, he still would. I don't think it's hit him yet. Her passing. He tried to find her for years. Even after he married Scarlett." He shakes his head. "I don't know what's wrong with him. He hit the jackpot with Scarlett, and still. First loves die hard, I guess."

Does this guy have a thing for Scarlett? Is that why he's so close to their son? I see the cracks in his friendship with Vince the more he talks.

"My mother legally changed her last name. To Zarra, with two Rs. And yeah, I heard Vince is no peach in the husband department." I scoff.

"Who told you that?"

Luke, but I obviously can't tell Chris that. "I just hear things, the more people I talk to."

"Vince turned out to be a stand-up guy for his son. Still, it was always Pepper he wanted. He proposed to Scarlett when he found out about her pregnancy, but I think that was because of a lot of pressure from his family. The family name, his father in local politics, all of that. He would've done it for Pepper, even at eighteen. He would've found a way to make it work. But I guess—well, I guess you're not his daughter anyway, so it doesn't matter."

I try to think what life would've been like if my mother shut her mouth and married Vince to keep up with appearances. If she would've told him she was pregnant, told him I was his, and married him. I would've thought my whole life that he was my dad, and I would've been wrong.

I hate my mother. If she were here right now, I'd scream at her. How could she do what she did to Vince, and never tell me about my real father? All kids need to know who their father is.

CONVERSATION BETWEEN PEPPER
AND ZOEY SIX WEEKS AGO

Zoey: You had an unplanned pregnancy, so you ran away. You could've raised me near my father.

Pepper: I wish I could've.

Zoey: All this time, you left me in limbo. I hate you.

Pepper: Calm down. You don't hate me. You're allowed to be mad, but you don't hate me. Look, we did fine. When I told you your father was an asshole, I meant it. Can you tell me, honestly, why all of a sudden this is such a sticking point for you? You never cared so much before.

Zoey: Because I'm pregnant. I have no idea who the father is. And kids deserve to know.

23

The front door opens, and bags rustle in the foyer. Heels click on the tile and then a woman, not much older than me, enters. She has big hair—very curly—and bangs that have frizzed, but underneath it, she's pretty. She just needs a flat iron, maybe one of those Brazilian blowouts. She stops at the entryway to the kitchen and looks at me, then tilts her head.

"Chris?"

"Hey, babe," he says as he stands and kisses her. "This is my girlfriend, Kelly," he says to me.

"Nice to meet you. Zoey Wilson." I hold out a hand, which she shakes after finagling the bags around and before Chris takes them from her arms.

"You're Zoey?" She eyes me suspiciously, nervously. "Is there anything we can do for you?"

So, they've talked about me. I look over at Chris. "Well, I'm sure you heard Vince isn't my father, so I still don't know who is. I know they were all friends in high school. I was just hoping Chris here had some answers for me. He doesn't."

She's standing like a deer frozen in headlights. "I—"

She's interrupted by the front door opening again, and I hear voices. I know them. All three of them.

Kelly looks at Chris. "I ran into them in the grocery store parking lot. They were picking up wine at Gulf Spirits, and I just told them to come straight here. I'm sorry. I didn't know—"

Scarlett, Vince, and Luke all walk into the kitchen. I close my eyes tightly because I know, I just know who's going to speak first.

"Zoey? Is that you?"

Yep. Luke says it first.

Scarlett and Vince both turn to him in disbelief. "Excuse me, how do you know her?" Scarlett spits.

Oh, he dealt me some drugs, no biggie. Luke looks at me nervously, his eyes darting between me and his parents and Chris and Kelly, who are also looking at him with interest now.

"We were at the same party last night," I say. "Actually, I'm glad to see you again, Luke. To thank you properly." I look at Scarlett in particular. "Someone got a little handsy with me last night and Luke stepped in. You've raised a fine young man." A fine young drug dealer who hates his father. Teenage angst, don't I remember. I can't get in the middle of whatever this is. "I've really got to go."

Scarlett blocks my passage. "What are you doing here? How do you even know Chris? Why have you been hounding my whole family?" Her finger points toward my face. "Stay away from my son."

"I just wanted to know if Chris had any information on my father. I know you were all friends back in the day."

"Well, as you can see, we still are."

"Don't worry, Scarlett. My plane leaves tomorrow night. You'll never have to see me again."

"Good."

"Scarlett," Vince says, a warning to his voice.

"Dad, Jesus, why are you being such a jerk?" Luke jumps in. "I guess a better question is, how do *you* guys know Zoey?"

Scarlett looks resigned, like she knows she has to tell him. I remember from last night that he said he overheard a conversation about this. He doesn't know it's me they were talking about.

"Because, Luke," Scarlett starts. "Your father dated her mother all through high school. She came here because she thought he was her father. We had a paternity test done. Don't worry, it's not him."

Scarlett really is vicious. Now she's resorted to hurting her son just to get to me?

And, out of nowhere, I start to cry.

It's all getting to me. The last two months. Everything about them. And here I am, in a house full of strangers that know something about me, and no one is saying a thing. I feel attacked, and in the state I'm in with my own pregnancy, I really can't deal with this.

"Look, I'm leaving," I say through sobs. "I just wanted to know who my father is. To tell him . . . to tell him he's going to be a grandfather. I'm pregnant, and I don't even know where I came from."

A silence hushes over everyone at the same time. I don't even have the courage to look up and see them all staring at me, because I know it'll be with pity. They'll all be thinking *poor girl with no parents, now a single parent herself.* When I lift my head, there's a softness on Scarlett's face.

Now, she sees her former best friend, not only in looks but in the same situation. Knocked up, unmarried, and too young. Or maybe she sees herself. The same damn thing happened to her, not much older than me. She got a ring and a family, flawed as it is. I have no one.

"Zoey, I really, truly don't know who your father is, if it isn't Vince," Scarlett says. "I swear she didn't tell me anything."

I nod. I believe her. Right now, I think she'd tell me the truth.

"I have to go," I say.

"I'm sorry we couldn't be more help to you. Take care of yourself back in New York."

Her voice is lower, less edge to it. I awkwardly look at everyone and actually throw up a hand and wave. There's nothing else to say.

"I'll walk you to your car," Luke says.

No one objects, because they can't right now. No one asked me to stay and have a barbecue with them, to act like some pseudo family, but they'll let Luke walk me out because it's the decent thing to do. The door closes behind us.

"Thanks for covering for me. With my parents," he says.

"Yeah, well, I wouldn't rat out my little brother," I say with a laugh, and he chuckles. I don't want him to know I knew who he was anyway. What point would that serve? "Don't worry. I didn't smoke any of that stuff last night. I was just trying to fit in."

"I hear you. And I'm sorry for what you're going through. If you ever just want to talk or whatever, you can call me. If I hear anything through closed doors about your father, I can let you know."

"Really? That would be great."

I give him my phone number, and we say goodbye. I get into the blue car and drive back to the hotel. I'm starving and decide I'll order room service when I get there. I've been out and about all day. Between the library, Detective Logan, and the pregnancy—and having to survive on decaf the past couple of months—it hasn't left me with a ton of energy.

My own baby's father could be anyone. Well, that's not true, but there are three candidates. Unfortunately, Tristan isn't one of them. I took that breakup hard, and here we are. I took Anna's advice of *The best way to get over someone is to get under someone else.* In one month, there were two Tinder hookups who I never messaged with again, and a party with a guy whose first name could either be Nick or Rick or Rich.

When I found out I was pregnant, quick math told me it's probably Tinder hookup number two. I guess I can try to contact him, just to let him know. He deserves to know, even if I've already made the decision. I just wanted to find out about myself first. A small part of me thinks maybe I'll change my mind and keep it. But I have no one.

Back at the hotel, I order room service and lie on the bed, staring at the ceiling.

Thirty minutes later, there's a knock on the door. I jump up and look through the peephole.

Oh fuck. It's not room service.

Fuck fuck fuck fuck fuck.

Three loud bangs on the other side. "Open the door, Zoey. I hear you moving around."

I lean my head onto the door to try to gain confidence. I open it, and she's standing there, and it's still like looking into a mirror.

"Hi, Mom. What brings you to Florida?"

CONVERSATION BETWEEN PEPPER
AND ZOEY LAST WEDNESDAY

Pepper: We need to talk about this. We need to come up with a plan, Zoey. You can't just run away every time I bring up the baby.

Zoey: I'm staying at Anna's for a couple of days. Don't bother me.

Pepper: Anna isn't going to help you raise the baby if you decide to keep it. I am. You need to let me in.

Zoey: I'm not keeping it, and I don't have to let you anywhere. You're still lying to me. I found a letter in that box of crap with your diploma. One you wrote to someone named Scarlett Kane. Months ago, you told me that you lied about something bad. The letter said you survived an accident and that's the only reason you kept me. I need some time away from you. You're a liar. A liar who didn't want me.

Pepper: Please, Zoey. Please just stop.

Zoey: I need to talk to that Scarlett person, or someone else.

Pepper: Don't you dare. No one in Florida needs to know where I am or what my life has been like.

Zoey: Fine. If I ever talk to anyone, I'll just tell them you're dead.

PART 3

A LOVELY LIE

24

PEPPER

The Uber turns into Gulf Sands and Suites, and I throw an extra five dollars at the driver because I huffed and puffed the whole way—this guy and his fucking speed limit. I told him I was in a rush; doesn't he know who I am? I open the door and exit in a mad dash after grabbing my small bag and the airport flowers.

Hotels never give out room numbers, they only connect you to leave a message, so I have to use my superb acting skills. Thankfully, Cara LaFleur, my character on *All My Children*, had to do something like this a decade ago. I'm still convinced they could've brought me back from the dead, or made me an evil twin, but of course the show got canceled.

The lobby is massive but not altogether busy, which is perfect for me. I dump my overnight bag at a utility closet door near the elevators and look around until I find what I want. There's a nondescript blue ballcap on my head with my hair tied up inside and I'm wearing a gray hoodie zipped to my neck. I go right to the concierge, to the man in the seafoam-green polo shirt, look at his name tag, and smile. I go into my character like the director is giving me notes. *Time to manipulate him and get what you want. Aaaaaaaaand action!*

"Hi, Hector." I place the flowers on the desk. "Delivery for a guest. Zoey Wilson. These need to be delivered to the room as soon as possible. My boss is going to kill me if these don't get there before six. It has to do with this whole surprise someone has planned for her. God, I think it's a surprise engagement or birthday party or something big. They have to be waiting at her door when she gets back. If you can just bring these up and leave them at the foot of the door?"

I give him that face, the one I perfected as a teen, the one that puts men in a trance. The damsel in distress face, and most men want to be heroes even though I'll be damned if someone thinks I need saving.

"Sure, no problem. I'll get one of the porters right away," Hector says.

"Great!" I'm so overenthusiastic, almost like I played a flower delivery person in a bit part once before, but no, I need better billing than that. "My truck is idling out front. Don't want to get towed! Have a great night, Hector."

I turn and go through the automatic doors, to the left by the smoking pole, take off the cap and unzip the hoodie. I'm wearing a lacy lime-green tank top underneath, something loud, something noticeable, something they'd never think the frumpy delivery girl just wore—*frumpy* was never a word used to describe me. I wait thirty seconds and come right back in behind a family who just got out of a cab. A mom, a dad, a skulking teenager, and a ten-year-old boy, face caked with ice cream. Requisite St. Petersburg paraphernalia on their loudly colored shirts from that Wings store this place has on every two blocks on the beach. I glance at Hector as he hands the flowers to someone, and the guy heads to the elevator.

I glide over, pick up my bag, and wait. When the door opens, I step in first and dig through my purse, making all sorts of *oh shit* noises. The guy uses his key card to access the guest rooms and presses the button for the third floor.

"Oh, thank God we're going to the same one! I can't find anything in here!" I exclaim, all too cheery again. I can act like a dumb blonde stereotype if I need to. I have professional training, for God's sake.

When the doors open, he gestures for me to go out first. I cross my fingers and make a right as he makes a left down the hall. I duck into the corridor with the ice machine and the vending machine, and even fish out a couple of bucks to get a bottle of Diet Coke, praying to God that Zoey has a minibar. It should be stocked with little bottles of rum, which better be fucking full because if she's drinking while pregnant, I'll kill her, even if she's not planning on keeping it.

I hear movement and the elevator bell ding, the doors opening, then closing, and the hum of it going back down in the distance. I exit the cubbyhole where I'm hiding and go down the opposite hall until I see the flowers.

I pound on her door three times. There's a shadow on the bottom, and I hear her inside.

"Open the door, Zoey. I hear you moving around."

She opens the door like we're back in Brooklyn and I need to use the shower in the only full bath in our apartment. Nonchalant.

"Hi, Mom. What brings you to Florida?" she says.

I push my way in and slam the door behind me, then drop my bag and put the Diet Coke on the neighboring desk. "Jesus Christ,

Zoey. I knew it. I knew you were here. Thank God I can still track your phone."

She crosses her arms over her chest. "Great, Mom. I'm not a little kid."

"Then stop acting like one. You think it's fun for me to run all over the place looking for you?"

She scoffs. "I can't believe you actually came here. Like, got on a plane and followed me here."

"I can't believe *you* actually came here, and you weren't answering my calls. I told you a million times to leave this alone and that you weren't going to find out anything. Pack your shit. I'm bringing you home. You have more pressing things going on in your own life than digging into my past."

"Holy shit, Mom. This is my past too! I came here looking for my father! If you would've just told me who he is to begin with, none of this would've happened. I want to know why you're lying to me."

Zoey's voice catches—she's upset. Does she deserve to know? Probably. But she's going to regret finding out for the rest of her life. I've been protecting her. Yes, I've also been protecting myself. I've been protecting a lot of people, even though I started it.

But at least she's here, in the hotel room. She's not out investigating. There are no journals or papers scattered about the room. She's tan. She's probably been giving herself a little vacation and trying to give me a heart attack in the process just to fuck with me.

"You didn't even find anything, did you?" I ask. "I told you there was nothing to see."

Zoey smiles, that wicked smile she uses when she's about to say something that would've gotten her punished in high school. "Oh, don't you worry. I talked to plenty of people."

I gulp. She obviously didn't talk to the right ones. If someone told her something other than what I told the cops, they'd have put a warrant out for my arrest, and I never would've been able to leave New York state.

So, I play her game and shrug. "Like who?"

"Like Vince Russo."

Shit. I know my face goes white at his name, and I try my best to fake it. I'm an actress, after all. By now, she knows he was the high school boyfriend. Jesus, she talked to him? He's still here. My throat is dry, and I eye the Diet Coke I put on the desk when I walked in. I can't grab for it. She'll know that I'm reacting to his name, and I can't let her know.

I shrug again. No biggie. "My ex-boyfriend from high school. That's nice. How is he?"

"He's not my father, I know that much."

No, no he's not; no matter how much I wish the opposite were true. I screwed it all up. "So, he's good, then?"

Her eyes narrow and she laughs. "Why don't you go find out?"

"Fine. I will. Where is he?"

Zoey turns to the desk, opens the Diet Coke, and swallows half the can.

"All that high-fructose corn syrup isn't good for the baby," I say.

"Yeah, I know. You've mentioned that before, and I told you it doesn't matter. This is diet, though." She takes the pen from its holder and writes something on a piece of paper, then folds it and hands it to me. "Go ahead. Go over and talk to Vince. He's single, so no one will mind. And not for nothing, Mom, he's super hot. You should see where that goes. First love, and all." She tosses me a stack of keys. "You can even take my rental. It's the tiny bright-blue, ugly-looking thing in the second row of the visitor's lot. Has a rental tag."

Typical for someone her age, she lies. She's lied about the stupidest things, sent me on wild goose chases when she was supposedly at this friend or that friend's house after school. Like I had time for her bullshit in between running lines. Didn't she know I needed to be in a zone to perfect my timing? I couldn't be blamed for wondering whether it was her fault I got canned from *AMC* when I missed my cues toward the end. She was already ten or eleven by then—old enough to realize that Mommy needed to do what Mommy needed to do, and she needed to be more independent.

Still . . . the chance to see Vince? This could be catastrophic for him, and for me. "How do I know this is really his house?"

She smirks. "It's a townhouse. There's a van in the driveway. It says *Parker & Russo Pools.* You should leave now; I know for a fact he's there."

INTERVIEW THE DAY AFTER
THE SENIOR PICNIC

Detective Logan: How well do you know Chris Parker?

Pepper: He's Vince's best friend.

Detective Logan: And?

Pepper: And? What am I supposed to say? Oh, yeah. He's Chloe's boyfriend.

Detective Logan: So, you've all hung out for a long time. Four years for you and Vince, huh?

Pepper: On and off. I told you Detective Long One, I'm single.

Detective Logan: Logan. And Chloe was a close friend?

Pepper: Right. Logan. And yes, Chloe was a close friend.

Detective Logan: You don't seem too broken up by her death.

Pepper: I'm an actress. I'm acting okay with it. Do you really want me sitting here crying?

Detective Logan: Why didn't you go to Chris's party again?

Pepper: Tired.

Detective Logan: That's all? Head cheerleader, and you didn't go to the biggest party of the year?

Pepper: I didn't know it was a requirement for my final grades.

Detective Logan: Any other reason you would've stayed away?

Pepper: What are you asking?

Detective Logan: You tell me.

25

PEPPER

I rip the paper with Vince's address out of Zoey's hands and take the keys and leave. Stomping down the hallway, my blood pressure is through the roof. Zoey thinks she can come down here and talk to Vince about me? What did she say to him? I'd drag her ass with me to admit to the lies she's probably told, but honestly, I'd rather see him alone. It's something I've wanted for a long time, although I've never admitted it to anyone. I have a lifetime of regret about what I did to him back then. I see that regret more times than not when I look in the mirror. When I think of the past, of who I was back then. The horrible things I did.

I close my eyes and deep breathe like I'm preparing for an emotional scene, which I kind of am. I walk calmly into the elevator. Method acting—I'm playing the stress-free mom who just found her daughter, and everything is going to be all right. Zoey should rest anyway, while I try to come to terms with the fact that I'll be a grandma at forty if she changes her mind and decides to keep the baby.

I, for one, know that you can change your mind on a dime.

I find her car in the lot immediately—all I had to do was look for something that a kid who makes $250 a week at a boutique secondhand clothing store could afford. Plus, she said it was bright blue and ugly, so it's hard to miss. It's shockingly blue. I'm almost embarrassed getting into it, but then I remember this is the western coast of Florida, where people don't care much about status. This isn't Miami. It's definitely not New York.

This is my old life. Back for an hour, and I already miss it a little. The way people look at you and smile and say *how are you doing?* and mean it. The January weather, the ability to wear flip-flops everywhere instead of designer heels. Most of mine at home are knockoffs and even less comfortable.

I miss lots of things. Lots of people. But I still shouldn't be here.

I put the address into my phone because of course the car doesn't have GPS, and I see the route it wants to take. I know the area and knew some kids who lived in this neighborhood when I was younger. It's been over two decades, so I'm sure it's been updated. I hate to think of Vince, who always did anything for me, living in a run-down complex.

Zoey said he was single, and I wonder if he ever married or if he's just divorced. With or without kids? Admittedly, I never looked him up. I couldn't let it derail my budding career. Where I was going with my acting, Florida was not the place for me. Instead, I'd built this fantasy about him and what our lives would've been like if I didn't do what I did. If I didn't cheat on him. What was I thinking? I wonder what he looks like—if he lost his athletic build, or if he kept up with the workouts. He's probably bald and has a potbelly. Even though Zoey said he was super hot, I convince myself he's aged poorly, like so many other ex-athletes. I can't believe I'm about to see Vince Russo, who was my first everything. I treated him unfairly. He didn't deserve that.

He didn't deserve what came after, either.

What if there's a spark? I can't stay here, in Florida. Too many bad memories, even if it's only one major one. It will always outweigh the good. He'd have to come to New York.

Look at me getting ahead of myself.

I turn down the street and drive slowly until I see the van in the driveway. *Parker & Russo Pools.* I internally cringe thinking about Vince being partners with Chris Parker, but I dismiss that immediately. Even though they were best friends back then, Parker is a common name, and I'd bet my last dollar that Chris took off and never looked back after his girlfriend was killed. He certainly had reason to, just like I did.

Getting out of the car, I smooth myself down and prop up my boobs. Just in case. My stomach warbles heading up the driveway. Man, I can't wait to see his face when he sees me after all this time. I ring the doorbell and hear *I'll get it.* So, there's more than one person here. Footsteps approach and the door opens. A teenage boy is there, and oh my God, he looks exactly like Vince. I tingle and try to hide my shudder of shock. I guess Vince is divorced. It's probably his weekend with the kids.

"Hi," I say and clear my throat. "I'm actually looking for your father? Vince Russo?"

His eyebrows knot. "O-kay . . ." He drags it out, then calls over his shoulder. "Dad, it's for you?" He says it like a question, like it's so unusual that someone would be at the door asking for him.

"Huh? For me? Here?"

It's undeniably Vince's voice, one I still recognize after all this time. All the *I love you*s, the promises, the sex and grunting, the begging to have me back. All the complying.

He turns the corner, and our eyes meet. Yes, it's definitely him. Vince Russo. My first love. And it all comes back—the love, washing over me like a hurricane. At first, I'm not sure he recognizes me, and I half smile and give a little wave, but his hand goes over his mouth. Then he falls to his knees, crying.

Damn, I meant more to him than I thought. Why would that be his first reaction?

"Dad, are you okay?" the kid asks.

Vince is still on the ground, and I don't know what to do. I'm about to invite myself in and help when—

"Mom, come here, quick!" the kid screams.

Oh my God. Mom? So, Vince *is* married? Or is this a weekend kid exchange? I mean, it's after four on a Sunday. It could be. Or did Zoey lie to me, again, just to get me into this impossible situation? More likely.

Mom comes from around the same corner and sees Vince on the floor. She immediately runs to him and asks the kid what happened. Vince looks at me again, his teary eyes saying something I can't figure out. His hand is still over his mouth, and I see the wedding band.

His eyes are saying regret. I see it because it's the same thing I see in my own eyes half the time. Then he points, and Mom lifts her head to look at me and I get a clear view of his wife and—

It's Scarlett Kane.

No fucking way.

INTERVIEW THE DAY AFTER
THE SENIOR PICNIC

Detective Logan: Tell me again how you got home.

Pepper: My best friend drove me. Scarlett Kane.

Detective Logan: Right. And you were walking for a while?

Pepper: No. I never said that.

Detective Logan: You weren't on Three Bridges Road?

Pepper: No.

Detective Logan: That's weird. Scarlett said you were there together.

Pepper: Oh, was that the name of the road we were on? I get confused. Yes, we were there, then.

Detective Logan: It's the road that leads to the park where the accident happened. I assumed you'd remember.

Pepper: Well, Detective, you know what people say about assuming.

Detective Logan: Tell me how you got there. Under what circumstances.

Pepper: Scarlett's car wouldn't start.

Detective Logan: Really? Then how did she drive you home?

Pepper: No, wait. That's wrong. She was too drunk, so she didn't try to start the car. My mistake. We were going up the road to see if we could find a ride.

Detective Logan: How did you end up back at the fair to get her car?

Pepper: We walked back. No one was on the road to help us. So we left.

Detective Logan: Is that all?

Pepper: Wait. One car passed us, but they just beeped the horn and yelled out the window, probably on their way to the party. Some guys from the team. I saw Jordan Kessler, I think John Nelson, and Kurt Hyatt was probably driving. I know his car. You can ask them.

Detective Logan: That sounds incredibly familiar. Almost rehearsed.

26

SCARLETT

Senior Picnic
June 1999

"**Y**ou shouldn't be smoking and drinking in your condition, Pepper," I say disapprovingly. "You know that, right?"

Pepper tosses her cigarette out the window and sips her vodka, whipping her long, dark hair over one shoulder before tying it into a side braid so her pink streaks poke through.

"Does this look okay?" she asks, ignoring the question.

She already told me she was taking care of it—getting an abortion as soon as she gets to New York. "I want the pink streaks to show. I want to be a unicorn." She points to the clock on the dashboard. "Ugh. We're late."

It's June, usually a rainy month on the western Florida bay, but the blurred lines of heat radiate off the pavement as I speed Pepper's chariot to the annual fair. It's her last time to be seen for how fabulous she is before she leaves me, and the other peasants of Florida, to win her Oscar.

Swerving right, I park at the far end of the lot where most people are gathered, and everyone is hiding their vodka in Poland

Spring bottles and mixed drinks in Snapple bottles. It's the usual group—the football team, the cheerleaders, and those they deign to allow near them.

Pepper looks at me between chugs of her own water bottle. I try not to *tsk tsk* her—but there's still a baby in there. "Ugh, I see Chloe. What a loser," she says.

Loser? She's one of our better friends, but Pepper's been fickle lately, about everyone. For the better part of six months, if I think hard about it. I take a long swig of the vodka, letting the slow burn descend to my belly. "Come on. Stop."

She scoffs. "Haven't you noticed that she's turning into a friggin' weirdo? I mean, what's with all those dreary clothes lately? And that dark boxed dye job? Ick. Like, let's face it, the girl needs some help in the mug department. She should be dressing to look better, not worse. She needs to keep the attention off her face. All of that black and purple makeup is *woof*."

Despite myself, I chuckle as Pepper barks like a dog. It's hard not to get swept up in her opinions. Vince may be hopelessly in love with her, but I do everything she says too. She plucked me from obscurity when she moved here at the beginning of middle school seven years ago and took me under her wing. Instantly popular, I never want to rock the boat with her. Plus, I'm more comfortable following. Always have been. Our friendship is an odd pairing, but it works. Like vodka and olives.

Pepper plays with her braid, and her eyes dart from left to right, her yellow cotton sundress clinging to her chest with hot-as-hell heat, making her look like a wilted dandelion. "So, you think Vince is here? I really don't feel like dealing with him after all the vodka."

Pepper dumped Vince, again, a couple of weeks ago, for the tenth time since Christmas. *"Whatever, Scarlett, I was, like, so over him,"* she'd said. *"I'm moving to New York anyway for school, like, where was it going to go?"* She's been telling the same story for the last six months, but somehow, they always break up and make up and break up again. Round and round. Although this time it will probably stick. She's not even going to tell him she's carrying his kid. She said it's her body, her choice, which I agree with, but I still think he deserves to know. But it's none of my business.

What she said is probably true, anyway. Pepper will never let herself be tied down, barefoot and pregnant, to some small-town football player from Florida, when she's about to embark on the kind of journey to the big city that people only dream about. Pepper plans on a mansion in the Hollywood Hills, a penthouse in Manhattan, and an on-call masseuse for both. To be on James Van Der Beek's arm for the Emmys, Matt Damon's for the Oscars.

I scan the crowd. "No, I don't see Vince yet."

Pepper opens her pack of menthols and releases a skinny stick to her mouth. "Well, of course, he's going to show up at some point. He wouldn't miss a last opportunity to make fun of everyone. You know what a dick he is." She glances into her open bag, and I wonder where her venom is coming from. "Where's my lighter? Did you steal it?"

I reach into my pocket and clutch the plastic and metal cylinder. "Steal is a harsh word," I say as I torch my own cigarette before handing the lighter back to its rightful owner. "And take it easy on Vince, will you? He's head over heels. Always has been. His heart is absolutely shattered."

Pepper scoffs. "Don't defend him right now."

"Sorry." I acquiesce. As usual.

Pepper leads the way toward the truck where our friends are gathered. Everyone talks about graduation the previous day and compares inventory of swiped Smirnoff bottles stashed away for Chris Parker's inevitable after-party. Other students from school pass

by; some stop and talk, but most nod and wave hello, uninvited to
the gutter of hatred and hierarchy Pepper presides upon. The queen
bee. The north star. She has more gravitational pull than the moon.

Vince finally makes his grand appearance a half hour after our
arrival. His puppy dog eyes shift toward us, and he nods at Pepper,
clearly heartbroken, and she turns away to make a show of laughing
into my shoulder, like a real uncaring bitch. I give Vince a soft wave
and try to look sympathetic, but still, I let Pepper dismiss him. He
ignores me, as usual. Despite him dating my best friend for four
years, he's never taken to me, like he still sees the nerd he's known
since elementary school.

Shouts ring out from the distance, and my eyes follow the sound.
Chloe and Chris are having a screaming match, and Chloe pushes
him and walks off toward the rides while Chris follows her, taking
long strides to keep up with her quick pace.

"More drama with those two," Jordan Kessler, the football team's
leading wide receiver, says loudly, then lowers his voice to a slight
whisper, as if what he is going to say is top-secret information. "I
heard Chloe cheated on Chris."

I whip my head toward him. "Who said that?"

"No idea where it came from, but it's been going around."

As our crew compares hallway gossip, everyone drinks. Vince,
mostly quiet, always staring at Pepper, drinks an entire six pack in
less than thirty minutes, which puffs up his bravado, and things
take a turn as the sea of black clothing and tattoos gets closer to
the A-list crowd.

"Oh look, it's a goth parade," Vince huffs as Julian Ackers and
some friends walk by.

Julian's head tilts up, like he expects to be harassed by his regular
tormentor. His long black hair is swept into a ponytail with just
the front falling loose over his eye. He sports multiple piercings,

and he wears a long-sleeved T-shirt most of the time despite the incessant Florida heat. Julian has bravely held his own against Vince and the rest of the popular crowd all through high school. It infuriates Vince that he can't intimidate the goth kid, and it shows. Vince's fists are always clenched, ready to strike, whenever Julian sasses him, which is often.

High school politics determines everyone's place in line, and Julian—he runs with a crowd that has no direction. He and his kind are often seen smoking pot in the far lot before and after school. They listen to The Cure and bands like Sonic Youth, unlike the rest of the herd that thinks Santana and the Backstreet Boys are the only things that make life worth living.

Julian nonchalantly takes a pocket watch that hangs from a chain out of his sticker-covered backpack, glances at it, then lifts his hazel-blue eyes to Vince. "You're obsessed with me, Russo. Do you ever wonder why? High school is over, so no one will know if you want to make out with me in the woods later," he says with a sneer, then winks at Vince as he and his friends stride past.

Vince huffs and throws an empty bottle in his direction. Julian shifts so as not to get hit. "Keep walking, zombie boy. Don't make me kick your fucking ass."

Undeterred by the flying glass, Julian makes kissy noises and gives Vince the finger as he walks by, his goth crowd dragging their wide pants and piercings with them as they follow. Then he turns around. "Hey, Pepper. Looking good."

That is not going to sit well with a beer-and-testosterone-filled Vince. And I'm right, because seconds later Julian's throat is in Vince's grasp.

"I'll kill you, you motherfucker!"

Pepper jumps off the back of the truck and gets between them. "Jesus Christ, Vince, stop it! I'm so sick of this bullshit.

Can't you ever let anything go? Be the bigger man, for fuck's sake."

Vince, clearly hurt by her words and castrated by her reprimands, lets Julian go, even though his friends will give him hell for it later. He always does what Pepper says. Still, he points at Julian, his hand shaped like a gun, and shoots. "You're a dead man."

Pepper and Vince stay on opposite sides of the group after that. The west coast sun sets into an inferno in the sky after another hour of drinking in the lot, and Pepper decides it's time to go into the fair. Like lemmings, everyone trails her one by one in a line. Near the rides, small children cling to parents' hands or to the new stuffed animal they've just won. The air is thick with the smells of manure from a nearby farm and sugar from the cotton candy makers in every direction. They all gorge on sweets and greasy hot dogs and play silly boardwalk-style games.

With all the socializing and drunkenness, I don't realize I've been separated from Pepper, and I don't know for how long. The vodka has made me sleepy, my eyes heavy. I drift from group to group, making banal conversation. Twenty more minutes pass when I see Pepper, clearly distressed, at the edge of the woods beyond the fair—that bright yellow sundress is a dead giveaway, even in the dark. She's pacing back and forth, her hand on her head. Something isn't right. I exit the rides section of the fair and go around the back of a different parking lot, not to be noticed, and tiptoe into the darkness.

"Pepper?" I whisper as I approach. "Are you okay?"

Pepper hurls herself into my arms and cries. Hyperventilating, she tries to get words to come out, but there are none, just sounds. Desperate, horrible sounds as the tears flow like her face sprung a leak.

"Sit down," I order, out of character for me when addressing her. "Let me look at you."

Shockingly, Pepper listens—there's a first time for everything, I guess. We sit in the tall grass, far away from the fairgrounds, so we can't be seen. I take Pepper's face in my hands and angle it toward the lunar light to expose abrasions on her right cheek. A strap on her dress is ripped. Her mascara runs down her face like clown makeup, and the tears keep coming, widening the black streaks that trickle off her chin like an oil drip. It's obvious that something terrible happened.

I hold her and stroke her hair to soothe her. "It's okay, Pepper. Shhhh. It's okay. I'm here."

There's what seems like a long period of silence as I wait in anticipation to find out what happened, but it's only about a minute or so until she speaks. "I'm going to kill him," she says matter-of-factly.

Pepper's face twists, and I still don't know what happened, but I know she is serious about what she just said. It's all in the tone. I knot my eyebrows together. "Kill who?"

She gasps for the thick, humid air around her, but she still can't fully breathe, despite doing her best to take a deep breath. "I told Jordan I would meet him back here to fool around."

I'm taken aback. "Jordan Kessler? Jesus, Pepper."

I can't keep the disdain from my voice. If Vince finds out someone from the team touched Pepper, he'll flip. She's really trying to burn every goddamn bridge she has left here. Of course, she's just throwing the match and slow-walking away from the explosion that is going to become of Vince and Jordan's friendship. And yes, it's on Jordan too, but I know from experience that Pepper likely started it.

"Don't lecture me about who I can and can't hook up with," she snaps, back in control. "Look, I'm drunk. I'm not thinking clearly. I was waiting for Jordan, and I saw Julian Ackers walking home. I tried to apologize for Vince, but . . ." She starts shaking again, and her voice catches. "I told him I thought he was hot."

"Really?" Senior picnic will rear its ugly head if Pepper said that aloud. Julian must've rejected poor Pepper; she doesn't exactly take it well when she doesn't get what she wants. She's created drama before. "So, what happened?"

She lifts her head to the moon again, so I can see her tear-stained face more clearly when she speaks next. "With Julian? He tried to rape me."

INTERVIEW THE DAY AFTER
THE SENIOR PICNIC

Pepper: What do you mean it sounds rehearsed? The truth doesn't need to be rehearsed.

Detective Logan: And Julian Ackers?

Pepper: What about him? He was a little goth asshole. I mean, I didn't know him well, and I'm sorry he died and all, but he was known to be aggressive.

Detective Logan: Was he ever aggressive with you?

Pepper: No. Not with me.

27

SCARLETT

A ghost. I'm staring at a ghost.

There she is, though, defying science. Defying every horror movie I've ever seen. She's not translucent, and she's not floating. Her arms don't reach out to try to steal my soul.

But it's definitely her. It's Pepper. It's Pepper, in the flesh, alive and well and standing on Chris Parker's stoop. It's Pepper, who's turned my husband into a blubbering pile of mush on the floor right beneath me. It's Pepper, my old best friend. She's alive.

Zoey lied to me—to all of us.

"You're alive."

The words don't come from me. They come from Vince. And I already know I've lost him to her. The last seventeen years disappear in a puff of smoke. It's my fault, really—he was never mine to begin with. I must've been kidding myself. I pull Luke closer to me.

Pepper's face twists, not understanding the scene unfolding in front of her. "Of course I'm alive. Why would you think otherwise?"

Vince opens his mouth to answer, and Pepper holds up a hand and stops him in his tracks. So typical, he's already taking direction from her, and she just crawled out of her grave five seconds ago.

"Zoey. She told you I was dead, didn't she?"

Vince stands and walks to her in slow motion. He takes her in his arms and hugs her. Nothing like the hugs I've gotten for the past seventeen years. This one is packed with relief, memories, and love.

"Who is that?" Luke whispers next to me.

Shit. I can't believe Luke is witnessing this. I swallow the lump down. "Her name is Pepper. She's Zoey's mother. She's your father's ex-girlfriend from high school."

"Oh." Luke looks uneasy watching his father show such obvious affection to another woman. "Why is he acting like that?"

"He thought she was dead. We all did."

Noises come from the kitchen, and Chris appears in the foyer. "What's going on?" he asks.

Of course he has to ask. He can't see the woman in the doorway because she isn't there anymore. She's still in Vince's arms.

"It's Pepper. She's here. She's not dead," I say.

"What the f—hell," Chris says after looking at Luke. Like Luke's never heard the word *fuck*.

Pepper lets go of Vince, and I see she, too, is wiping tears. Kelly comes from around the corner to investigate, and now the whole front of the house is in chaos. Pepper looks at me and gives me a weak smile, and I can't help it—I grab her into a hug. It's Pepper. It's the girl I worshipped, the girl I loved, the girl I always wanted to be. Like Jesus Christ himself, it took her three days to die and resurrect, and to me it's an even bigger miracle.

"Pepper," I whisper. "Oh my God. What are you doing here?"

Her hug is stilted, stiff. She doesn't melt into me the way she did with Vince.

"I'm surprised to see you, Scarlett," she says as she pulls back.

"Where did you come from? How did you know we were all at Chris's house?"

Her lips slightly purse. "This is Chris's house? I thought Vince lived here. Zoey told me—" She looks back at Vince, who I try to ignore, and he's *still* staring at her in awe. "Oh . . ." she says in a knowing way, her eyes glowing with relief when she looks back at me. "Zoey lied to me, as usual. And holy shit, did you end up with Chris after all these years? I got confused. For a second, I thought you were with Vince. Like that would ever happen." She chuckles.

I may as well have downed a vial that says *DRINK ME* the way I shrink at her words. I lift my head and look at Vince, and he's still staring at her. It's quiet. Like, super quiet—until—

"Dad. Tell her."

It's Luke to the rescue. He shifts so he's standing in front of me, and I feel the love radiating off my son. Protection. Just like that, in this moment, he's transformed into a man right before my eyes. He has the courage to step in and say what his weak-ass father doesn't.

"Why don't we all go sit down?" Vince says. This time, he's not looking at anyone. He shuts the front door as we all walk through the foyer and head to the kitchen.

As soon as we get there, Pepper whips around and looks at me, then Vince, then Luke. She scowls, then covers it up with a tight-lipped smile. Her head swivels toward me in slow motion, the way you see the evil doll do in the horror movie before it starts to talk out of nowhere and makes you shit your pants.

"Scarlett, you married *my* Vince? Wow."

Yep, she's evil, and I'm about to shit my pants watching her doll lips move. The first things I think to say are *No, you have it wrong* because I want to appease her and then *It's not what you think* because I don't want to upset her and then *I'm sorry* because

I want her to like me. Instead of blubbering it all out incoherently, I'm intimidated into complete silence. The same way I was at eleven when she came into my life. The same way I was at thirteen, and fifteen. *Do whatever Pepper says.* Well, I told that lovely lie when I was eighteen, and I've regretted it ever since. It's almost twenty-two years later. Not this time.

I go back at her, for the first time in my life. "Yes, I did. And this is our son, Luke." My arm is still around him, and I don't recognize the sound of my own voice. I'm sure everyone can see right through me. Like I said, Vince was never mine. "We've been married for seventeen years." My voice cracks.

"Huh." It's a statement, not a question. She looks at Vince, seeking an explanation, and he looks away. Coward. "Vince?"

"We ran into each other downtown after college," he spits out faster than a racecar. "We were drunk. She got pregnant."

How dare he do that right in front of Luke.

You son of a bitch. All bets are off. How about I remind you who your perfect little girlfriend is, darling husband? She cheated on you and *got pregnant* by someone else.

"Hey, Pepper," I say. "Zoey told us she came here looking for her father. We thought it was Vince, but the paternity test said it wasn't. Who's her father?"

INTERVIEW THE DAY AFTER
THE SENIOR PICNIC

Pepper: Are we about done here, Detective? I don't feel like talking anymore.

Detective Logan: Oh? Why is that?

Pepper: I'm tired, I don't feel well, and people died last night. I have nothing to offer you regarding this situation. I went to a fair with my friend, we drank like everyone else did, we went home. Nothing else exciting or noteworthy happened. I don't understand wanting to talk to a bunch of teenagers over a car accident.

Detective Logan: You're my last interview. I have to say, no one has been as dismissive as you over this. Well, that's not entirely true. Your boyfriend seemed rather dismissive too.

Pepper: How many times do I have to tell you: Vince isn't my boyfriend.

Detective Logan: Right. So you'd have no reason to protect him, then?

Pepper: Protect him from what?

Detective Logan: That's what I'm trying to find out.

28

PEPPER

Well, shit.

I think back to the last few months of senior year, when I took the pregnancy test. When it came back positive, I was thrilled. Beyond thrilled. I saw it as a way that we could be together forever. High school was ending, and I'd be on my own in New York. No one would be around to judge, to stare, to point out how it would never work between him and me. I was in love, head over heels in love, and nothing would ever come between us.

Truth be told—I'd planned to disappear on Scarlett anyway. She never would've understood my new life. So, when it slipped out that I was pregnant and Scarlett grilled me, I let her assume it was Vince's. And everything that happened at the senior picnic—I had so many emotions swirling inside after that encounter with Julian in the woods when Scarlett found me, broken and crying and tossed to the ground after being used like a sex doll. In those scant few hours, I survived more devastation than most get in a lifetime. I knew my only real escape was to run away.

Zoey's father was supposed to come to New York with me. I was devastated when he told me that he'd never planned on it and that our relationship wasn't that big of a deal anyway. Meanwhile, I had been excited to start our lives together.

Stupid, silly girl.

Then the accident happened. I realized what a shit I was to Vince, and I wanted him back. But I had to go to New York first and get my shit together. I'd be back for him by Christmas—that was my plan. But then I changed my mind and kept Zoey, because a part of me still wanted to be connected to her father. I stayed in New York and let Vince go. I had to. I loved him enough to not hurt him anymore. I swore I'd never return to Florida.

And now, here I am, in a place I never thought I'd be again, and my best friend is married to my boyfriend.

I take Vince in—all of him. He's aged wonderfully, his blond hair silver only near his sideburns. Still tall, tan, and fit. I think of all the times he told me he loved me, the way he dropped everything for me. The way he didn't care if he looked corny in front of the team, as long as I was happy.

The other thing he did to save me that night. Our little secret.

And now—now Vince is with Scarlett Kane. Ahem, Scarlett Russo.

Pepper Russo sounds better. It just does.

"Who's Zoey's father, Pepper?" Scarlett asks me again.

"None of your business," I shoot back. I haven't seen any of these people in over two decades. I owe zero explanations, especially to her. "Why do you think you're owed any sort of insight into my life after all this time? I haven't seen you in twenty years."

On second thought, I should tread carefully with her. I *do* remember what she did for me that night—vividly. It's hard to forget, after I browbeat her into not only repeating my lies but believing every single one I fed her. She'd do anything for me.

But so would Vince. They always did. They both did illegal shit to protect me. I get it. That isn't going to stop me from reminding them both who I am. I wonder how far I can take this.

Scarlett, happily married to Vince Russo, with a kid. She's living my life. Does she really think she can compete with me?

INTERVIEW THE DAY AFTER
THE SENIOR PICNIC

Pepper: What makes you think Vince did anything?

Detective Logan: Call it intuition. I feel like if you were in trouble, he'd be there for you.

Pepper: Of course he would. He loves me.

Detective Logan: Do you love him?

Pepper: I thought this interview was about the accident.

Detective Logan: Why are you deflecting?

Pepper: Why are you asking stupid questions?

29

PEPPER

Senior Picnic
June 1999

The first emotion I feel is rage. At Julian Ackers, and what he did to me tonight. I've known him since middle school. He's changed through the years, all right—he runs with a crowd of drug-dabbling losers now—but I'm shocked at what's happened. He will have to pay.

Surely not knowing how to react to a situation like this one, Scarlett nurtures. "Let's get you cleaned up." She tries to control the circumstances and gingerly lifts me up off the ground and ties the broken strap from my sundress into a small knot to keep it fastened. "How did it happen? I'm taking you to the police station right now," she says.

I morph right back into being in control because I already know how this is going to end. I said as much. *I'm going to kill him.* "We're hammered. They'll say it's my fault, that I asked for it because I started the conversation. They'll arrest us for underage drinking."

"Underage drinking should be the least of their concerns. I think having Julian arrested for sexual assault and sent to jail is worth it."

"Scarlett, no. I'll deal with it. I always deal with everything. I'll be fine."

"He tried to rape you! In your condition! We can't let him get away with it. How did you even fight him off?"

I look toward the darkness. Damn right he's going to pay, but not the way Scarlett has in mind. Jail for assault is too good for him. He tried to take my body, but he can't stop my penchant for vengeance.

I turn my head toward the fair. "I told him Jordan was on his way, meeting me at that exact spot in the woods, and I guess he got scared and bailed. Is everyone still in there?" I ask, nodding my head toward the lights. "I don't want anyone to see me like this. Please, let's just go home. Can you take me home?"

"No, I'm taking you to the police station," Scarlett says with purpose, my upper arm in her clutch.

"You're not." I exaggerate the *T*. My statement is final. Honestly, who does she think she is right now? I need to tread carefully; she needs to believe I'm still in shock for the rest of my plan to work. I've recovered quite nicely if I do say so myself. Compartmentalization. *Remember the faces from that low-rent acting camp you went to last summer. The expressions. You have to make her believe you. Aaaaaaaand action!* "No cops—they'll do a pelvic examination, and they'll find out I'm pregnant. I can't let my parents know. Please."

That seems to stifle her.

On wobbly legs, we hoof across the grass and into the parking lot. I lean on Scarlett's shoulder, wounded and broken, a thesaurus of hurt emotions. We walk together in stride. Right foot, left foot. Right foot, left foot. Stepping over the beer bottles and greasy napkins and condom wrappers that litter the lot as evidence that sex is on everyone's brain. A burning sensation of bile lingers in my throat at the thought of what Julian just did to me.

192 JAIME LYNN HENDRICKS

Then, like I'm injected with an adrenaline shot, I snap out of my woeful demeanor when we pass Chloe's Dodge. Like a bat out of hell, I run full force to the front and kick one of her headlights in with the heel of my shoe, sending shards of glass in every direction around us, flickering like twinkle twinkle little stars against the night sky.

"Fucking whore bitch!" I scream. Hey, I'm full of rage. Why not?

"Pepper, what are you doing?" Scarlett stares in shock.

How's this for manipulation? "She deserves it. She took Chris away from you!"

"What? That was over a year ago. We were never even a couple. Stop it!" she yells as I bang on the hood of the car. "Stop!" She grabs me and hugs me, as I decide to play on her by crying into her arms for the second time that night.

Again, like nothing terrible has happened, I compose myself. "Actually, you're right; we're too drunk. Let's go thumb a ride up the road."

Scarlett is incredulous, but I don't have time for her shit. Damn Goody Two-shoes. She may as well be wearing a bonnet. "What? I can't leave my car here. My dad will kill me." She motions toward the mess I just made of Chloe's car. "See what happens when vehicles are left unattended?"

It's dark, and I look toward her car, mostly alone at the end of the lot. The garbage littered from car to car is a path of everyone's indignity, fortunately made visible only by the moonlight, but the stench of stale beer and heartache hangs in the grass around us. I persist.

"I'll find someone to get us home. Just stay at my house. I'll drive you back here to get your car in the morning. Your parents won't even know."

I know she'll do what I say. If she only knows what I'm really planning. She longingly looks back at her car, the vessel she thinks can ferry us to justice, but she follows my orders, as usual, and I walk away. Her footsteps pound behind me. Because of course.

The butter-colored path is lit up the hill, the moon telling us that it's the right way to go, our very own yellow brick road. Neither of us are wearing shoes fit for the occasion, and we drag our clunky wedges along the back road until my feet blister. Scarlett suggests going to the hospital and the police over and over, but I bounce between happy hitchhiker and miserable assault victim. I need to think about the endgame.

We walk almost a mile, with about five to go when a car slows as the driver spots us.

Perfection.

"Look, it's a car with a busted headlight," I say.

"So?"

"So, you know who drives a car with a busted headlight, don't you? At least that fucker is busted now. How could you forget already? Remember, we kicked it out earlier tonight?"

Fine, *we* is a stretch, but I confidently walk into the middle of the road and put my arms up, turning my body into an X. There is no fear on my side as the car rolls toward me, yard by yard, and it eventually slows to a halt in the middle of the road. I go to the open driver's side window and lean inside while Scarlett lags behind.

"Hey, Chloe!" I say with a smile, as fake as the pink streaks in my hair. "We need a lift. Take us home?" I ask as I circle around to the passenger side and open the door without a proper invitation. "Come on, Scarlett, get in."

Scarlett hesitates. She's way too drunk, we've both walked too long, and we're both too tired. But it's a perfect plan, really. I get in and close the door and shoot Chloe a look and my evil *Don't cross me* smile, my pursed lips. "You don't mind, right?"

"No, come on in," Chloe says, and rummages her right arm into her back seat to move away the garbage from earlier in the night. "Sorry, I wanted McDonald's before we went to the senior picnic. To soak up the alcohol. I was planning to go to the party at Chris's house. But get in. What could go wrong with a little detour?"

Indeed.

INTERVIEW THE DAY AFTER
THE SENIOR PICNIC

Detective Logan: So you saw the car full of guys. And that's it?

Pepper: That's what I said.

Detective Logan: And you're sure? A hundred percent? You were on the road to the park. Anything you saw could help our investigation.

Pepper: We saw no other cars. No other people. Cross my heart and hope to die.

30

VINCE

Pepper is back. The love of my life.

Only Chris knows how much the shock of her death hit me. Truth be told, I talk about Pepper all the time with him. Always have, for the last twenty-two years since she left. When her cell phone was cut off. When her parents refused to tell me anything that time I banged on their door, scaring the hell out of them and her little brother, Hunter. The way I've obsessed about looking for her on social media. I did everything short of hiring a PI. Chris had to stop me—literally, with force—from going to the airport and booking a ticket to New York. I was eighteen and had no endgame there; I just planned to walk around until I spotted her. She's my fate, and I knew I'd find her.

Chris thought otherwise and tackled me and took away my keys. We snuck a couple of beers out of my parents' fridge and sat in the driveway drinking, where he convinced me to forget about her and go to college. When he said she was just a piece of tail, I tried to hit him, and he tackled me again. Sat my ass down, told me that she left for a reason, and that after the way she treated me, I was better off without her. He may have been right. I know she used me, and then she fucking bailed on me. After everything I did for her.

Still, the memories of her . . . they haunt me. Seeing her in my English class freshman year, when she walked in with that red lipstick and that shiny dark hair and those fucking legs—the ones she wrapped around me a month later, and I was gone. It was love at first sight for me, but the fact that she talked to me and dated me, that we lost our virginity to each other—it still blows my mind. We had sex all the time—*all* the time. She was a little firecracker, that one.

Three and a half straight years of passion and love. Then senior year, right after Christmas, she started acting weird. Didn't pick up her phone. Took forever to call me back. Unexplained absences. The first time she dumped me, it hurt so much I thought I'd been shot. When we got back together, I said I'd never let her go, and I meant it.

She dumped me one, two, three, four more times. Embarrassed me in front of the team, my parents, my siblings, my teachers—she had no shame. She seemed to get off on it. That only made me want her more. Nothing else mattered—not my family, not the guys, not my grades—nothing. It was so corny for a fifteen-year-old boy to fall in love the way I did, and stay in love, but I honestly loved her with everything I had.

With everything I have. With everything I am.

There are so many things I can't admit out loud to Scarlett. I can't admit when I saw her downtown at the bar all those years ago, I beelined to her for one reason only. I asked her if she heard from Pepper, and she said she hadn't since the senior picnic. Pepper was still a ghost. So, yes—I fucked Scarlett. It was like having Pepper again; they were best friends, after all.

My father heard me on the phone with Chris, complaining about Scarlett's pregnancy, and demanded I propose, because how would it look if his son had a child out of wedlock? I can't believe she said yes. I'm glad for Luke and I love him more than life itself, but Scarlett is just where I ended up. And we're a family for my son. But with him off to college soon, and Pepper alive, I can't promise my marriage will last.

I can't admit that the best I've felt since Pepper was when I had the affair with Lila, and that the only reason I started it was because she slightly resembled her. That every time I close my eyes during sex, whether it's with Scarlett or Lila or any of the girls I fucked in college, that I picture Pepper on top of me. I'm not super proud, but there were a couple of one-night stands over the past few years too. With closed eyes, my hands can slide up any woman's abdomen to their breasts, and just like that, I'm fondling Pepper again.

I can't admit that when I slept on the couch the last two nights, I cried myself to sleep over Pepper's death. All the things I never got to tell her. All the things we never got to do together. I think I even called out her name, and I wonder if Scarlett heard. I don't particularly care if she did.

I can't admit I wanted Zoey to be mine. Something that belonged to just Pepper and me.

But she isn't mine. And now Pepper is standing in front of me, and I have to remember I'm Scarlett's husband, not hers, no matter how much I wish the reverse were true. And Scarlett won't stop asking her who Zoey's father is.

That's a goddamn good question.

INTERVIEW THE DAY AFTER
THE SENIOR PICNIC

Detective Logan: I need to know if you'd lie for anyone. That's all.

Vince: Man, you're going in circles.

Detective Logan: I have a knack for this sort of stuff. I don't think you've been honest with me.

Vince: I honestly don't care what you think. Can I go now? I have to make a call.

31

PEPPER

I can't even look at Vince right now. He must be devastated knowing that not only was I screwing someone else while I was with him, but that I had a kid because of it.

Whatever. He married *Scarlett*. Jesus.

Still, everyone watches me expectantly, and my past stares me in the face. Scarlett, Vince, and Chris. And Vince's kid, and some other girl who came from outside. Are my feelings back for Vince? They never really left. First love and all. I'm the one who torched our relationship. It's all my fault.

And my confusing feelings for Zoey's father are back too. There's nothing I can do about that now. When you fixate on someone like that, it never goes away. I'm sure it's how Vince still feels about me.

I can't be here.

"I have to leave," I say. "Zoey—she needs me." My liar daughter who told everyone I was dead.

"Wait, Pepper, wait," Vince says and takes a step toward me as Scarlett glares. Then he shakes his head and lets out a light laugh. "Man, you destroyed me back then. I'm glad you're alive. How long are you in town?"

"Just until tomorrow. I only came here to drag Zoey home. I'm sorry she caused so much trouble. She's—she's got a lot going on." I turn to the door. "I have to go."

"Pepper."

This time the voice is Scarlett. Before I look her way, I have mini flashbacks of times in middle school and high school. Sleepovers, cheer practice, driving lessons, and talking about boys. I talked to her about Vince for almost four straight years, and now she's married to him. She has a kid with him. With *my* boyfriend. I don't want to hate her, but I do. I really do.

I turn around and smile. "Yes?"

"Can we have lunch tomorrow? I work at the hotel where Zoey is staying. Just come and get me at the concierge desk at noon. I think we should talk."

About this dipshit situation, or senior picnic? Chloe. Julian. The sexual assault. The accident. The fallout. The lies. What happened after.

The truth.

There's so much that Scarlett doesn't know about that night. She's blissfully unaware of what happened after she dropped me off at home. Even so, now that she knows I'm "alive," I guess I have to appease her. If she goes to the cops now, I'm fucked.

"Sure. It would be great to catch up. I'll see you tomorrow, then."

"Great."

She's smiling, but I see through it. It's my smile. The *keep your friends close and your enemies closer* smile. Maybe she wants to do girl talk so she thinks I'll feel bad if I go sneaking around her back with her husband.

I won't. Feel bad, that is. He's mine.

"I'll walk you out," Vince says.

"Dad," the kid says urgently. "I need you to show me something on the grill. Uncle Chris was having trouble with the rotisserie rod."

Uncle Chris. How strange. I guess Vince and Chris are still inseparable. BFFs, business partners—they've shared so much. *So much.* The more things change, the more they stay the same. And this kid thinks he's slick saying what his mother won't. *Don't go with her.* There ain't a goddamn thing wrong with that rotisserie rod and we all know it.

"I'll be back in a second, pal," Vince says, oblivious that his son is trying to get his attention. I own Vince's attention like I saved up for it and bought it on sale.

We walk out, and I can only imagine what's being said behind that closed door.

"I thought you were dead," Vince says.

His eyes tear, and I notice that even though he looks the same, he looks forty. Little crinkles around his eyes, and that dark tan that permeates your skin when you've spent your whole life in Florida—a little leathery, but it looks good. He must work outside, evidenced by Chris's work truck in the driveway. I should admire Zoey for being so much like me, but I'm going to kill her for making me think this was Vince's house and that he was single. She had to know he was married to Scarlett.

"I'm sorry about Zoey. She's been a handful." We walk awkwardly, neither of us saying what we want to say. So, I'll start. "I can't believe you married Scarlett." I can't keep the sarcasm out of my voice. It boils over like too much water in the pot. I even hear the sizzle.

"Yeah, well . . . you know how it is. I wanted my son to have a real family."

"How did you two even—"

He interrupts. "I always wondered what would've happened if . . . if you didn't leave. You left me. Pepper, who is Zoey's father? It's been killing me since we got the call yesterday. I have to know."

I walk a little faster. "No, Vince, you don't. It's ancient history. Plus, I feel like Zoey deserves to know first."

"Are you going to tell her?"

"Yes, I am. Now. Tonight."

"Are you going to introduce her to him?"

That stabs me in the heart. "Yes, I'll bring her to him."

"Did you love him?"

Shit. At the time, I was infatuated with him the way teenagers are. And love makes you do crazy things. Looking back, I feel like an asshole for thinking it was more than it was. My love for Vince was real. With Zoey's dad, it was just obsession. I don't know what to say to Vince that will make him feel anything but hurt. We stop at the car.

"Thanks for walking me back, Vince. It really was good to see you." I mean it.

"Can I see you before you leave?"

"I don't know how that's going to be possible. I have to be with Zoey tonight. And I have lunch with your wife tomorrow." We both need the reminder—Vince is married.

I'm not sure that will stop either of us.

He looks back at the house, where Scarlett is watching us from the bay window in front. She's not even trying to pretend to do anything else. Then he looks at the pool truck. "My cell is the second number listed on the truck. Text me if you change your mind."

He comes in for a hug again, and I grab him back, even settling my head into his chest. It feels good; familiar. I know if I don't detach, he certainly won't, so I pull back and climb into the car, stick the key in the ignition, and leave. I see him go back into the house through the rearview mirror. When the door closes, I turn around and take his cell number off the van.

Back at the hotel, I'm nervous to talk to Zoey, so I grab a bottle of wine in the gift shop in the lobby. I wait until I see people near the elevator since I still don't have a key to go up, so when a group hovers, I wait with them. In the elevator, I don't know if the warbling in my stomach is due to the motion or the conversation I'm about to have. I'll tell her what she needs to know, and that's it. She can never know the rest. I get off on three, walk down the hall, and tap on the door. She opens it immediately, wearing that snarky little shit-eating grin.

"Very funny," I say.

"What?" she asks innocently, like she didn't just set me up to be humiliated. "Did you see Vince?"

"Yes, I saw Vince. And his wife, Scarlett, my old best friend. At Chris's house, where you sent me. Why would you do that?"

She shrugs, and I walk past her and set the wine bottle down. I rifle around near the minibar until I find a corkscrew. There are little Styrofoam cups wrapped in plastic, and I take one out and uncork the bottle, then pour the wine. *Glub glub glub.* Fantastic sound. I take a long, hard swallow.

"I know why you're acting out. And I've thought a lot about it. I'm going to tell you who your father is."

Her eyes widen. "Who is it?"

"First, let me tell you how I met him."

32

PEPPER

Senior Picnic
June 1999

In the fair, I discard Scarlett like yesterday's news and sneak out. It's dark and I walk quickly, already a little late. Looking behind one last time to make sure no one can see me, I creep into the woods. The crumpled blanket is still there from when we met a few days earlier. I pick it up and dust it off before placing it back down. A twig breaks behind me and I gasp, then a hand clasps over my mouth from behind.

"Shhh. We don't want anyone to hear us," he says.

Comforted by his voice, I turn around and we embrace.

"Oh God, Julian," I say, out of breath already. "I love you. I missed you so much."

The whole thing with Julian happened by accident, really. It was about six months ago, and I had to pick up Hunter early from a birthday party because he didn't feel well. I appeased him as much as I could on the ride home until he threatened to puke in my car. I immediately turned into a restaurant parking lot and drove behind the building and let him out.

Under the streetlight, I saw a young man wearing a baseball hat, taking the trash to the receptacle behind the restaurant. He paused to remove his shirt, and my jaw dropped at the cut physique. He wiped his neck with the shirt, then discarded it and grabbed a clean shirt that was hooked onto his belt loop and put that on. I glanced at Hunter, who was trying to throw up. Whatever, he was eleven, he could take care of himself. I went into flirt mode and approached the stranger.

"Excuse me, can you help my little brother? He's sick. Can you grab him some water? I'd be eternally grateful," I said, batting my lashes.

He turned around and took off his hat so his dark hair fell onto his face. That was when I saw it was Julian, but he didn't look like I remembered. Long gone was the strange emo punk dressed in black. And it was the first time I noticed he had hazel-bluish eyes.

"Look at this. Pepper Wilson needs my help," he said with a smirk.

I wanted to jump into damsel-in-distress mode, but first I had to remind him who I was, just in case he forgot about the social pecking order. We might've been outside of our hallowed hallways, but I still needed to pull rank. "So, you recognize me? Are you really going to make me go inside by myself? My brother might be dying."

I knew I was laying it on pretty thick, as subtlety was never my specialty. Julian put his shirt back on, much to my dismay, and slow jogged back inside the restaurant. He came out in two minutes with a pitcher of water and two glasses, and also a roll of toilet paper and some mints reserved for exiting patrons.

"Thanks, Julian. That's very kind of you," I said as I took them.

"You know my name?" he asked.

I rolled my eyes and made a scoffing noise, and he laughed under his breath. He took a pack of cigarettes out of his left back pocket and lit one. Through the white tufts of smoke, he watched me care for my brother. I wanted to deal with Hunter before resuming my conversation—I wanted to at least look empathetic even if I didn't give a shit what Hunter was going through. Next time lay off the cake, buddy.

Hunter puked for five straight minutes, while I had my back to Julian. When he finished, I made him sip some water, then wiped his mouth with toilet paper and gave him a handful of mints. I whispered to him to go back to the car so I could try to get a minute alone with Julian. When I turned around, he was gone.

In math class the following Monday, Julian ignored me, and I fixated. Algorithms be damned, I'd spent the entire forty-three minutes staring at him. He sat two rows to my left and one row in front, so I got a good view. I'd never noticed his perfect profile before, his clear skin and the way it glowed below his dark hair and intense eyes. Now that I'd seen his naked broad chest, I wondered how I'd never noticed it before. Even with the long-sleeved T-shirts, his muscles were clear as day. I watched as he listened to the teacher and wrote things down in his sticker-covered notebook. He was smart; I knew he was smart. He never looked confused, and he never stared into space like everyone else in class. My own tank top began to cling to my chest with heat as I fantasized about his lips. I only broke out of my trance when the bell rang and he stood up and packed his notebook into his black knapsack. I noticed how tall he was. How tall, strapping, and hot he was.

I followed him out of class and into the hallway and opened my mouth to shout to him, but Vince got there first. I was behind Julian, and Vince walked toward us. His face lit up when he saw me, and he held his grin until he reached us. Before he could even say hello to me, he shoved an unsuspecting Julian—hard—into the wall of lockers, screaming asshole this and that, and then laughed as if proud of himself.

"Hey, gorgeous," Vince said as he planted his sloppy wet lips on my face. "Come over after school. I have to get to gym. I love you."

He attempted to slobber on me again, and I rebuffed him. "Ew, Vince, gross!" I squealed as I wiped my mouth and brushed past him.

What a Neanderthal. Why did I suddenly think that? I took a deep breath and walked toward poor Julian, my heels and toes racing against each other to see which could get there first. My heart felt like a jazz snare drum—*ding-da-ding, ding-da-ding*—as my anticipation grew. My breath was short and labored as I tingled all over, like my whole body had spent its life asleep and had just been released from a vise, blood rushing everywhere to dance with my veins and nerves and cells. Life flowed back into my body when I finally reached him, so close that I could pick out his brand of soap. *Mmm, Irish Spring. His smell.* He stood up and refilled his bag with books that had scattered across the hall floor.

"Hey. Are you okay?" I asked, my palms clammy as my lunch-time diet soda bubbled in my stomach.

He stopped loading his pack and turned to face me, boring his gorgeous eyes into mine, and my knees buckled. How had I never noticed him before?

"Yeah, like you care," he said as he tossed his backpack onto his shoulder and walked away.

I skipped to catch up. "I do care. That's why I asked. I'm sorry he's such a jerk." It's not like Julian was going to go back and tell Vince what I just said.

Julian continued to walk in the hallway as I beckoned silently next to him, almost speed walking to keep up with his long strides. "You know, people can see you talking to me," he said.

"So? I wanted to thank you for the other night. You were gone by the time my brother finished. I left the pitcher and glasses and stuff by the back door. I didn't want you to get in trouble."

"You're welcome."

He kept moving, quickly, as I tried to stay alongside him.

"I actually wanted to know if you could help me with math later today. I kind of spaced out today in class. I noticed you're pretty into it."

"I thought you had plans with Vince after school? Go bang your boyfriend."

Mortified, I stopped walking. Julian kept going. Was he walking away from me? I wouldn't have that. I caught up again.

"Julian, I'm sorry about him. Don't listen to him. And really, I'd like to see you after school. You can come over to my place. No one is home."

"I have to work later. I don't have time to drive to your part of town."

There was a definite his side and my side. His side consisted of inlets and row houses, mine of mini mansions on the bay with private wet and dry docks. The haves and the have-nots.

"Then I'll come to you." I realized I sounded desperate. "Please?" *Oh God, stop whining!*

"Just meet me back at the restaurant, then. I'll see you later."

He disappeared around a corner and left me nowhere near my history class, as I had followed him like a lost puppy, not taking my normal route. There I was, the incredible Pepper Wilson, and he just didn't care. I would have to change that.

During our first tutoring session, I worked quickly, placing my hand on his knee, and he didn't even notice. A few days later, I stopped to talk to him in the hall when he was near his locker, and I made body contact again, this time in the form of exaggeratedly falling into him when someone brushed past me in on their way to class. He didn't even bother to steady me. His indifference toward me was a new feeling. I obsessed over him. I imagined scenarios about him, about us, in my head.

The third time, I was determined to take matters into my own hands and slashed his tire in the school parking lot. I innocently drove past as he cursed and banged his hands on his trunk, and I offered him a ride. I made up a story about needing to stop home to change my shoes because of aching feet, and we went to my house. He reluctantly went inside as I changed my shoes. Then I complained that it was too hot and took off my top. He didn't know what to do. Then I unhooked my bra and approached him. He did the rest.

We hid our relationship from all our friends, because no one would understand—the goth kid and the head cheerleader simply didn't run in the same circle. He liked skateboards and piercings, I liked hair clips and pom-poms. We stopped talking in school, just sneaking heat-filled glances and getting away with an occasional brush of the hands if we passed each other in opposite directions. Eventually, the double life became too hard for me, and I dumped Vince. I thought it would make the transition to Julian easier for those around me, for the few months I had left in Florida, anyway.

And I wanted him around me, all the time. Our stolen time together was passionate and hungry, usually clandestine meetings in dark parking lots or parks. I became addicted to him, the thought of leaving him so distressing that I thought I had convinced him to move to New York with me. The things he did to my body had me frenzied even when I wasn't with him; just the memory of his lips and his tongue and his fingers gave me chills. I had told him I loved him time and time again, although he never said it back. It wasn't like him, and that was okay; deep down, I knew how he felt.

Now, in the woods behind the fair, I lace my fingers through each other at the back of his neck as I kiss him. "I love you," I whisper again. I rock myself back and forth against his chest. "I love you."

There's something in his kiss that hesitates, even as his lips cover mine. They're stiff and dry, like overcooked steak.

"Is something wrong?" I ask.

He chuckles, takes a step back, and yanks his cigarettes out of his back pocket. He taps the bottom of the pack until one slides out of the open top, then lifts it to his mouth and lights it. Swiping his hair out of his face, he taps another cigarette out, which I take, even though I prefer menthols. He holds a lighter close to my face and I inhale the smoke, using the gasp of toxins to calm my nerves. He takes four silent drags before he speaks. Well, not really silent. He accentuates the sounds. Inhale. Suck. Blow.

"I've been thinking about something," he says.

"Oh yeah?"

"Yeah." Another drag of the cigarette, but no more words.

"Are you going to tell me?" I nervously blow smoke out of my nose. Something is wrong. There's a tear pooling at the bottom of my eye, and I hope the moonlight doesn't catch it. I don't want him to see.

"I don't think this is a good idea—any of this stuff with me and you, really. Not anymore."

INTERVIEW THE DAY AFTER
THE SENIOR PICNIC

Detective Logan: First let me say, I'm sorry for your loss. A twin brother. That's got to be awful.

Juliet: Can we make this quick? I need to be with my family.

Detective Logan: Of course. Can you tell me anything about last night that stuck out as strange?

Juliet: My brother was an enigma, Detective. He dresses strange—I guess we both do. Our kind usually sticks together, so I don't know what he was doing with Chloe. But I saw them together.

Detective Logan: When?

Juliet: Once like a month ago, then again last week.

Detective Logan: How do you know they weren't just friends?

Juliet: Well. The last time I saw them together—it was at my house. In his room. I walked in on them by accident. They were definitely more than friends.

Detective Logan: I see. Did you ever talk to him about it?

Juliet: Yeah, after she left. I knew she was dating one of the guys from the team, so it was weird to see her with Julian. All he said was it's complicated. You know, now that I think about it, he wasn't acting the same the last month or so.

33

VINCE

I vibrate as I walk back to the shitstorm that's waiting for me inside Chris's house. I'll give Pepper some room, but I really need to know who she was cheating on me with. My feelings resurfaced tenfold when I thought she was dead. Now she's alive. She's here.

Scarlett is in the window, glaring at me. She's disgusted. I can tell because it's the look she's worn for half of our marriage. I don't really know how she feels now that Pepper is back. They were best friends; she thought she was dead too. She's got to be relieved. Or maybe not. I know more about Scarlett and that accident than she thinks. I know she was there. And she knows nothing about *me* and the accident.

But she's got to know I still love Pepper, especially after all the shit that's happened in the last few days. She must've always known. Our marriage has been the most un-fun threesome in history. There were always three.

The door creaks open and I close it behind me. Everyone is standing near each other, everyone silent. Kelly, who never knew any of the story, is clutching Chris's arm. Scarlett is clutching Luke's, waiting for me to say something first.

"Sunday funday, no?" I say. So stupid. But I don't know how to approach what just happened.

"What the hell?" Chris says. "What's wrong with that girl, Zoey? Why would she lie to us and tell us Pepper was dead?"

"I don't know. She always wanted to know about her father." I glance quickly at Scarlett, whose eyes don't meet mine, and then back to Chris. "I don't know why she thought saying Pepper was dead would help." Why she'd totally fuck with my emotions, even after thinking I might be her father. It doesn't make sense.

"I don't feel well," Luke says. He even grabs his stomach in an exaggerated manner, proving to me that he's lying. It's the same move he'd use to get out of school if he didn't finish his homework or forgot to study for a test. A father knows.

"Right. We should go home," Scarlett says, then looks at our hosts. "I'm sorry, guys, can we rain check the barbecue?"

I hate myself for making Luke feel like he has to protect his mother. That's supposed to be my job. But Luke can sense the same thing Scarlett can, I guess. I pat the pocket of my jeans and know my keys are in there. "Let's go, then."

We say goodbye and drive the ten minutes home, in silence. Luke grunts every once in a while, overplaying his role, and Scarlett stares out the window, watching the bungalows on the strip as we head into Pass-a-Grille.

Once inside the house, Luke heads straight to his room, giving his mother and me the privacy we need. I find myself wishing it were soundproofed because I have a feeling this conversation is going to get loud. I drop my keys on the table by the garage door and grab a beer out of the refrigerator. Scarlett watches my every move with laser focus. The way she acted for years right after she found out about Lila. Like I'm hiding a girlfriend in my pocket.

I'm not. I'm hiding her in my heart.

"Well?" she finally says.

I take a deep breath. "Well, what?" I know it's going to start the fight.

She just shakes her head. Grabs those damn cigarettes and goes outside. I finish my beer, contemplating my next move in the time it takes her to come back inside. I quietly get up and grab another beer.

"So, what now?" she asks.

"I don't know." It's one of the first times I'm totally honest with her.

The silence is broken by my cell phone chatter. It's a text that gives me a hard-on.

Zoey just left. Can you come to the hotel where we can be alone? I need you.

"Who's that?" Scarlett asks.

Why she asks, I have no idea. She knows. I place my half-full beer on the table and don't meet her eyes when I walk down the hall and grab my keys. "I have to go."

34

ZOEY

My father is dead.

All these years, asking questions, hopeful, getting the runaround—all this time, she knew. She knew, and she didn't tell me.

"You bitch," I say. She tilts her head like she's going to object, but she keeps her mouth closed. What can she really say? "Why didn't you tell me Julian was my father? After I found that letter?"

"Because, Zoey. It was a hard time in my life. I didn't want to relive any of it either. He—Julian—he knew I was pregnant. And he dumped me that night. It was a shock to me to hear the next morning about the accident. And that he was seeing Chloe. I was confused. I thought I loved him. But I was wrong. I made a lot of mistakes."

I don't believe her. She thinks I don't know her, but that eye shift she does when she's lying is right there. I see it, along with the slumped shoulders and one hand on her hip. She might think she looks assertive, but I can tell she's just pretending. She's an actress, after all—and a terrible one at that. No wonder her career never went to the next level, if these are her performances.

There's more to that accident. The detective said as much. She couldn't be involved in my father's death, could she? Is that the secret everyone is hiding?

"I talked to Juliet, Mom. I talked to Vince and Scarlett and Chris. I even talked to that Detective Logan dude. No one—not one person mentioned you with Julian. Why should I believe you? How do I know he was really my father? I mean, it's not like we can get a cheek swab."

"I told you, our relationship was a secret."

"Are you kidding me right now? And then he died the next day, and you still never said anything? Not even to the detective?"

"Why would I? What point would that serve?"

I eye her suspiciously. "Because you're lying about something."

"No, Zoey, it's because I was in high school. I was a stupid kid." Her eyes tear, then one pools over, and she wipes it away. "A stupid kid who got knocked up, dumped, and then he died. I didn't know what to do. I realized I still loved Vince, but . . . I just wanted to go to New York and get it all over with."

Holy shit—what a callous, uncaring, selfish bitch. "Stop with your crocodile tears. Get it over with? You mean get your abortion and get rid of me?" But she didn't. She didn't do it because something happened that changed her mind. And it wasn't falling down a hill. "What were you talking about in that letter?"

The silence between us speaks volumes. She's not going to tell me. Or, she's going to lie, and lie, and lie. Well, now I'm armed with more information, and if anyone knows anything else about that night, I have something else to say about it. Julian is my father. People need to know that.

I grab my keys. "I have to get out of here. I need some air."

I exit the room at warp speed. After pressing the call button for the elevator fifteen times in a row like a crazy person, I turn around and take the stairs down. I don't want to be anywhere near my mother right now.

I find the bright blue splotch at the end of the parking lot. I don't even know where I'm going, but I need air. I roll down the windows and pull out of the lot and head right down the beach.

Juliet Duncan, who I met the other night, is my aunt. My family. I have a whole other family. Aunts, uncles, cousins. Another set of grandparents I never met. And I think they're all here, in Florida. In this town. I want to see Juliet again, but I don't even know what to say to her without sounding like a freaking lunatic. The way she spoke of my mother, I don't think she'd be so happy.

Then again—maybe I'm the key to her feeling like she can have her brother back. I'm half of him, after all.

I pat my belly. My father was a twin—God, what if there are two of them in there? I kick myself for not telling the father, the random Tinder hookup. I kick myself for my behavior over the entire last six months—I've been careless and reckless, and I'm going to end up just like my mother.

According to the signs, I'm near Clearwater, and I park the car to watch the sun set over the Gulf of Mexico, contemplating my life. As soon as I get home tomorrow night, I'm going to call him. Joseph. That's his name—the baby daddy. He deserves to know. I need to decide what the hell I want to do with my life once I step off that plane. At six weeks along, I'm running out of time. Finish college and be a reporter, or drop out and be a mom?

Just like *her*. At this point, that's the least appealing option.

The sky is dark, and I get into my car to leave. Yet the wheels don't turn toward the hotel when I pass it. They go to another

familiar spot. Armed with my new info, I have a feeling if I mention Julian's name, I'll get more of the true story. Everyone is lying.
I can pretend I know more than I do. That's a journalism tactic
I learned in school to get people to say more than they want to.

I pull into the driveway, fly out of the car, and ring the bell. The
door opens. Scarlett looks upset, her eyes rimmed red.

"Zoey. What are you doing here?"

"I need to know something before I leave. My mother told me
about her and Julian."

Her cheeks droop and her mouth gapes. Her hand quickly flies
over to cover it, and it's weird how much I know her after only
forty-eight hours. Oh yeah, she knows what I'm about to say. She
must've always known that he's my father, and now that I've got her
where I want her, maybe I'll find out the truth about the accident.

"Oh my God." Now her hand is on her head, and she looks
white as a ghost. "She told you that he tried to rape her the night
of the accident?"

Wait. What?

INTERVIEW THE DAY AFTER
THE SENIOR PICNIC

Detective Logan: Julian was acting strange, how?

Juliet: I don't know. I thought he got Chloe pregnant, to be honest.

Detective Logan: Why would you say that?

Juliet: I heard him on the phone alluding to something like that. Can you find out if Chloe was pregnant? If she wasn't, there was something else going on with him.

35

PEPPER

Senior Picnic
June 1999

T here's no way Julian is breaking up with me.

Every hope I have has just fallen off a cliff and died. While I still don't understand Julian's last statement, the shock and betrayal I feel is instant. I'm not used to losing control, and I'm definitely not used to having someone dump me. Someone lesser than me; not the goth kid. No way.

"You said you were coming to New York with me." My voice cracks at first, then comes out in an insecure whisper instead of my usual confident tone. Dammit, don't fall apart in front of him. "We're having a baby. We're going to be a family."

Julian takes another drag of his cigarette. "I told you I'm not ready to be a father, and what I think you should do. New York? It's not happening. It never was."

No. No no no no no. "But you let me go on and on about it, and you never said a word."

He shrugs. "Yeah, my bad. The last few times, you seemed pretty serious, like you actually thought I was leaving Florida and moving with you. But like I said"—he takes another drag—"not happening."

Does. Not. Compute.

I love him; he loves me. "Why, Julian? Tell me why." I get right in his face; I need him to tell me why he's ending us like this. "Tell me!" I throw myself at him in an attempt to kiss him, and he in turn pushes me off, his lip curled and his jaw set. I fall to the ground, where I stay. The pain from the twigs that dig into my bare backside is nothing compared to having my heart ripped from my chest cavity, still pumping. "Please, Julian. Please don't do this. I love you. I'll stay. I don't have to go to New York."

I'll give it up. I will. For him, I will.

"Love? Pepper, do you even hear yourself? I'm eighteen, for fuck's sake. I never told you I loved you."

No, he's never said it, but I know it. I won't accept a different answer—I've had the scenario in my brain for months. We are going to be together and live happily ever after—there is no alternative. "We said forever."

"*You* said forever. I had my dick in the head cheerleader. At what point was I supposed to disagree with you?"

He stands tall, his moonlit shadow like one of the trees around us. He doesn't move, and he doesn't speak; I hear him taking drag after drag of his cigarette. Inhale. Suck. Blow. Insignificant sounds, but ones I cling to out of the fear that they are the last ones I'll hear from him. Still in the dirt, I crawl over to his lower leg and wrap myself around it.

"I know you love me," I whisper. "You can't fake that."

He scoffs. "Faking it. That's all you've been doing—your whole life is make-believe, with your little worshippers and your asshole boyfriend. You've done nothing but play a part, so quit crying. You love being the queen of the school. Come on, Pepper. You can't possibly think I was ever into that stuff."

Inhale. Suck. Blow. The cigarette finally comes crashing down too close to me, and he stomps it out with his free foot.

"I dumped Vince for you so many times," I whisper. Panicked. Poor Vince will never take me back knowing I slept with Julian. That he got me pregnant. I'm going to lose everyone and end up alone.

Julian's eyes go dark. "You're fucking obsessed. What's wrong with you? We're not in a relationship—we fucked for a few months. I never said I was going to New York. You imagined a love story that didn't happen."

To have Julian say that I imagined our love hurts beyond comprehension, and I have trouble processing it. I feel like he's holding me underwater. Do I stop fighting and give in? Die right here while clutching his leg?

No. Rage takes over. His words cut deep, but not deeper than what he says next.

"There's someone else anyway. Someone I actually like."

I open my mouth to say something. No words come out—I've been rendered completely and utterly speechless.

Just like that, the switch flips. This isn't going to end well. For him, anyway. Julian must be scared when I tip my eyes north toward him from the ground and show him my evil. He takes a step back as I rise like a monster from a horror movie, which is what I'm about to become.

"Who?" I say slowly, my voice unrecognizable and deep.

He smirks at me. I'm at my lowest point in my life, and he doesn't care. Why doesn't he care about me? Instead, he pulls another cigarette to his mouth and lights it, the tip glowing red like eyes from said horror movie. Inhale. Suck. Blow.

"Haven't you heard the gossip? That Chloe is cheating on Chris?" He stops and takes another drag of his cigarette. "She is. With me. There, you know the truth. *Now* will you leave me alone?"

Rage.

I go at him full force, flailing my arms in the air, trying to hit anything. He puts his arms up defensively, but lets me slap him, acting as calmly as if he's reading a book. I realize I can't rattle him and stop acting like a maniac. For now. I won't be passed over for Chloe, someone lesser. Nope. Not Chloe. Not now, not ever.

"Chloe?" A million scenarios go through my head and come out at once. "She won't be faithful." My cries herald on desperate; I can't lose Julian. "Not her, Julian. She's a whore."

"In the best possible way." Inhale. Suck. Blow. "You're not as great as you think you are. Get over yourself. Really." He looks at his watch. "I have to meet her over in Rockland Park soon. So, I guess this is goodbye."

"Why are you telling me this?" I ask. "Are you purposely trying to hurt me?"

"Jesus Christ, Pepper. It's the only way to get you to understand. Finito." With his index finger, he slashes his own throat ear to ear as he says it. *Finito.* His eyes come to life as he dismisses me, but all I see is his imminent death as he raises two fingers in the air. "Peace. And don't try to come after me for child support. I told you to take care of it."

My head spins. I'm going to kill him. I am. I really, truly am.

His cigarette butt lands right next to me, and he turns to leave. Just like that, he walks out of the woods, and out of my life. I scream at the top of my lungs as I watch him walk away. I sit crying in the darkness as his frame gets smaller and smaller, the distance between us wider and farther. I find myself crawling through the brush, twigs catching on my legs and sundress, as I cry soulless, gut-wrenching coughs.

When I finally focus, toward the fair, I see the silhouette of my best friend in the distance.

I can't let Scarlett know what just happened—she has me on an invisible pedestal. If Scarlett sees me, rejected and tossed away by Julian Ackers, of all people, the entire persona I've built for seven years will come crashing down. I have to think fast, and make Julian pay for what he's done to me.

As Scarlett gets closer, my crazy, storytelling mind jumps into play. Jordan. *Say you came to meet Jordan. She'll believe it. Deep down, she knows you'll fuck your ex-boyfriend's friend.* I plot my story, wipe more dirt on myself, and tear my own dress strap. Next are the crocodile tears; I taught myself to cry on command. Julian was right—I'm as fake as a three-dollar bill.

But the rage is real.

"Pepper?" she whispers as she approaches. "Are you okay?"

I give her the whole fake story that I made up about meeting Jordan Kessler and seeing Julian. That asshole.

"Really? So what happened?" she asks.

I know what I spill next will get her to do anything I say for the rest of the night. And my night is just beginning. "With Julian? He tried to rape me."

INTERVIEW THE DAY AFTER
THE SENIOR PICNIC

Detective Logan: Juliet, anything you can tell us could be helpful. Between you and me, I'm not exactly convinced this is an accident. The scene was too clean.

Juliet: It was in a park. I don't understand.

Detective Logan: If Chloe was with your brother the way you say and saw him when she entered the park, we'd see different tire marks, like she tried to stop. But that's not there. It's almost like she accelerated. It's not sitting right with me. If someone hurt your brother, wouldn't you want to know why?

36

ZOEY

"**W**hat do you mean, Julian tried to rape my mother?"

This can't be right. My mother just told me an entire story about how much she loved Julian, how they were together in secret for months, and then how he lied to her about their future and dumped her, and effectively me. My mother loved Julian with her entire heart back then. Scarlett has no idea what she's talking about. He did no such thing.

"Do you want to come in?" Scarlett asks and holds the door open.

I nod, tears in my eyes. Either Scarlett is lying, or—God, was my mother lying to protect me? Was my father a rapist and she doesn't want me to know the truth, that I'm a product of a rape? The emotions inside me whip forward and back like a boat in a hurricane, and I hold back wave after wave of nausea.

Inside Scarlett's house for the second time in as many days, I feel different. Now, I feel like we might be on the same side. Through my conversation with Luke, I know that Vince cheated on her. And now, I know the woman is in shock because *I'm* the one who lied about my own mother being dead and she had to see her former best friend resurrected. The first time I was here, I was a smug little shit, intent on making her talk. I didn't like that she lied to me about Vince, and I thought she knew more than she let on about the accident.

Now I'm sure of it. Nothing has added up since my plane landed. "Where's Vince?" I ask.

She looks defeated, tired. She shrugs. "We left Chris's right after your mother did. Luke is resting upstairs; he said he doesn't feel well. Who could blame him? Vince and I had an argument, which I'm sure you meant to cause, and then he got a text message and left. I don't know where he is. But I have a pretty good idea."

Scarlett could be right in her assumptions on where Vince is—my mother is a monster. He's probably with her. She probably called him the second I left the hotel room. She has no boundaries and she's a liar. God only knows what additional lies she's feeding to Vince.

I'm a monster too. I feel like I've ruined this woman's life. For what? Ugh, being raised by a narcissist rubbed off on me in the worst way, and my chest tightens. We sit down at the kitchen table, and Scarlett pours a glass of white wine and looks toward me.

"You want some? Or red?" she asks, then pulls the bottle back. "Oh, shit. I forgot. You're pregnant." I nod. She grabs my hand. "Oh, honey."

It's maternal instinct. She's a good mother, and I feel even worse about my antics. Tears brim my eyelids as the room blurs. I grab a napkin out of a dispenser on the table and blot.

"It's why I've been so obsessed with finding out about my father and who he is. I'm sorry for causing all this chaos in your life. I just had a talk with my mother, and she finally told me who my dad is."

This time, Scarlett's eyes go glassy. I don't want to betray my mother's trust, but what Scarlett said about Julian—Dad— whoever, doesn't sit right with me. Rapist?

"Do you want to tell me?" she asks, not pressing.

"Yes. She said Julian was my father. And you just told me he tried to rape her. Am I a product of rape?"

I wait for a reaction, and she shakes her head, insistent. "No. No, Julian assaulted your mother that night of the senior picnic. She was already pregnant for a month when that happened."

Time to pop the Perfect Pepper bubble. "No, I don't think you understand. My mother lied to you. She told me she was in a rela- tionship with Julian. That she loved him, and it's why she dumped Vince. She said he told her they'd go to New York together, but then he dumped her that night, saying he wasn't ready to be a father. And that it crushed her."

"No!" Scarlett pounds her fist on the table and makes it vibrate, scaring me, and I push my chair back a little. Now her eyes are wild. "That's not right. Julian—he assaulted her. She got away. He—she—" Her voice cracks, and then her hands go over her face, trying to cover the realization that she's been lied to. She's trying to hide her crying, but the blubbering is obvious, and I let her get it out for a minute or two. The anguish on her face is heartbreaking. "Oh God, what have I done?" she whispers.

I stand, approach her side of the table, and crouch down to hold her and pat her shoulder. Something obviously has her shaken up. She finally grabs one of the napkins, blows her nose, and leaves it on the table, then takes another and does the same. She rubs her temples, and her face is strained as if she has a migraine.

"What's wrong?" I ask.

She sniffles. "Julian is your father? Are you sure?"

I nod. "Yes, that's what she said. My father is dead. He died that night in the accident."

She's quiet. In shock. Continues rubbing her temples in disbelief. "Why should I believe you?"

"Well, you can ask her yourself, for starters. I'll call her right now."

Scarlett stares blankly ahead, like she's focused on something farther in the kitchen. I turn to see if she's staring at anything in particular, but all I see are appliances and clean dishes piled up in a rack on one side of the sink. I look back at her and she's still fixated, and I realize she's looking at nothing. She's just trying hard to not look at me.

She knows something. I was right the whole time.

"If that's true, I'm sorry you'll never get to meet your father," she says, her voice low and sympathetic. Then she finally looks directly at me, and her tone becomes more assertive. "But make no mistake. That was no accident."

"What do you mean?" Please, please, please tell me what I've been dying to know.

She stands and paces. "Your mother—she—well, for starters, she lied to me."

"I'm sure," I say. "But what else did she do?"

"It's about what she made *me* do, because of her lies."

INTERVIEW THE DAY AFTER
THE SENIOR PICNIC

Detective Logan: You're the last interview I have. I know it's been a long day for both of us. Are you sure that's all?

Pepper: Yep. That's all. I'm sorry you think something bad happened. If it did, I hope you catch them.

Detective Logan: I intend to.

37

SCARLETT

Senior Picnic
June 1999

We pile into Chloe's car, Pepper riding shotgun and me in the back, even though I'm guilt ridden about Pepper going bananas and kicking in the headlight. But I can't judge anything Pepper's been feeling. I'm torn apart that she wouldn't let me take her to the police station and report Julian Ackers for assaulting her.

"What happened to your car? Did you know one of your headlights is busted?" Pepper asks. She always did read my mind.

"Yeah, I saw," Chloe says. "There was glass around the front of the car. I guess someone was drunk and thought it was funny."

"Funny. That's a good word."

Chloe doesn't answer, and as the stale french fry smell from the McDonald's bag hits my nostrils, my throat closes like I'm going to be sick. Pepper, on the other hand, is having the time of her life. She puts on her seatbelt, rolls down the window, and sticks her right leg out, letting it hang over the side of the car door like wet spaghetti as Chloe slowly gets back on the road.

"I'm taking one of these," Pepper says as she reaches into Chloe's fresh pack of cigarettes. She hooks one into her mouth and then pulls out another and tucks it behind her ear for later. She looks at me in the back. "Here, have one," she says as she tosses yet another cigarette.

Chloe side-eyes her, but she doesn't dare say a word. In fact, a lighter materializes in her hand, and she lights Pepper's cigarette with one hand while the other steers. Pepper takes a huge puff, accentuating the sound in and out.

"Mmm, nothing like a smoke. Right, Chloe?" she says.

"Mmhmm," Chloe mumbles as the car accelerates.

"Why are you speeding?"

"Just trying to get you guys home."

Pepper tears the lighter out of her hand and faces me in the back seat to light my cigarette, but the flame keeps going out. I take the lighter away from her and roll the silver disc with my thumb at least ten times, with no luck.

"Close the window, Pepper. It's not lighting. There's too much wind," I say, but then another wave of stale fries hits my nose, and I clamp my hand over my mouth. "I think I'm going to be sick."

"Oh, stop being so dramatic. Take a nap," Pepper snaps.

I *have* had an awful lot to drink and I *am* exhausted, so I don't think twice as my eyes close. Caught in that moment of hazing in and out of consciousness, I only hear bits and pieces of the conversation in the front seat.

"So, what are you really doing out here, Chloe?" Pepper asks.

"I was going to the party. Weren't you?"

"Really. Huh. Because if I were you, and thank God I'm *not*, but if I were, I'd have turned left onto Wainscott about a mile back. Takes you right to the highway. It's only a couple miles from there, but this is the opposite direction. Are you going somewhere? Big plans? Hot date?"

"No."

"Where's Chris?"

"I don't really feel like talking about this," Chloe says with a wavering voice.

"Looks like we're near Rockland Park. Pull over."

The car slows, and Chloe pulls to the side of the road, the engine softly purring like a kitten. "What do you want from me, Pepper?"

"You were coming out here tonight anyway, weren't you? Just take the fucking car into the park. Like you planned."

Well, now I'm wide awake. Something is happening and I rub my eyes. "What's going on? Where are we?"

"Go back to sleep," Pepper scolds.

I shake my head back and forth, thinking maybe I can shake the alcohol out of me, like a dog ridding itself of water after it jumps out of a pool. My brain is clouded, and I don't understand where we are, or why we've stopped, or why they're fighting. Pepper curls her leg back inside and straightens herself out.

Chloe unbuckles her seatbelt and turns toward Pepper. "Pepper, please," she begs.

"Please what? You're so fucking jealous of us. You went after Chris knowing Scarlett liked him. You steal men. Well, not this time. Not him. I won't allow it."

Is she talking about Vince? I'm trying to focus, but the old vodka stifles me with double vision. That's why I can't react when a shadow appears in the distance. The next part happens in seconds. Pepper flings her left leg into the driver's side bucket as she puts the car in drive. Then she hits the gas. Hard. The car lurches forward, and the shadow becomes Julian Ackers.

Oh no.

Pepper doesn't take her foot off the gas. In fact, her rage takes the wheel and aims as I brace myself. The next thing I know, we're stopped. I pick myself up off the floor of the back seat—I rolled off at impact and have no idea what just happened. However, when my vision becomes clear, I scream.

In the driver's side seat, Chloe's head bleeds over the steering wheel, the visible skull-shaped crack in the windshield telling me what I clearly missed in the chaos. Chloe's eyes are closed, hot blood trickling from the middle of her temple, pooling onto the dashboard.

"Chloe! Chloe, are you okay?" I say when I sit up, and then rub my own neck. The pain is piercing, a thousand hot knives stabbing into the stem of my skull. "Pepper? Are you okay? What happened?"

"I don't know," Pepper says, her voice weak. "Chloe freaked out."

I know I've had too much to drink, but I also know I didn't hallucinate what happened in the front seat. Pepper took the wheel. "No," I try to shake my head to signal no, but I can't move my neck.

"No. There was something going on with you guys. Who were you talking about? You guys were fighting."

"Ah, fuck!" Pepper screams when she tries to maneuver her way up. "I'm pinned, and my fucking arm hurts."

I lift my gaze to the front of the car, where the one headlight left gives off enough light to see Julian Ackers slumped over the hood of the car, between the entrance boulder and the bumper, not moving. The shriek that emerges from my mouth is a sound that I didn't think my body was capable of making. My hand still on the back of my neck, I adjust my eyes to the darkness and attempt to look around the seat.

"Where's my bag?" I say. "I need my phone. I have to call nine-one-one."

"Don't you fucking dare call nine-one-one," Pepper orders.

"What? What are you talking about?"

"I'm not throwing away my future because of this whore. She *was* cheating on Chris. I found out she fucked Vince. Look, that's why I dumped him. I was too embarrassed for you to know the truth, that he cheated on me, with her. But this—" She waves toward the rock, to the lifeless rag doll of broken bones and blood. "He tried to *rape* me, and almost got away with it too. We could be accessories to this. To murder. *Murder*, Scarlett."

Murder. Visions of orange jumpsuits dance through my head. "No. It was an accident. It wasn't murder." Right? Wait . . . I know what I saw. Pepper's foot on the gas. Pepper's hand on the wheel. "What did you do?"

Her eyes go wild. "We have to get out of here. No one knows we were with her. Get your shit and let's get the fuck out of this car."

"Wait. What? You're not making sense. We have to get help. Chloe needs help."

"Chloe's dead."

"No," I say as I shake my head, then wince. "No. Look. She's breathing." I squint past her. "Julian too. Look, his hand is moving!"

Pepper looks over at Chloe. Although faint and labored, there is definite movement in her back, like her lungs are fighting to get any squeeze of air that they can. Chloe's visible eye opens and although neither her head nor her body move, the sound is discernible. It's Chloe's voice.

"Help me."

Before I can say another word, Pepper takes over. "Get out of the car," she demands. "I'll save her. I need room."

I never challenge Pepper, ever. And the girl's complete dismissal of the event that just took place shocks me. Sure, Pepper's been acting strangely for the past few months, and I know she's traumatized between the attempted rape and now the front-row seat at the accident, but her composure in the situation doesn't sit right with me. So, I stand firm.

"No, I'm not going anywhere. We have to help Chloe."

Pepper's eyes shoot poison darts into me, and I'm immediately subdued. "Get out. Didn't you practically fail those CPR lessons we had in ninth? I'll try to revive her. And don't touch that fucking phone, I'm warning you." None of it is a request.

I revert back to myself, meek little Scarlett who does whatever Pepper says. I get out of the car and crawl away. I make it about twenty feet or so when I see movement in the front seats, the silhouette of Pepper trying to help Chloe, possibly breathing into her mouth. Something is going on, I'm just not positive what. Damn vodka, I swear I'm never drinking again. After a minute, Pepper slides her body out of the open front passenger's side window, cradling her arm.

"Chloe's dead. I tried to save her, but she started spitting up blood. Then she just stopped breathing. I checked her pulse on her neck and on her wrist. She's dead."

My life flashes before me. While all our other friends are going to be rushing sororities and getting degrees and starting families, we're going to be rotting away in a prison cell for manslaughter.

"What about Julian? He's moving."

She swivels her head over to him and pays attention for about three seconds, likely contemplating the situation, and then turns back to me. "He'll never survive. He's probably got internal bleeding. The car hit him front and center. Come on. We have to go."

"Pepper, Jesus, are you crazy? He's suffering."

"Good."

It's ninety degrees, but I'm shivering. The sweat around my hairline and down my back is cold sweat. It's got to be from the shock. Of the accident, and of what Pepper is trying to make me do. We can't *leave* the scene of an accident where two people are going to die. "What's wrong with you? Oh my God. We did this."

Pepper is as callous as can be, pointing back at the car. "*She* did this! Neither of us were driving. She wasn't wearing her seatbelt, that's not our fault. Look at this crash. Chloe would've died way before anyone would've gotten here to help her. We're in Rockland Park, for fuck's sake. It's the middle of nowhere. Why do you even care? She stole Chris, *and* Vince. How do we know that Julian didn't already rape a bunch of girls, or that he was planning to do it more? Now, we've got to get out of here." She's already dragging me across the asphalt, away from the car.

I tug my arm away from her. "What are you talking about? We can't leave!" Despite the pain, I shake my head vigorously. "We have to tell someone what happened here. And about what Julian did to you."

"No, we're not going to tell anyone. This is the story, so pay attention."

This is the story. Those words are going to be on her damn headstone. Every time we'd gotten in trouble the last seven years, Pepper always fixed it with "this is the story." Excuses for being late to class, sure. Leaving the scene of an accident where two people are going to die is quite something else, and I'm not prepared.

"This is the story. We tried to thumb a ride up on Three Bridges Road—we'll stick with that in case anyone saw us near here. When we couldn't get a ride, we sobered up and went back for your car. We were never in the car with Chloe. No one saw us with her."

Pepper tucks into her bag and yanks out a Poland Spring bottle laced with vodka. She wipes it down, then creeps back to the car and pours what little remains over Chloe's face and lips. She wipes the bottle down again and places it under Chloe's left hand, still dangling, into the foot bed of the car. Her head swivels back to me.

"Chloe was drinking and driving. It's a shame, really. She meant to stop but hit the gas by accident. Alcohol dulls your senses, you know."

She stands in front of me, the menacing moonlight making her face gray, and continues her charade.

"I mean, she had what was coming to her. She stole your boyfriend. Mine too. I didn't even realize what was going on with her and Vince, right behind my back. And Julian, *that rapist*, was probably out here getting high like he always did. Possibly creeping on a girl he was hoping to find alone. All I know is that we can't be involved. Think about it. Do you really want to have to delay college for a murder investigation?"

"It was an accident," I say softly. "It was just an accident." Now, I'm saying it to convince myself, fighting my knowledge of what I saw against *this is the story* like a heavyweight match. Pepper has a way of making me believe what she wants me to believe, and I'm KO'd in an instant.

"I'm not sure that's how other people will see it," she says. "I mean, think about how it will look. Not just for me, but all of us are involved. Chris hooked up with you and then went right for Chloe. What if people think you were jealous? Do you really want to throw your life away? Trust me, it's easier this way. Let's just go back and get your car. We'll never mention this again. Deal?"

She says it like a used car salesman. *Deal.* That's it. Handshake and a note on a cocktail napkin. "How are we supposed to explain my neck? And your arm?"

She shrugs. "We were drunk and fell. Wouldn't be the first time."

I look back at the destroyed car, my heart not matching what comes out of my mouth—it's not enough to explain my feelings. "Oh my God. I can't believe this." It sounds blunt and dry, not awake and liquid, like how I really feel. I can barely keep my head above the ocean of lies I'm submerged in, and I just know I'm going to drown.

Pepper faces me and shakes me, despite the pain in her arm, and despite the fact that she knows by now she's causing pain to her best friend's neck. "You need to look at me. Focus. You need to listen. I need you to repeat what happened. What's the story?"

This is the story. I repeat everything she just told me. "No one is going to believe us, though." I turn to look at the crash again but close my eyes immediately. I can't bear further witness to the mess that I'm involved in. "I don't even know who you are right now. Making me lie about this. Our DNA is going to be all over her. In the car too."

Truth is, I don't even know who *I* am right now. Why am I going along with her? Why? Because I'm Scarlett Kane, and that's just what I do—whatever Pepper Wilson says.

"Come on. You're just in shock. And we've been in her car a hundred times, she even drove us after graduation yesterday. It's not like she cleaned the car. You see what a pig she is—old McDonald's bags? Gross. And we were all hugging earlier. If a stray hair is on her, no one will care. Our prints are all over the car, along with half the high school. No one is going to look. It looks like a drunk driving accident."

My face is blank. Complete and utter shock at the train of thought that's going into this deception.

"You seem to be forgetting what happened to me tonight. Julian deserved to die. You know what that fucker did to me!" The tears she cries seem real this time, but she composes herself quickly again. "Are you sure nothing fell out of your bag? You have everything, right? Nothing can tie you to that car?"

I look in my bag on demand. Cell phone, keys, cigarettes, wallet, lighter, sunglasses, ChapStick, leftover ride tickets. "Everything's here," I whisper.

"Good. Let's go. We were never here. Do you understand? *We were never here.* We can't ever talk about this again. I mean, you have to promise me." Tears well in her eyes again. "Promise you'll keep this secret forever!"

"I will." Why? *Why, why, why, why, why?* I ask myself a million times. "But what about them?"

"Someone will report them missing. Some idiot will be jogging or walking their dog in the park tomorrow morning and see it. Either way, it won't be a long search, we're only a few miles from the fair. Everyone saw them both there. But you and I—we have to go, and we have to go now."

INTERVIEW THE DAY AFTER
THE SENIOR PICNIC

Detective Logan: Are you sure you have nothing else to say?

Scarlett: Nope. That's about it. Good luck with everything.

Detective Logan: I'm sorry about your friend.

Scarlett: Thank you. Hopefully she didn't suffer.

38

SCARLETT

The whole scenario comes crashing back.

Wait, bad choice of words.

If what Zoey just said is true, then I was right back then—not only was it murder, it was cold-blooded murder, and why? Because Julian dumped Pepper? He didn't deserve to die for that. She aimed that car at him—most of the night is fuzzy, but I remember that—no matter how she tried and tried to convince me otherwise. And poor Chloe ended up dead for no reason. She never saw college, marriage, career, kids, grandkids—all because she was in a relationship with someone Pepper claimed to hate.

Chloe had won. She beat Pepper and paid the ultimate price.

Worse—I was there. I lied to the cops, because Pepper told me Julian assaulted her; that she saw red when she saw him at the park entrance and needed to get her revenge. Only none of it was true. She knew he'd be there the whole time. She marked Chloe's car with the busted headlight, so she knew who to stop on the dark road.

Isn't that called premeditated murder?

The memories wash over me like a tornado, destroying everything in its path—my confidence, my self-worth, everything. The last twenty-two years, I've carried the guilt over the lies, but I had convinced myself I did it to protect Pepper. My poor, pregnant, violated friend.

That bitch.

But now, here we are. I'm sitting in my kitchen with the daughter of my dead-but-resurrected former best friend, who is vulnerable and pregnant. I can't fight the urge that things need to be done differently this time. While I'll make sure Pepper pays for what she did, right now my concern is for the young girl before me. I won't tell her exactly how wretched her mother is—it's not fair. A minute ago, I was ready to tell her everything, but now, I have to change course.

"Your mother lied to me about Julian. She never showed interest in him. It's a shock to hear they were together. Let alone for him to be your father."

She frowns. "You just said it wasn't an accident. What happened that night?"

Shit. Of course she hasn't forgotten. It's half her reason for being here the last forty-eight hours. Her eyes are teary, hopeful. But this isn't my story to tell. Hell, I don't even think I know the real story. All this time, burying the secret for Pepper's benefit. I didn't tell Zoey even when I thought Pepper was dead. What kind of hold does this woman have on me? Still?

"Can you call your mother? See if she'll come over? To be quite honest, Zoey, I feel like she owes me an explanation too. I was also lied to. Maybe we should see what else she has to say."

The look she gives me this time is something I haven't seen from her since we met. It's solidarity. She nods her head slightly, and there's a small smile as she pulls her phone from her bag. I chew on my nails as I watch her swipe and connect the call. Pepper answers—I hear her voice on the line, but Zoey presses the phone hard to her ear as she talks so I hear nothing except for her side.

"It's me . . . At Scarlett's . . . Yes . . . I—we—we need to talk to you about something . . . Let me finish . . . I told her about Julian being my father . . . I don't care . . . Yeah, well, she said something disturbing that I think you need to explain . . . Why, though? . . . I don't care . . . No. You come here. It's just the two of us . . ."

It's quiet on Zoey's end for a few seconds when her face goes white and her eyes divert. My heart turns into ice because I know what Pepper just said to her. I know it in my bones, the way I know I love Luke. Pepper is with Vince.

Zoey continues. "You're a piece of work. Just leave . . . Honestly, Mom, if you're not here in twenty minutes, I'm dead to you. Just like my father."

Zoey disconnects the call, and I don't hate her anymore. In fact, I kind of like her. Still, the lump in my throat is there, the one that developed the second Vince walked out after getting that text an hour ago. The one he didn't let me see. The one I knew was Pepper.

"She's with Vince, isn't she?" I ask.

Zoey doesn't hesitate. "Yes, she is," she says with conviction. "I'm sorry. God, she always does this. She loves taking what belongs to someone else. She's so fucking insecure. She never got what she wanted—first Julian, I guess then Vince, even her acting career is bullshit. She has no morals. None."

No shit, huh? My fists clench so hard I know I must be drawing blood. I blow out a breath of air, pour more wine. Sit back down. Take gulps. "Oh well. What am I going to do?" I say, dejected, accepting my loss. "I guess he never really loved me. He never got over your mother."

"That can't be true," Zoey says, but I'm already waving my hand in her face, showing her not to bother with the lies to try to make me feel better. "If he didn't love you, he wouldn't be here after this long."

It takes all my strength not to laugh hysterically. After this long, he's not here because he loves me. He's here to fulfill some fatherly obligation. I know our marriage will be over after Luke graduates, and I'm convinced Vince believes the same thing. At this point, I honestly don't know how I can fake the next five months.

I'll do it, though. I'll do it for Luke.

"Vince has always had one foot out the door. There was another one. Her name was Lila. It was a decade ago." I sound weak, stupid. A doormat. "God, I should've divorced him then. I had proof. It was an easy out."

Why am I telling this to Zoey?

Why? Because I have to get it out. All the excuses I made to my friends, and to my sister Hannah, when I called them crying. *We have to stay together for Luke. He said he's ending it with Lila.* What a punching bag I must've sounded like. Of course, Pepper groomed me to be that way—to take shit from people who tell me they love me, even if their actions say otherwise.

I'll never regret Vince because I have Luke, but if I had any kind of spine and left him after Lila, maybe I'd be in a different loving relationship right now. Maybe even married to someone else. My relationship, my marriage, has never been filled with warmth or the kind of love you read about. The only time I've felt real love in seventeen years is every time I look at Luke.

Plus, the more I think about it, the more I have to admit—I don't think Lila was the only one. And none of us will ever compare to Pepper. And now she's back.

VOICEMAILS FROM SCARLETT TO PEPPER
THE DAY AFTER THE SENIOR PICNIC

Scarlett: Hey, it's me. Did you know the cops want to talk to everyone? Call me back.

Scarlett: Where are you? My mom is bringing me down now. Call me back.

Scarlett: I said everything you wanted me to say. I don't think I messed up, but the guy kept asking about my neck and the end of the night. He was acting like he knew something was fucked. Call me back.

Scarlett: Where are you? Have you gone in yet? I need to know what you said. Call me back.

39

PEPPER

"**S**hit."

Now it's time to panic. I can't believe Zoey told *Scarlett* of all people about Julian. Since when the hell are they BFFs? I'm going to have to explain what happened. To everyone. I throw the phone down on the bed. Vince was right, I shouldn't have answered. We were about to start something, and I wouldn't have had any regrets. He's oblivious to my distress as he comes close again, trying to reignite the spark.

I texted him as soon as Zoey left. I know it's selfish, but whatever. Admittedly, part of what's happening now is jealousy. I can't wrap my head around the fact that Scarlett is married to him. It's not fair. He was always mine. Not hers.

"That was Zoey," I say to him. "She's with your wife."

I say that in lieu of saying her name. Not that the words *your wife* roll off my tongue any easier.

Vince's face falls. "What is she doing with her?" He opens the minibar and takes out, well, everything. He unscrews a cap on the small whiskey bottle and downs it.

"Zoey and I had an argument before she left. She—God, Vince, this is so hard."

I sit on the bed, and he sits next to me and takes my hand. "What?"

My eyes tear. "I told her about her father, and she just told Scarlett. We have to go to your house. Now. Things are—complicated."

His face hardens, and he gulps, making his Adam's apple visible. I always loved that about him. "And? Who is it?"

I have to tell him now. I can't dump this all on him in front of Scarlett, especially since I lied to her. To him, too. Shit. He's going to kill me. I have to sell this the best way I know how. *Channel it, Pepper. Make him believe your lies. Aaaaaaaand action!*

"Vince, I know this is going to be hard for you. Not just because of the teenage cheating, but because of who I was doing it with."

"I'm listening."

I take a deep breath. "It was Julian." It comes out barely above a whisper. "Julian is Zoey's father."

His eyebrows dent, confused. "What? How? You told me he almost raped you." Then his eyes go wide. "Oh God, Pepper. Did he? Is that what this is? Is Zoey because of—of that?"

His voice is loud, and I'm afraid if someone is passing in the hallway, they'll hear him. I wave a hand at him and shush him, indicating to keep his voice down. Even though what I say next is going to kill him.

"No." My voice is still low. "No, that's not what happened. I had a lot of secrets back then."

"Secrets? What secrets?"

It's time, and I turn to face the wall, because I'm a coward and I can't even look at him. I can't even act my way out of what I'm about to say. "Julian. And me. It was going on for a while."

Vince drops my hand, stands up, and walks across the room, back to the minibar, where he makes another small bottle of whiskey go bye-bye. His breathing is harder and faster. He's alternating between clenching his fists and letting them out to rub his hands over each other, reminding me of a petulant child who was told they have to turn off the cartoons. His cheeks are red and puffy, like he's holding his breath. I know he's about to blow. Some things never change.

"You were screwing that asshole behind my back? I can't believe you, Pepper." He's angry. Pacing. "What was the fucking point of calling me that night and saying he tried to rape you?"

I needed that favor, that's why. And I knew it would make him mad. I wanted attention after Julian dumped me. It's not like anyone could've asked Julian to prove he didn't try to rape me. He was dead.

I knew Vince would never break my trust, either. Even though it was all a lovely lie.

"I was scared after the car accident, Vince."

"Why did you even tell me about that either? I don't understand what the point of any of this is."

I lower my head. "I thought I loved him. I was a kid. You were the one I loved. I was just confused."

"Did he assault you? Answer me."

"No, he didn't. I was upset, and I wanted you to hate him even more. So, I lied."

He bangs his fist on the desk. "God damn it, Pepper! Do you know what you've done?"

Vince still thinks that Chloe was drunk and hit Julian by accident. He lied to the cops to protect me, because I asked him not to mention I was there, at the site of the accident.

To protect himself for being there, after.

His face is white as a ghost and his hands are trembling. Then he looks at his hands. First the back, then he flips his palms up, and then back down again. He never takes his eyes off his hands.

"Your plan worked. I hated him even more. I wish you hadn't called me that night about your keys. You have no idea how much damage you've caused." Now he's unscrewing a small bottle of vodka. Apparently, he's finished the whiskey.

I don't want him blaming me for any of this. I want him to see it as I did—that he saved me. So, I get up and go to him and lean into his chest. At first, he's rigid, but then he exhales and wraps his arms around me. Tightly. There's something more behind it—maybe it's our shared misfortune. But it feels good, and I feel like a teenager again. When Vince was mine.

Vince *is* mine.

I tilt my head and our eyes lock. I can feel his slight hesitation, and it's like a slap across my face. He's married to Scarlett.

"I'm sorry, Vince. I'm sorry I cheated on you. I'm sorry for everything. I wish we could just go back to when we were us."

His fingers are interlocked with each other at the small of my back, like he used to hold me back then. "Why didn't you ever reach out to me? How could you just leave without a trace, babe?" Now he looks embarrassed and flushes. "I mean . . . I don't know why I called you that."

I smile. "You always called me that. And I couldn't. I had Zoey, and then . . . I didn't want to burden you. You were better off without me, and I wanted you to have the life you deserved. But I did still love you. I do still love you. I never should've taken up with Julian."

He stiffens against me at the mention of Julian's name.

"We have to go," I say, thinking of Zoey. "I have to be honest with Scarlett about what happened. With Zoey. And with you. Give me your keys, you've had too much to drink."

He nods, pauses. He's staring. I look at his lips. He moves closer and kisses me again. Harder. More passionate. His hands are everywhere.

It's just a love scene. You know what to do.

I mean, who wastes a hotel room?

CONVERSATION BETWEEN PEPPER AND VINCE THE NIGHT OF THE SENIOR PICNIC

Vince: Hi, babe.

Pepper: Are you drunk? You're slurring.

Vince: I'm at Chris's party. Are you coming here? I miss you. I want to get back together. Please take me back. I love you, babe.

Pepper: I need a favor.

40

PEPPER

Senior Picnic
June 1999

We pull into my driveway, and I give Scarlett a longing look, one I learned in drama class. She doesn't look at me as she puts the car in park. Frowning, I tug at the handle, and the car door creaks open when her fingers clutch around my forearm. She finally says something.

"I can't let this ruin my life." Tears track down her cheeks. "I want to go to college and meet the love of my life and get married and have kids and never have to think about this again." She wipes her nose on her bare forearm. "I'm normal. Boring. I'm not like you. I'm not going to New York to be an 'actress.'" She uses air quotes around my dreams like she's never heard of such a thing.

What's *normal* for me is taking Scarlett's devotion and twisting it in my favor. I lunge for her across the console and hug her so tightly she gasps, but I feel her chest pumping as she tries to fight the hysterical tears. So I do the same. Acting, and all. *Pepper, the director needs you to show just how sorry you are. Aaaaaand action!*

"You listen to me," I say as I take her face into both of my hands, "no one will ever know we were there. I promise. Have I ever let you down?" She shakes her head softly. "I have to get inside. I'll call you when I wake up tomorrow. Promise." It isn't the first nor last time I lie.

I jump out of the car and she speeds off, likely wanting to get as far away from me as possible, back to her little twin bed and her stuffed animals, unaware of what she really helped me cover up. I walk up my driveway and reach in my bag for my house keys.

Only, they aren't there. I feel around the fabric in the dark, and there are no sharp edges, no jangle. I dump my bag on the porch. Three lip glosses, my wallet, my phone, and my sunglasses. No house keys.

Holy shit. They must have fallen out during the crash. Which means they're still there. In Chloe's car. *No no no no no.* After berating Scarlett to make sure she had everything, leave it to me to fuck this all up. I have to get back there.

There's no time. And if I make Scarlett go back, she'll surely call the police.

Panicking, I flip my phone open and go all the way to the bottom of my contacts, where I see Vince's name. I know he'll still do anything I ask, so I connect the call. When he picks up after two rings, I hear people in the background.

"Hi, babe."

Of course he still calls me that. He sounds like he's underwater. "Are you drunk? You're slurring."

"I'm at Chris's party. Are you coming here? I miss you. I want to get back together. Please take me back. I love you, babe."

It's always the same thing, every time I see him, every time I call him, and it's doubly so when he's been drinking. I can use this. "I need a favor."

"What? What do you need?"

I start to cry. "I'm in trouble, Vince. Can you go somewhere private? This is important."

"Are you okay? What happened?" His voice is completely clear this time, like all it takes is saving me for him to sober up. "Hang on."

His phone must be in his pocket because the party sounds are muffled, though I do hear music, screeching girls, and chants that are probably happening by the keg. Then nothing.

"Vince? Are you still there?"

He doesn't answer for another minute. "I'm here, babe. I'm outside, a little down the block. What's wrong? Why are you crying?"

I really need Vince to help me. The director who lives in my head starts talking again. *This is the part where you use your manipulation!* "Something terrible happened. I need you to promise me you won't say a word about this. Promise."

"Babe, I swear on anything. I love you. Just tell me."

I take a deep breath. "Julian Ackers assaulted me. Tried to rape me."

He doesn't hesitate before he screams into the phone. "I will fucking kill that fucker!" My heart drops when the sound muffles again, but I hear "Chris! Chris, get the car!" He comes back on the line. "Where are you?"

"God damn it, Vince! I told you not to say anything. Shut the fuck up."

"I'm going to kill him. He dies tonight. Dead. A dead man. I'm going to kill him."

Vince continues rambling, but I need him to calm down. "Listen to me, Vince. He's already dead. I really need you to help me. To calm down, and to help me."

"What do you mean, he's already dead?"

Vince assures me that no one heard him scream for Chris, and that no one came outside that wasn't already there. I tell him about the accident, and about Chloe driving drunk and causing it. Because acting. He's devastated about that, for Chris, but he agrees to keep quiet and retrieve my keys at the site and meet me back at my house. He swears he can get to Rockland Park and to my house in twenty minutes, and tells me to stay put. Like, where am I going, anyway?

I sit on my ass in my driveway and rock into myself, reliving the night. I think about what an idiot I've been. How could I ever do what I did to Vince? Look at him—one mention of needing help, and he's going to a crime scene for me. I never deserved him. I know he'll take me back, but I've ruined everything.

Still, this baby is growing inside me—Julian's baby. I just got into a car wreck, where I had a hand in killing this baby's father. Could I be responsible for death again?

Maybe I can do this. Be a mom. Keep one part of Julian. Tonight, I had rage, but tomorrow, I'm sure I'll be filled with regret. Vince can never know the truth, about me, about the baby. I may have loved him for the last four years, but I don't want to burden him with *me* right now.

It's the least selfish thought I've ever had. And I know it's because I truly love him.

I have to leave for New York as soon as possible, and not let Vince know where I'll be. Get some distance. Figure my shit out. I'll be back at Christmas, after my first semester, when everything will be taken care of. We'll get back together. We'll get married.

But for now, I need a clean break. I'm just dying to see him first.

CONVERSATION BETWEEN PEPPER AND VINCE THE NIGHT OF THE SENIOR PICNIC

Pepper: What took you so long? It's been over an hour.

Vince: I was being extra cautious, that's all.

Pepper: Why aren't you wearing your jersey?

Vince: It snagged. I took it off hours ago.

Pepper: Thank you so much for doing this, Vince. For everything.

Vince: Anything for you, babe. Are you sure you're okay?

Pepper: Yes. Are you? After seeing them?

Vince: Felt half good, I won't lie.

Pepper: Vince, you have to swear to me, if you ever loved me—

Vince: I do love you. With everything I am.

Pepper: I'm just saying, if you really love me, you have to swear to take this to the grave. Everything that happened tonight. With Julian, with the accident, with me being in the car. Everything. You swear?

Vince: I promise, babe. How did you get home, anyway? You didn't walk here from the park, did you?

Pepper: Don't say anything about this either. Scarlett drove me home. She was in the back seat of Chloe's car.

Vince: Typical she just dumped you here. I don't know what you see in that girl.

Pepper: I don't want to talk about Scarlett. In fact, I don't want to talk at all. I just want you to hold me for a little while before you go back to Chris's.

Vince: I don't have to go back there. I'll stay with you. I love you.

Pepper: You have to go back. You can't let anyone know you left. For your own protection, as well as mine.

Vince: I'll do whatever you want, babe. Can I kiss you? I miss you so much it hurts.

Pepper: You can do more than that.

41

SCARLETT

I've been through some real shit in my life. Some things I caused myself, and some things I thought were punishment for the past. I harbored hot-blooded anger toward my parents when they weren't supportive of my pregnancy and quickie marriage. Then there was that time I was passed over for a promotion, for Davina of all people, who was probably screwing our boss, Frank, on the side. That made me angry. I remember constantly looking at the gymnasium doorway, waiting for Vince to bust in—already too late—to watch Luke win his swimming championship a decade ago, only to discover he wasn't coming at all because he was at the doctor with his miscarrying side piece.

All valid reasons for violent, shaking, stabbing rage.

Then there's this time, when a rumpled Vince walks into our home with a rumpled Pepper after Zoey called her.

I see it on his face, on both their faces. The infidelity. The guilt. The I-got-caught-in-the-cookie-jar. It's amazing that I spent seventeen years with this man compared to Pepper's four, and here we are. I look away with disgust because that's the only emotion I have left for either of them.

He excuses himself to the bar cabinet and pours something dark—probably whiskey or bourbon—and drinks it down in one gulp without ice before pouring another, this one twice as big. Then the asshole actually goes and stands next to her again. *Her.*

The realization hits me like I just ran into a brick wall. My devotion toward Pepper never went away when I was her young little sponge, soaking up all the attention she gave me, no matter how passive-aggressive it was. She was right; I was always second. One-one-one versus two-two-two—even our birthdays nailed the hierarchy of our lives. That was rammed into me every day all through middle school and high school, when most young girls are searching for their self-worth. My self-worth was wrapped around how Pepper saw me, and that was it. My time with Vince was me trying to *be* Pepper. To *be* number one.

His time with me was probably doing the same. Being *with* Pepper.

What is it about her? Now the woman is standing in front of me, too close to my husband. Her boyfriend. Ugh, I need massive therapy.

"You guys having fun?" I ask through gritted teeth.

"You really suck, Mom," Zoey says. "How could you?"

Zoey sees it too. Again, I realize I like her. A lot.

"You don't know what you're talking about," Pepper snaps.

Really? Why all the anger then? Well, she's here for one reason only. To tell us the truth. To tell *me* the truth. I look directly at her, like Vince isn't even standing next to her. To me, he's a ghost right now, and he can dis-a-fucking-ppear for all I care.

"Julian Ackers is Zoey's father? Is that right?" I ask. Wait. I decide to twist the knife, and I look at the man I married seventeen years ago. "She lied to us. She told us he assaulted her. She was in a relationship with him. Cheated on you with him."

"I know," he says quietly, then twirls the liquid around in his cup before taking another sip. "I just found out."

"Great, she told you. So, you guys were bonding. Wonderful," I say, my mouth spitting out the sarcasm. Back to the bitch. "You lied to me. I know what you did, causing that accident. And now I know why. Do you think I'm going to let you get away with it? You got Chloe killed for no reason."

Zoey swings her head back and forth between us, cautiously, like she expects a cage fight to break out. "You caused it. I knew it," she says.

Pepper's face pinches the way it did when she got caught without her homework, then it relaxes the way it did before she charmed the teacher with her excuse, which they always bought—hook, line, and sinker.

"It *was* an accident," Pepper says.

However, I'm not a teacher she can charm. "You liar."

"Hey, calm down," Vince says. To me. In the history of the world, a man saying those words has never made the situation better.

We all talk rapidly over each other. "You weren't there, Vince. I was. You don't know what really happened."

He finishes the drink, then slams the glass down, rattling the table. His hands go up, like he's a lawyer in a courtroom trying to drive his point home. "Chloe was drunk. Everyone knew that. We all saw her drinking. Even her blood test said she was hammered. It was an accident."

Zoey laughs loudly, and we all shut up and look at her. Now she looks at Vince like he's the stupidest person on the planet. "You'll really believe anything she tells you, huh? I knew there was more to this story. Did she tell you Julian dumped her that night? For that girl, Chloe? Something tells me dear old Mom was mad, and now Chloe and my father are both dead. Go ahead, Mom. Tell him."

Vince shifts away from her ever so slightly, and his face goes dark. "What?" He turns to Pepper. "Julian dumped you for Chloe? I knew you were in the car that night when she hit him, but . . ." His voice trails when he looks at me. "And I know you were too. What happened?"

Well, how the hell does he know that? Pepper. Fucking Pepper told him. But when? How long has he known my secrets? I know none of his. None.

Our Mexican standoff needs at least one gun, and if we had three, we'd all be pointing them at each other like the end of a Tarantino flick. The betrayals are all out in the open. Only, I'm not sure we all know what they are. We've all been lying, and we've all been lied to.

"Pepper?" Vince says, his voice cracking.

Zoey is smiling at the table, enjoying the moment. Understanding her victory, her vindication, knowing she was right all along. She's going to make a great reporter, though I think private detective for hire is a better fit. She uncovered all of this in two days. Things I didn't know for twenty-two years. She's got us all pointing fingers. Exposing each other.

Pepper, always the drama queen, puts her hands over her face and whimpers. Crocodile tears. Acting.

"Cut the shit," I say. God, she's so fake. All those years I wasted on this piece of plastic in front of me. She's not human. She's been playing a part her whole life. I look at Zoey again. "Yes, we were in the car that night too. She's the one who aimed the car at Julian. She killed your father *on purpose*. It was never an accident. She got me to lie about it because she told me earlier in the night that he assaulted her and that he deserved it. But now we know it's because he dumped her." I look at Vince. "She even told me that Chloe was sleeping with *you*. That she stole you. That's how she got me to go along with it. She wasn't used to being second. Chloe died for being chosen first."

Zoey's face registers complete and utter shock as her mouth hangs open and she looks at her mother, demanding her to contradict what I just said.

"Stop, Scarlett. That didn't happen."

The statement doesn't come from Pepper. It comes from Vince. Defending her right to the end.

"What's the matter, Vince? You don't want to believe your precious Pepper is a murderer? Hey, how do you think your best friend Chris would feel about that? That his girlfriend's death was because poor, dumped Pepper couldn't handle not being number one? She lied, Vince. To everyone. She did what she always did, what she's doing now. Lying and playing on our emotions to get what she wants."

Vince rubs his hands over the two days of stubble on his face, then he rubs the top of his head and down the back of his neck. He's uncomfortable. I've seen this before. Like when I told him I was pregnant.

"The whole thing was an accident!" Pepper shouts.

"Really?" I say. "If that's true, then why did we leave the scene? Why did you force me to leave? I wanted to call the cops, but you said it was hopeless because Julian was going to die anyway, and that Chloe was already dead."

I look at Vince. I don't know why I'm trying to convince him that she's evil. She can have him.

"She told me that to other people, it would look like we wanted revenge if we were there. For Chris. For you. And she said that

Julian was a rapist who deserved it. She manipulated me, and she manipulated you. She's still doing it, right now."

I look at her blank face. She's trying to figure out how to turn this on me. No way.

"Right, Pepper? Go ahead, tell us. If it was an accident, why didn't you let me call the cops? Why did we leave? I'll tell you why. Because you planned it. Julian dumped you for Chloe, and *you're* the one who wanted revenge."

Vince has now stepped a full foot away from her, and Zoey's eyes are filled with tears.

"You killed my father on purpose?" Zoey asks, still absorbing what she heard as we all bicker.

"No, I didn't," Pepper insists. She lies. Pepper *lies*. "Like, I mean, yes, we were in the car, but Chloe was driving drunk and the car swerved—and. Well. I—I was worried about the underage drinking. I didn't want to get caught. I didn't want to be delayed going to New York—to college. I—it was . . ." Her voice trails off as she attempts to gather more of her bullshit lies.

"You're lying. Why would you let Julian die if you loved him?" Zoey asks.

Pepper looks at Vince. "You believe me, right?" she asks as she reaches out to touch his forearm.

Vince's face hardens as he inches away from her outstretched hand. "I don't know, Pepper. You told me he assaulted you that night, and an hour ago, you told me you were in a relationship with him and that he's the one who knocked you up." Not *got you pregnant*. Knocked you up. A dirty little secret. Vince's house of Pepper cards is tumbling. "If what Scarlett is saying is true . . . I mean . . . you remember what happened that night. After."

After?

Apparently, there's more to that night that I don't know. We're all staring at Pepper, waiting for her to make up another story, but she stays quiet. Zoey is still crying. Her mother is a lying monster who killed her father. We're all partially guilty for his death by keeping quiet.

"After?" I ask.

"Yes. After." Vince looks at Pepper, his face reddened with rage. "I could kill you right now."

42

VINCE

Senior Picnic
June 1999

F ocus.

I swipe Chris's keys from the hook by the garage door and tear the fuck out of there. He'll never even know his car is missing. He's so fucking hammered, thinking Chloe cheated on him after all this time. He might be banging half the girls' soccer team at his house right now, but he's not going to take this well. Chloe being dead. Hand to God, that shit upsets me, but Pepper needs me. I'll be back to his house in under an hour. No one will even realize I'm not there with over a hundred people at the party.

Maybe after this, Pepper will see how much I love her, and I can get her back. That's all I want.

Lie. I *want* to see Julian dead. That'll be fun. That motherfucker.

Still, what good would it be if I died on the way. I'm fucking hammered too. I keep widening my eyes, trying to focus, then the streetlights hit, and I quickly shut them tightly, then remember I'm driving and open one eye. It keeps happening, over and over.

It doesn't help that I was half passed out in Chris's basement when Pepper's call came in.

Focus.

Where the hell am I? Oh, right, I took the road to go into the back end of the park. That's where the big parking lot is, next to the basketball court and that spray park for the kids. The park is closed, and no one will be there.

What time is it? I glance at the digital clock but the numbers all blend. Double. Triple, even. Damn it, those lights. I see a one. Could be ten-something, eleven-something, or one-something. I have no idea what time I even got back to Chris's house from the fair. I just know I've been driving for almost ten minutes. I've got to be close. I promised Pepper I'd be quick, but I'm going to need more time. Going in the back way means a trek through the woods to get to the boulder on the other entrance, where the accident happened. But I don't want anyone to see me driving into the main entrance.

Did I just miss the turn? No. I strain my open eye. I see that metal fence indicating the corner of the lot. Or is that the second corner? Where's the opening?

Focus.

Ah, there it is. I shut the lights off, turn the car into the lot, and park it as far as I can next to the woods. I pop the trunk and grab that mini flashlight Chris keeps there after the time we got a flat coming home from a party. Changing a tire in the dark—I don't recommend it. Especially after a twelve-pack.

The grass is taller than it should be and it tickles my ankles as I try to imagine my way to the other end of the park like my brain is a compass, which it's not. I know it should only be about a quarter to a half a mile, so I break into a swift jog, dodging branches that smack into my body all around me. There's no real trail. Just woods.

After five minutes, I see where the trees end and there's a clearing. I stop.

Focus.

I hear nothing. No birds, no bees, no joggers *shush-shushing*, no sirens approaching. Still, I stalk to the edge quietly. Once I'm in the open, I see the car to the right, about fifty feet away. It's pitch-black; the headlights are out. The moon has moved over to the other side of the trees, so I'm really on my own. Me and my trusty flashlight, which I've turned off because I'm not a fucking idiot and I know my ass can't get caught here. I approach slowly, half looking away. I don't want to see Chloe dead.

I want to see Julian dead.

First things first. I take the handle of the passenger side door under my jersey and wrangle it open. It's a little stuck and takes a few pulls, but eventually it opens. Opening my eyes wide, I try to zero in on where I should be looking.

Chloe's right arm is slumped onto the console. There's a spiderweb crack in the windshield.

Fuck.

Focus.

I reach my arm into the passenger side bucket and feel around until my fingers clutch Pepper's keys. Thank God. I jam them into my pocket and crouch down. I have to use my hip to jimmy the door shut from the bottom. It makes a loud cracking noise and I instinctively pause, hoping no one is within earshot to hear it. Or to see me here.

Now I stand. I want a good look at that motherfucker at the other end of the car.

I see nothing.

I widen my eyes again, but I see nothing.

Focus.

I turn on the flashlight and point it toward the front of the car, near the boulder. There's blood, but there's no Julian.

Fuck.

I see dots of blood to the left of the car. It's almost like a trail, which I follow, careful not to step on any of it. Ten yards away, I see his body near the trees.

Wait. Is he moving?

He's turned onto his right side, his right arm outstretched while he slowly pulls himself across the grass beyond the asphalt with his left hand, inch by inch like the fucking worm he is. Now his head is turned, facing the light source. It's in front of my face, in the dark, so he can't see me.

"Vince? Is that you? Help. Please help me."

I look down at my number-four jersey. Of course he knows it's me. I walk over. Slowly. He's clutching his abdomen. There's not a whole lot of blood. It seems to just be coming out of his head. And his mouth. He's probably got massive internal injuries. Good.

"Does it hurt, you piece of shit?" I say.

He coughs. "Vince, please. There was an accident." His voice is weak, staggering. "That's Chloe's car. Can you check on her? Call for help. My phone is crushed."

"Fuck you." This asshole thinks I'm going to help him? "I know what you did to Pepper tonight."

"Vince, I'm sorry for ever fucking with Pepper. Can we put that aside right now?" His voice shakes. Good. "Please, don't let me die. I need help."

Put that aside? This asshole thinks he can assault my girlfriend and I'm going to let him live? Yeah. That's not going to fucking happen. I shut the flashlight off and place it on the ground. His breathing is already anemic, just like the rest of him, so by the time I snap his nostrils closed with one hand and press my other hand over his mouth, he knows he won't get away with what he did to her. He doesn't have the strength to fight back. Good.

When he stops breathing, I drop his head. My hands have blood on them, literally and figuratively. Without thinking, I wipe them on my jersey.

Fuck! What do I do now?

Focus.

I pick this puny piece of shit up and bring him back to the car and wedge him in the spot he must've crawled out from. Startled at my own actions, I step back and gasp. I killed him. Fuck. I take off my jersey and wipe my hands down. I grab the flashlight and run into the woods, back where I started.

He would've died anyway. No one was there. It's not my fault. I put him out of his misery.

Focus.

Thank God for littering assholes because I find a plastic Publix grocery bag hanging on a branch. I finish wiping my hands and ball up my jersey. I put it in the bag and tie a tight knot across the top. Twice. I run more.

Focus.

I stop when I can almost see Chris's car. Then I dig. Like a fucking polar bear, I'm smashing the earth below me, and once I'm two feet in, like a dog hiding a bone, I drop the bag in the hole and cover it up. I spread some needles and branches over the fresh dirt.

Focus.

I go to the area by the spray park, where there's always a drip, and I spend as much time as I need scrubbing my hands. When I'm satisfied, I get in the car. On my way to Pepper.

I quickly realize that yes, I'll do anything for her.

Focus.

43

PEPPER

"Everyone just calm down," I say, especially to Vince.

He needs to keep his mouth shut. He can't tell Scarlett that he went back, that he saw them there, that he's always known we were there. I don't blame him for hating me right now, but it wasn't his fault, it was mine.

"What? What was after?" Scarlett asks him. "What else did she make you do?"

"I left my keys in Chloe's car," I say quickly, stopping Vince from talking. "Vince went back and got them for me."

Scarlett's head whips to Vince. "Are you fucking serious? You knew about this the whole time? That we were there? You saw them, dead, the same night?"

"Guys!" Zoey screams. "Can we get back to what actually happened to my father?" She's looking at me, but also flits her eyes to Vince and Scarlett. But then, back to me. "Mom, please. What really happened? Everyone is telling so many lies, I don't know what to believe."

She's crying. My daughter is crying. She's the one who went looking for the truth, and now she can't handle it. Scarlett's face is completely purple, Vince's face is nothing like it was a half hour ago, and me . . . well, I'm just fucking caught.

Come on, Pepper, tell the story with conviction! Believe it! Aaaaaaaand action!

"This is what happened, Zoey," I say, and take a deep breath. "I was cheating on Vince with Julian. I thought I loved him, and I thought he was coming to New York with me."

Vince makes a noise, and disgust is reflected all over his face.

"I was embarrassed when Julian dumped me, so yes, I made up a lie and said he tried to rape me to cover up why I was crying. To Scarlett, and later to Vince. It was just to save face, and I realize that makes me an asshole. Neither of them knew the truth until today. It's not their fault. But yes, Scarlett and I were in the car. Chloe was drunk and hit him." I have to keep that lie, not only for myself, but for Vince. I already feel him slipping, and I can't let him know what I did.

"That's a lie, Pepper. You're lying. You took the wheel. I remember it all," Scarlett says. "I'm going to the cops. I'm going to tell them what really happened. What you really did."

"Stop!" Now it's Vince. "Scarlett, come on. What's the purpose now?" He looks at Zoey, hands up defensively. "Look, I'm sorry for what happened to your father." He looks back at Scarlett. "Going to the cops helps no one. It just fucks up all our lives."

Scarlett isn't having it. "*Our* lives? To hell with that. I'm thinking about Luke, and no one else. That's what a real parent does— sacrifices for their child. Picture him in this situation. What if Luke was killed by a jealous ex, and Beth lied to all her friends, sullying his reputation, the way Pepper did with Julian? What happened that night is not okay, and Pepper, I'm sorry, but you need to pay for your part in this. Juliet needs to know. She needs to know Zoey is her niece, too." My heart literally jumps into my throat when Scarlett picks up the phone. "I'm calling the police."

"Stop!" Vince shouts again, and she looks at him but doesn't dial. He grunts and yells and doesn't make any sense as he refills his glass again. "Scarlett, wait. It's not Pepper's fault."

She rolls her eyes. "The hell it's not. No, nothing is ever Pepper's fault when it comes to you. I've figured that out. I don't care if I get in trouble too. Pepper needs to pay."

She's talking about me like I'm not here. I guess to her, I'm not.

"Scarlett." Vince's spoken word has enough emotion behind it that we all stop talking. "She didn't kill him. I did."

The whole room goes silent until Zoey speaks.

"What?" Zoey finally asks. "What are you talking about?"

"Vince, no," I say, my voice cracking. I can't let him lie for me.

He takes another huge gulp, finishing his drink, and faces me. Looking into my eyes, he takes both of my hands in his, then gently touches my face. He still wants to protect me.

"I don't believe this," Scarlett whispers, shaking her head.

He turns to face Scarlett, and she's not even crying. In fact, her expression is stoic, dismissive. It's acceptance. She knows he loves me, and she's not even upset. She's done with him; I can tell. I may not have seen her for over two decades, but I know this girl. This woman.

Vince sits down at the table and places his hands over his face, rubs the top of his head, then hides his face again. "Oh, Jesus." When he uncovers his eyes, tears roll down his cheeks. "I went to get Pepper's keys," he says. "Julian wasn't dead."

Yes, Julian was dead. I took the wheel and aimed at him. It was me. I killed him.

"Vince?" I say.

He looks at me and softly shakes his head. "It's okay, Pepper. It's the truth." This time, he looks at Zoey. Avoiding Scarlett. He's done with her too. "I'm sorry, Zoey. I didn't know anything about what really happened. When I went to get your mother's keys, Julian was still alive. Badly injured, but alive. Your mother didn't kill him; I did. I thought he tried to rape her, and I snapped, and I suffocated what was left of him. I put his body back from where he crawled out. And I swear, I didn't know Pepper was pregnant. I wouldn't have killed a father, I just thought . . . I thought Julian was getting what he deserved."

Zoey looks at me, and I've never seen so much hatred directed at me before. "My father could've lived? Vince could've helped him. But no, he's dead because of your lies. How could you live with yourself? How could you ever look me in the face and tell me you loved me? You're a fucking monster."

"No, don't do that," Vince says. "She didn't *make* me do anything. It was all me."

"She put him there!" Zoey points at me, then looks at Scarlett. "I believe you. Call the police."

Scarlett picks up the phone again, and I nearly shit myself. She's really going to turn all of us in.

"Wait, wait," Vince says. "Put the phone down, Scarlett. Before we all fly off the handle, we need to sleep on this. There's a lot at stake. For everyone."

Zoey's open mouth closes, and she looks down, right before she looks back up at me. "I hate you. Get out. I never want to see you again."

Look at her, trying to order me out of someone else's house. She has no authority here. Have we had mother/daughter trauma before? Sure. Who hasn't? She's never looked at me with such venom. I want to shrink, to fall into a crack in the floor and never come back.

But I can't; I have to stay, and we all need to figure out together what happens next. I reach for her, but she pulls away with disgust.

"I think we should all put our tempers aside," I say. "We need to be logical about what happens next. We're all adults. And Scarlett, if you're really thinking about your son, you don't want him to lose his father. Or his mother, for that matter. You don't know what the fallout will be for lying to the cops. This is a serious matter. We need to keep our emotions in check right now."

"It's obstruction of justice. I know that much from my criminal justice class," Zoey says, looking directly at me, the heat of her stare melting my face. "I'd have to check the laws specifically for Florida, but I really doubt there's a statute of limitations when murder is involved."

I look at Scarlett—she's really the one who's going to choose the outcome, because she has the least amount of blame. I hate to admit that she *is* telling the truth. Everything she did, I manipulated her into doing. She followed it because she was obsessed with me and afraid of me, and I did nothing but use her to get the adoration I so craved. But now, the lies are out and I've all but stolen her husband.

All bets are off. She has no reason to do as I say anymore.

And Vince—Vince killed someone. For me.

"Can we please all just sleep on this?" I suggest. "Digest what's happening? We can talk about it at lunch tomorrow. I just don't want anyone to do anything rash. Vince is right; there's a lot at stake here. Let's meet at your desk at noon tomorrow. We can all talk it out."

Just when I thought I'd never seen such a look of hatred from Zoey, Scarlett doubles it—if looks could kill, I'd be deader than Chloe and Julian.

"I wish I never met you," she spits. "I want you out of my house." Then she looks at Vince. "Both of you. You two deserve each other. I can see it all over both your faces, what happened between you at that hotel. I'm done."

Vince says nothing, just holds his head in his hands, listening to his life spiraling out of control. Does he want me? Sure, that much was evident an hour ago. But I'm afraid that right now he's weighing his mistakes—there's Zoey, Luke, this mess, Florida, New York, and Scarlett. Would he leave his son and come to New York? Doubtful. Would I move back here? Jesus, no way. And be in the middle of all this, forever? It's why I left.

"Did I stutter? Get the hell out of my house," Scarlett says.

My face is burning hot, and I'm not a hundred percent sure I can trust her not to call the cops after I leave. I look at Zoey. "Come on. Let's go. We all need a good night's sleep. We can all talk about this tomorrow at lunch."

Zoey skids back in her chair, not to stand but to get farther away from me. "Don't touch me. Get away from me."

"Zoey," I warn.

"What? Go, leave with him," she says in loathing, nodding in Vince's direction, then looks at my nemesis. "Can I stay here tonight? I promise I won't be a bother; the couch is fine. I just don't want—"

"Yes," Scarlett says immediately. "I'll make up the spare room. And the two of you can get the hell out."

"What about my son?" Vince says.

"You certainly didn't give a shit about him when you missed half his childhood having affairs and fathering other children. You didn't think about him an hour ago when you were fucking your ex-girlfriend. You've never thought about anyone but yourself, and you don't deserve him. You never deserved me. You two deserve each other. Now, like I said, both of you can get the hell out."

I panic when Zoey turns away from me. Won't look at me. Vince throws me his keys.

"You drive. I've had too much."

And he walks away from his family, for me, just like that.

44

ZOEY

When the door slams behind them, Scarlett is staring at the space that her husband occupied a minute ago. The big, empty space.

This is all my fault.

Although, to be honest, she's so much better off. I've obviously known my mother my whole life, and she's a narcissistic bitch who has zero regard for anything or anyone but herself. And Scarlett, well, I've known her for three days, and even I know she'll survive this and be better on the other side of it. I'm not sure what type of witness I'd make to the police, but I heard everything my mother and Vince said. I'll do anything I can to help Scarlett.

I head straight for the wine on the counter and pour a glass, then place it in front of Scarlett and sit next to her. "I'm sorry."

She takes the wine and gulps it down. "You didn't do anything."

"I'm the one who came here and started all this. If my mother would've just told me the truth, then—"

"Then what? Then I'd still be lying to myself about my marriage." She shakes her head. "He's not only an adulterer. He's a murderer. Jesus Christ."

Did I open this woman's eyes? Or am I convincing myself of that to make myself feel better? Am I just like my mother?

No, I'm not. I feel genuine remorse.

"What are you going to do?" I ask.

She runs her hand through her strawberry-blonde hair, pulling it over one shoulder, and shrugs. "They were right. I can't be emotional about this. I have to think of Luke. Shit. Luke."

"Where is he?"

"He said he had an upset stomach, but I think that was a ruse to try to get us to leave Chris's earlier. Hang on, let me check on him and make up the spare room for you. Give me a few minutes."

With that, Scarlett disappears down the hall and up the stairs. A door opens, then closes a few seconds later. Then another, and another. In less than five minutes, she's back downstairs at the table, in tan sweatpants that hang off her hips and a black hoodie with a decal for The Deck Bar and Grille in the middle.

"I just made up the spare room and put fresh towels on the bed," she says.

"Thanks. How's Luke?"

"He's sleeping. Thank God, he always sleeps with his headphones on, blaring something. I guess he wasn't faking being sick. We'll see once it's time to get up for school tomorrow." She looks at the refrigerator, then back at me. "Have you eaten? I'm starving."

I shake my head left to right, and she smiles at me, then opens the refrigerator door. "I have some chicken cutlets that I can bread and fry up, if you like that sort of thing. Or we can throw some burgers on the grill. If I can figure out how to turn it on." Then the door slams shut with a thud, and she leans her head on it and lets out a huge sob. "God, I can't even turn on the grill. And I'm going to be on my own at forty."

I stand and go to her, and when I turn her to face me, she cries into my shoulder. I let her.

This is all my fault, and I feel like the biggest asshole on the planet.

"God, what am I going to say to Luke tomorrow?"

Crap. "I'm not a parent, but after everything that happened the last few days, I'd just tell him the truth."

Right after I say it, my own truth hits me. I'm not a parent. Except that I am. I have a baby inside me. And like she's reading my mind, Scarlett inquires about my situation.

"What are you going to do when you get home? Does the father know?" She pulls the cutlets out of their package and grabs a bowl from the cupboard. "If I'm being too nosy, just tell me to shut up."

"No, it's okay."

The truth is, I haven't really talked to my mother about this at all. The only thing I've said to her is that I'm getting rid of it. But I found out a month and a half ago, and I haven't done it yet. I don't want to wait much longer.

"I wanted to find out about my own father first," I say. "That's why I've been all over this stuff since I got here. Now that I know . . . I think I'm going to tell the guy. I'm embarrassed to say it's the result of a Tinder hookup. You know what Tinder is, right?"

"Jesus, Zoey, I'm not that old."

I chuckle. "Well, I was going to just get rid of it, but so much has happened in the past few days. I feel like this guy has a right to know." I pause. "Joseph. His name was Joseph. He was nice enough, but it was what it was, and here we are. All I know is I don't want to end up like my mother. Young, pregnant, and alone."

Scarlett shrugs. "You could end up like me. Though I'm not sure that's much better. If this Joseph character wants to do the right thing and proposes, make sure he's not hung up on his ex from high school." She cracks an egg into one bowl, whisks it with more vigor than probably necessary, dunks the cutlets, then dips them into a bowl of breadcrumbs. "To be honest, I think you're going to make a great reporter. You got to the bottom of the story better and faster than anyone else."

I hold back the tears. "Thank you. My own mother has never said as much. I think she just wants me to do anything that means I could get a real job and move out so she could have her own party." I want to make Scarlett feel better about being on her own. "You're still young. Forty isn't what it used to be. Forty is the new thirty, as they say."

She pours oil into a pan and begins frying. The smell of the hot oil and the chicken first makes me nauseated, then my mouth waters. "Well, she probably didn't want you to investigate, at least on this story." She's quiet for two minutes. She's at the pan, flipping the cutlets, and then she looks at me. "I'm sorry. I'm really going to try not to speak ill of your mother to you. It's not fair. We always had a complicated relationship, but this—tonight—Vince, everything else, I just . . ."

"I get it. Don't worry about it. You're not going to say anything I don't feel already right now."

She throws together a quick salad too—nothing fancy, just lettuce, baby tomatoes, and cucumbers with olive oil and balsamic vinegar on the side. As we eat, I tell Scarlett a lot about myself, growing up in Brooklyn. I tell her about my best friend, Anna, and about my breakup with Tristan because I caught him kissing someone else. Talking about it—with her—makes me realize how trivial it all is. Here she is, her marriage ending because of my mother, and I was crying about some loser I dated for a year kissing some skank at a block party. I really need to put things in perspective—it was no reason to go on a rampage and sleep with every stranger I came across.

Scarlett also tells me a lot about Luke, and how he was growing up. About her marriage, and the Vince who never grew up, still going to bars with his friends until the middle of the night, while she took care of the baby and most of the responsibilities. She dips into Vince's other affair, the one she knew about with someone named Lila. He knocked her up too, but the woman miscarried. I think the only reason Scarlett cries when she talks is because of how much she had to lie to Luke when his father didn't show up to his championship swim meet, and how she's had to lie to him all the time after that, telling him that Vince was an upstanding man so their son wouldn't hate him.

I don't tell her that Luke doesn't think much of him anyway. She'll probably find that out soon enough.

She clears the plates and insists that I stay seated, and I see the mother I never had as she stacks the dishwasher and puts every-thing away. My grandparents did most of the cooking and cleaning and, well, *raising*, because Mom was acting or partying.

My mother and Vince are going to make a great couple when all is said and done. Selfish is as selfish does.

45

SCARLETT

I feel like I've told Zoey too much, but at least she gets it. She understands what I'm going through, because while I was married to Vince, she was raised by his counterpart. And she saw the whole thing come undone in real time, like I did. I don't have the courage to tell my friends or family what's happening to my marriage right now, so she's a great option.

I show her upstairs to the spare room. It's not much—a full-size bed, a small desk, and a chest of six drawers. It's a place for Luke's friends to crash, or for the rare occasion when my sister Crystal blows through for a day from Paris. We let Luke have a hand in the decoration when he was younger, and mostly it's his old toy graveyard. The dresser is piled with his Legos and his Thomas the Tank Engine, and all the crafts he used to make from clay and Play-Doh when he was a kid. Predominantly dinosaurs. The bedspread is navy blue to match the curtains, and there's a circular throw rug under the foot of the bed over the hardwood floors to hide the scratches. We really need to have them sanded.

We, we, we. We'll never be a "we" again, except when "we" talk to our divorce lawyers, and possibly our criminal defense lawyers.

I need to pound this into my brain. I'm on my own. I'm single. I'm starting over.

I move the towels from the top of the bed and place them on the desk. "The bathroom is right across the hall. We keep spare toothbrushes in the middle drawer. Help yourself."

"Thank you," Zoey says.

"Do you need to use any of my stuff? That bathroom is a teenage boy bathroom. He doesn't exactly have eye makeup remover and moisturizers at the ready."

She smiles and nods, so I go into my bathroom and grab a small trial size of a cleanser and a moisturizer, and also a shampoo, conditioner, and body wash for the next morning. I have dozens of them from the hotel—it's the same line we use in the spa, so it's good stuff. I place all of them in one of the little white mesh sachets with the seafoam-green drawstring from the hotel. I also pack in some cotton pads and Q-tips and a nail file, also things the rooms at the hotel are stocked with. I put in everything short of the mini sewing kit. Then I find a clean pair of loose comfy pants, black ones with a white strip down the sides of the legs, and a black V-neck T-shirt for her to sleep in. I place the sachet on top of the clothes and hand them to her when I walk in.

"Courtesy of the Gulf Sands and Suites," I say. "You can keep all the products."

"Thank you. This is great." She takes everything from me and presses her lips together. "I'm really sorry again. Three days ago, I never would've seen this coming. Me finishing my last night here, while my mother . . ."

"I know. Me too. Then again, I thought she was dead," I say with a chuckle. "Get some rest. One of us should. I'm sure I'll be up all night, thinking about it."

"About them? Together?"

No, not until she just said it. Ugh. "About how we're going to get justice for Chloe and Julian."

She nods. "I'm sure you'll think of something. Good night, Scarlett. And thanks again."

I return to my room and close the door. Stutter-stopping when I see the bed, I go around to the left, crawl into my side, and lift the covers up to my chin. Then I kick the sheets around, my legs working double-time like I'm riding a bicycle, and I roll to the middle of the bed.

The whole thing is my side, from now on. Vince doesn't have a side of the bed anymore. Not in this bed. In Pepper's, sure. Not here.

I place my hands behind my head and stare up at the ceiling, at the ice-blue shadow lines the moon makes when it cuts into the blinds on the window. Am I going to have to move? Is Vince still going to pay for Luke's college? Hard to do that from prison. I do okay as the concierge manager, but Vince, for all his faults, has been a great provider. When I think of something good about him, I make my mind immediately replace it with the knowledge that he's probably fucking Pepper, right now. Maybe for the second time. The third. And I picture her smug face, winning over me. Again.

I swore I wouldn't call the cops until we all had a rational, nonemotional discussion, but it's getting harder to resist. I knew it would; it's why I left my phone downstairs. Instead, I toss and turn, and throw Vince's pillow to the floor. It smells like him, and I'm sad and angry all at once again.

The alarm goes off, waking me, so I must've slept some, even though my head feels like it weighs twenty pounds and my eyelids thirty. The last thing I want is to go to work, but that's where we're all meeting for lunch. I can't call out. Plus, things need to be normal for Luke.

He's already in the shower, earlier than normal, so I propel myself out of bed, throw on a robe, and head downstairs. Most times, Luke is frenzied in the morning, but he probably slept a full twelve hours. I decide to reward him with a big plate of scrambled eggs and bacon.

By the time he rumbles down the steps, I'm spooning everything onto his plate.

"Morning," I say. Forced smile. Don't let him see. "Feeling any better?"

"Much," he says. He kisses me on the head, opens the fridge, and then asks, "Where's Dad?"

I can't lie one hundred percent; the kid isn't a fool. "We had a fight. He went back to Uncle Chris's. Probably sacked out on his couch again."

He takes out the orange juice and pours a glass. "Well, who's here? The spare room door is closed, and there's a toothbrush and some of your minis in my bathroom."

I take a deep breath. "Zoey's here. She also had a fight with her mother, so I told her she could stay."

Luke narrows his eyes. He's figuring it out. Shit.

I shove his plate on the table. "Eat." Cheery smile. Nothing to see here.

I try to make small talk with Luke as I nibble at my plate. I have zero appetite, and now he's in one of his one-word answer moods. If Vince fucks up my son because of his Pepper/murder bullshit, I'll never forgive myself. I should've left a decade ago. Then I'd never know what I know now, and ignorance really is bliss.

When he's finished eating, he grabs his knapsack and heads for the door. Then he stops and turns around. "Love you, Mom."

He rarely says that before school. He knows I need it. "Love you too."

My boy.

46

VINCE

'm walking on the bay, holding her hand, but something is wrong. My whole body feels like it's filled with lead, my movements sludging along. The sky is black, ominous, with red stars above me, red as blood. They stare as they snarl, showing fangs. What the? Something isn't right. I physically can't turn my head to face her, like my conscience won't let me see what I've done.

"Why, Vince?" she says.

I'm filled with dread, and I break the force keeping me from facing her.

It's Scarlett.

I wake up, drenched, naked, in an unfamiliar spot. In bed next to me is a naked woman with dark hair. Where the hell am I?

Wait. Wait. That's Pepper. I whip my head around, taking in the area around me. Now I remember. We're in Zoey's hotel room. The Gulf Sands and Suites, where Scarlett works. The clock reads ten-thirty. Shit. I plop my head back down on the pillow, rub my forehead, and last night comes back to me in bits and pieces. Too much alcohol. Being here, with Pepper, polishing off half the minibar. Being at my house, with Scarlett, polishing off half the bottle of bourbon. Fuck, I told them I killed Julian, because Scarlett wanted to turn Pepper in. I've totally screwed myself. Then . . . then Pepper and I came back here. Finished the minibar. Fucked all night. Best feeling I've ever had.

Which I needed, because the worst feeling I ever had was right before that. I walked away from my wife and my son. Holy shit, what's wrong with me?

These feelings I've harbored for Pepper are valid; I know that. But all that alcohol clouded my judgment. What I did for her back then was out of love, but she lied. Not only that, but she also cheated on me, got herself pregnant by someone else, lied about it to get my attention, and drove me so fucking crazy that I killed the poor kid. Then, she disappeared on me like I meant nothing.

All I've thought about since she "came back to life" was how much I always loved her and missed her. It took over—I've been a zombie, bitten by Pepper. My Pepper, who has been on a pedestal for almost three-quarters of my life. I haven't processed the lies and the terrible things she's done. It's hitting me now. What she did. And Jesus, last night I told my wife about what I did for Pepper.

Murder. Fucking *murder*.

All it took was one weekend to ruin my life. Scarlett's going to divorce me; that I know for sure. She might've forgiven me for Lila because, as bad as that situation was, I didn't rub her face in it. Last night, to her face, I chose Pepper and walked out with her. Scarlett's finished with me, and who the hell can blame her?

Regret consumes me, so much so that when I look to my right again and see Pepper, angelic, sleeping, absolute perfection—it makes me sick. That lying, cheating bitch manipulated me to the point of murder. My head is clear in an instant, and I know what Scarlett said is true. Pepper manipulated her too. And how did I handle it? By sleeping with the enemy.

I jump out of bed and search for water, but there's nothing but empty plastic bottles littering the floor. We certainly worked up a sweat last night. I head to the bathroom and drink from my cupped hand straight from the faucet. Then I stare at my stupid face in the mirror. The wetness fills the dry cracks on my tongue and throat, but it does nothing for the headache. Scarlett always has cucumbers in the fridge, says that works better than aspirin for a hangover because of electrolytes or some shit, and she's right.

Scarlett.

She's always taken care of me, and our son. Gave up her dream of being a wedding planner so she could raise Luke, and now she books Midwesterners on windsurfing trips. She makes restaurant reservations. She places orders on Ticketmaster. Why?

Because of me.

She should've left me ten years ago, but she didn't, because Luke came first. She's probably lived in complete misery for a decade because she loves that boy so much, and what have I done? I cast her aside, for Pepper.

For one night with Pepper.

I can't be with her. She's a liar.

In the mirror, I see her turn over in the bed and sit up. She runs her hand through her hair, rubs her eyes, and stretches her arms over her head with a long yawn. Pepper still has perfect tits. She gets up, stark naked, and I don't even get a hard-on as she gets closer and wraps her arms around me from behind.

"Hey, sleepyhead," she says.

Ashamed of my own nakedness, I grab a towel and wrap it around my lower half as I gently push her away, off me. "Not now."

She frowns. Sticks out her bottom lip. Things that mesmerized me in high school and yesterday turn her into a Medusa right now, and I refuse to look for fear of turning to stone.

"What's wrong?" she asks.

I push past her and go back into the room. I find my boxers, my jeans, my sweatshirt, all scattered in different places. I dress quickly and silently as she stares, the stare that used to turn me to mush and stop me dead in my tracks. I grab one sneaker and put it on, and I'm literally hopping toward the door on one foot trying to balance myself as I shove the other one on.

"I have to go."

"Where are you going?" Her eyes flare, her jaw clenches.

That's a goddamn good question. I'm not welcome at my own home.

"I'll meet you downstairs at Scarlett's desk at noon. She and Zoey will be there. We still have to take care of everything from last night. I have to see what I can do about saving our freedom right now," I lie.

I don't wait for an answer. I exit the room, fly down the stairs, and bolt out the side door before Scarlett, or any of her coworkers, can see me in the lobby. Once I get to my car, I find my phone in the console and it's out of juice. I start the engine, plug it into my charger, and wait a couple minutes for it to power up.

Scarlett never called. She never texted.

Chris did, though. Many, many times. I log into our system from our custom app and track him. He's at someone's house in town, likely on a service call, doing the work I was supposed to do. I call him.

"Well, well, well, where the hell are you?" he answers.

"Are you almost done? Can you get back to the office or your house? I'm in trouble, man."

"Yeah. I can be home in a half hour. Everything go okay after you guys left last night? I can't believe Pepper is alive."

"No, man. Everything is fucked. I'll bring the coffee and bagels. I'll tell you the whole story when I see you."

And I do.

We sit at his kitchen table, and he asks me to recount all of it. I tell him everything. From the senior picnic, right to picking up the bagels in the friggen coffee shop fifteen minutes ago. When I say I tell him everything, I mean it—including what I did to Julian.

"Jesus Christ, Vince. What the hell are you going to do?" Chris asks, concerned.

He knows his best friend is a murderer. But he's such a good friend to me that he's more concerned with my future than what happened to Chloe. It was a long time ago. She's the past; he knows that.

"Scarlett is going to leave me. Luke is going to hate me." He raises his eyebrows in a *Well, do you blame them* move. He's turned on me too. Good. "I don't know what I'm going to do, man. What's going to happen with all this."

"Fuck, Vince. Scarlett was the best wife you could've asked for. You got lucky with her. If I wasn't already engaged to Jennifer when we all reconnected, I may have ended up with her." Salt in the wound. Was my best friend pining for my wife for seventeen years? "Was Pepper really worth it?"

Back then, yes, I would do it again in a heartbeat. Because I was a stupid, hormonal teenager in love.

"She's not worth losing my family." Too little, too late; I know this.

"Scarlett's got a will of steel for staying with you after Lila. Not for nothing, but I agree with you. I think she's outta there," Chris says.

My elbows are on my knees, my hands forming a tepee over my mouth as I shake front to back in the chair. "It's a tough ask, but can I crash here for a few days until I figure out what's going to happen? Scarlett will slam the door in my face if I go there. I don't belong in that house."

He nods. "Yeah, you know you're always welcome here." He says it because he's been my best friend for thirty years and it would be shitty to abandon me now. Or, maybe, everyone I know is a better person than I am. I totally suck. "What about Pepper?" he adds.

Fuck Pepper. She deserves to go down for this as much as I do. I shrug. "I guess I'm about to find out."

47

SCARLETT

My leg has been shaking under my desk since I sat down this morning. I know he's up there, *they're* up there, legs twisted together in a knot, naked, spooning, exchanging *I love you*s. How could my life have gone up in smoke like this?

I should've called the cops yesterday. I should've called this morning. I can't let them, together, as a couple, steamroll me into lying down and taking it. Again.

Married to a murderer. All this time.

Unable to avoid the shitstorm I know is coming, I Google local divorce lawyers in between servicing customers. Of course, it's Monday, and people who just got in for the week want to know everything about everywhere. I'm explaining the new sights on the Pier and the free tram car to someone when I catch sight of Zoey walking in. I debated waking her up when I had to leave for work, but instead I let her sleep. Left a note in the bathroom to meet here at my desk at noon, and a quick glance at the clock reads eleven-forty. That was the plan yesterday, and as much as I don't want to see either Vince or Pepper, a decision will be made today. Before that bitch gets on a plane and walks away from it all for a second time.

Zoey catches my eyes and nods, pointing to a chair in the lobby. She'll wait until I'm finished with the customer before coming over.

Ten minutes later, brochures for John's Pass and the Pier in hand, Mr. and Mrs. Socks-and-Sandals leave, and Zoey comes over and sits in the chair in front of my desk. Her eyes are red, sagging, indicating a lack of sleep.

And I'm glad to see her. I circle back to last Thursday when she came in, smug, a stranger, upending my life. How I hated her. And now—now I feel like she's my friend.

"Hey," she says. "Thanks again for everything last night."

I nod. "You're welcome. How did you sleep?"

"About as good as I expected to. What a mess."

"I know. Have you thought about what you want to do about this?"

She straightens up in the chair, more assertive. "Have you? I mean, my God, Vince left with her and didn't even come home, did he? I hope you divorce him."

I chuckle, out of sheer nervousness. "I wrote down a couple of names this morning. Divorce lawyers. Something I should've done long before this." My eyes glass over when I say, "Poor Luke. The poor kid is going to be blindsided. He worships his father."

She opens her mouth, as if to say something, then closes it and presses her lips together. "He'll be fine. He's a good kid."

I feel like she wants to say more, but I don't ask because Pepper emerges from the elevator bank. Her hair is in a high bun, and she's wearing jeans and a black ribbed tank top. Basically, it's what I'd wear to run errands, but for some reason everything on her turns to glamour. My stomach lurches at the thought of Vince with her, but she's alone. And, in her usual confident stride, without a care in the world, she saunters over to my desk and plops herself in the seat next to Zoey. Zoey shifts her chair away and refuses to look at her mother.

"Sleep well?" I ask Pepper.

She shrugs. "I'm tired, to be honest."

"I bet." I don't hide the disdain in my voice. "Where's Vince?"

"How should I know?" Now she won't meet my eyes. Instead, she turns her gaze toward Zoey. "Are you okay, peanut?"

"Oh, Jesus," Zoey says sarcastically. "Now I'm 'peanut.' You haven't called me that in ten years. Stop sucking up. I'm not speaking to you."

Pepper's eyes widen and then roll, like what Zoey is saying is the most ridiculous thing she's ever heard. We sit in awkward silence for two minutes until Vince walks into the lobby from outside. He's in yesterday's clothes with bags under his eyes, but his hair looks wet and combed back. He slowly walks over to my desk, eyes all of us, and stops on me.

"Hi, Scarlett."

One look at that bastard puts me in tears, in front of him, Zoey, and *her*. This is the last thing I want to do. I thought I shed my last tear over Vince. He doesn't deserve my time. But the tears are sorrow, because Luke looks so much like him, a real mini me, and I have second thoughts about turning him in. For my boy, and him only.

I grab a tissue and blot my eyes. "We should go to the café. Let's not do this here."

I stand and turn toward the small, casual grab-and-go restaurant on the other side of the lobby and stop to fill a coffee cup. Zoey leads Vince and Pepper to the back table in the corner, farthest away from the door, where we can have privacy. After I pay with a swipe of my employee card, I join them. I face the entry, my chair not pulled in all the way to provide distance.

"Who's going to start?" I ask.

Vince lightly raises a hand. "Me. Thank you for not calling the cops yesterday," he says. "We need to be rational. We have to think about Luke."

"People need to know what she did," Zoey says.

"I didn't do anything! It was an accident," Pepper says, less confident than yesterday.

The bickering and squabbling continue. This is never going to be finished. No one is ever going to agree on what to do.

Turns out, we don't have to.

Three men walk toward us. Well, one tall Black man, who I recognize from Saturday morning as Detective Watson, and with him are two cops in blue. He's heading in our direction. When he nears our table, Vince and Pepper try to shush us, and it's dead silent when the detective reaches us.

"Vincent Russo?" he says as he looks at Vince.

"Yes?" Vince's eyes are completely panicked.

"I need you to come with me. You're under arrest for the murder of Julian Ackers."

"What?" He looks at me. "You turned me in?"

I'm floored. As much as I wanted to, I didn't call the cops. "I didn't. I swear. I—"

Zoey. Zoey did it. Vince killed her father. She got the story. She's getting justice. Saving the day.

"Mr. Russo, will you stand up please so I can read you your rights?" Watson says.

Vince is white as a ghost as he pushes back his chair. The whole time, he's looking at Pepper. He's probably waiting for her to stand up and defend him, which she doesn't do. She doesn't even look at him.

Did Pepper call the police to protect her own ass?

I get my answer when Watson looks at her. "Pepper Wilson? You're under arrest—"

"It's Zarra. Pepper Zarra. I'm an actress. Don't you know who I am?"

She's panicked, and she's finished. She can't get out of this.

Watson continues. "You're under arrest for leaving the scene of an accident that resulted in death. It's a first-degree felony. We're also hitting you with obstruction charges for lying to the cops. Will you stand and place your hands behind your back, please?"

Pepper turns toward me, her eyes burning a hole through me. "You're next."

I am. I'm next. Now I know Zoey called the cops, and I deserve what's coming.

The men in blue Mirandize and cuff Vince and Pepper and guide them out. Detective Watson looks at me and throws his card on the table. "Give us some time to process them. You can call me later regarding the details."

"Wait!" I say when he turns around to leave. I won't be Pepper and manipulate him like she did to me. I will accept my fate. "You didn't get the whole story. I'm involved."

"We did, Mrs. Russo. We have a recording, and to have complete access to it, we already cut a deal to keep you out of this. We'll talk about it later." He knocks twice on the table. "Call me."

He follows the cops out.

I'm in awe that Zoey not only recorded them, but turned them in. Her own mother.

"That was great acting," she says to me. "You should've been the actress, not my mother."

I knot my eyebrows together. "What are you talking about?"

"*You didn't get the whole story. I'm involved,*" she mimics. "Wow. Cutthroat. You turned in your own husband."

I shake my head. "No, Zoey. I didn't. I swear. I thought you did it."

"Me? I didn't know what the hell was going on last night. How could I have recorded it?"

We stare at each other in a game of chicken, both waiting for the other to admit it. We were the only ones there. It had to be her.

Until a thought passes in my head.

My boy.

Luke did it, for me. That's why I got the unprompted *I love you* before school this morning. But how did an underage boy convince the police to cut a deal for his mother?

My phone rings. It's Chris. When I answer, all he says is "We need to talk."

48

CHRIS

M y phone rings. It's just after six a.m., so I know whoever it is, it's an emergency. No one ever calls me this early. I look at the screen, and it's Luke. Oh shit, something is really wrong. I kind of expected it after that shit show last night, though.

"Hey, buddy. Everything okay?" I answer.

"No, Uncle Chris, things are fucking far from okay. I need you to listen to something."

I get out of bed, where Kelly is sleeping next to me, and go into the bathroom and shut the door. "What's up?"

"Everyone was here fighting last night, and they all said some really messed-up things. About Zoey's mom's other boyfriend or something. And your girlfriend. The one who died."

I hold my breath. That whole night was so messed up, and I never processed it. I know she was "just a high school girlfriend," but the fact that she cheated on me with Julian, and then they both died in that accident—it was a weird time in my life. Zoey appearing, and then me and Vince subsequently talking about it the other night, was strange. Pepper reappearing yesterday was worse.

"What did they say?" I ask.

"Someone named Julian is Zoey's father. Pepper caused the accident, and my father killed Julian."

Nothing he says makes sense. Nothing. Chloe drove drunk and hit Julian in the park. It was an accident. "What are you talking about? That's impossible."

"I hate him, Uncle Chris. He left with Pepper, and I'm sure he spent the night with her. Mom threw him out. He's always been terrible to Mom, but this is enough. I want him gone. I recorded the whole thing. Can I send it to you?"

"Yes. Send it now."

∞

I listened to the recording five times. Five. The first time, it was because my ears deceived me. There was no way that the whole night went down like that. But there it was, all of them admitting it. Julian dumping Pepper for Chloe—that hurt. Pepper running the car into Julian, killing Chloe. That hurt more. Vince committing murder for that lying bitch. Poor Scarlett being manipulated into everything. The whole thing was a cover-up from beginning to end.

How did no one ever figure this out?

Now, rage consumes me. I've bro'd before ho'd my entire life for Vince, but not this time. He's going down, and so is Pepper. She got my girlfriend killed. Vince is a murderer. Scarlett and Luke don't need this.

I shoot Luke a text.

> **Me:** *Hey. I'll take care of this. Act normal today.*
> **Luke:** *What are you going to do?*

What am I going to do? Seek my own justice for my dead girl-friend. No one will take a kid seriously.

> **Me:** *I'll figure it out. Then I'm going to the police.*
> **Luke:** *What about Mom?*
> **Me:** *Your mother was manipulated. I'll take care of it. I promise, Luke, you know I wouldn't let anything happen to you or your mother.*

It's the truth. I'm going to protect Scarlett with everything I have. I should've told her when Vince started the affair with Lila. Of course I knew, but bros before hos. However, this changes everything. I won't let Vince hurt her anymore. He's made his choice—that lying skank over his wife and kid. Chloe died because of her.

Now he'll face the consequences.

ZOEY

M y mother didn't do any time—she had a good lawyer who pled her down to a third degree, since my mother still insisted that it was an accident. Scarlett was a credible witness at the trial, but her being drunk at the time of the accident left her testimony up in the air. And since Vince was charged with the murder, the jury took pity on my mother. After all, she *was* pregnant with Julian's kid. Me. The whole thing was painted as Vince being a jealous boy-friend, with dear old Mom proclaiming her innocence. In Florida, they couldn't take Luke's secret recording as evidence, but Chris testified. So did Luke, against his own father.

There is a new baby in our lives. A girl, named Faith. I tried not to laugh at the sarcasm that my mother actually named her second kid *Faith*. To pay homage for her mistakes, she said. Faith was born while her father was serving time in prison. Vince pled guilty and cut a deal for less time. I helped my mother in the beginning, only out of obligation to my half sister.

Vince has seven more years, but he'll probably be out in less than five—I did my research about good behavior and overcrowded prisons, and they'll always let the white guy out first. Then my mother, Vince, and Faith can be a happy family, the way she likely intended when she got herself knocked up in Florida.

If Vince ever had thoughts about leaving her, well, she made sure that wouldn't happen. We all know what happened to the last man who rejected my pregnant mother.

I moved out a year ago, and I've only seen her twice since then. The first time was a week after I left, to grab the last of my things when she wasn't supposed to be home. I've moved to a basement apartment in Alphabet City, paying through the nose but doing it on my own. Another time, I ran into her at Trader Joe's, about two months ago. I was picking up some organic wine to bring to Anna's house. My mother's hair was shorter, and Faith was walking. She looks more like Vince than like me.

I miscarried as soon as I got home from Florida. The stress of that whole situation probably did my pregnancy in, keeping me from having to make the decision. I ended up getting a great job after I graduated, and that's what I want to concentrate on—being an investigative reporter. Detective Watson wrote a great letter of recommendation for me, praising my skills. I'm still earning my way up at a New York City newspaper, but I'll get there. I'm young. I have my whole life ahead of me.

I'm glad Scarlett found happiness again, I think as I descend the escalator at the airport. I'll be staying with Aunt Juliet in Florida for the weekend. As I hoped, she was thrilled about me being her twin's daughter, and I've gotten to know what side of my family pretty well in the last couple of years. I'm lucky.

Luke is holding a sign that says *Wilson* by the baggage claim, and I laugh when I see him.

"Dork," I say.

He hugs me. He's happy about the upcoming festivities. "What's up, sis?"

I call him bro, and he calls me sis. For the time we almost were. We talk, email, and text all the time. An unlikely friendship. Our common sister, whom Luke refuses to meet for now, keeps us tied together as family.

"Are you excited for tomorrow?" I ask.

"Yeah. I'm glad you made it, too."

"Wouldn't miss it," I say, and mean it.

"Well, let's get your bag and get you to your aunt's house," Luke says.

On the way, he tells me about college. He's still with Beth. He got off the waitlist and into UF and stopped rebelling and selling drugs, because he needed to be there for his mother as all of this was going down. Although Scarlett ended up with her own support system, one that was in place long before Vince.

When we get to Aunt Juliet's, I get out and grab my bag, run around to the driver's side, and kiss Luke on the cheek. "See you tomorrow, bro."

"Wait. Don't forget this," he says, and hands me the envelope that fell out of my purse.

The invitation for the wedding of Scarlett Russo to Christopher Parker.

ACKNOWLEDGEMENTS

As always, the first will always be a million thanks to agent extraordinaire, Anne Tibbets. Thank you for always trusting my writing and having my back.

To my team at Scarlet: These books would never be complete without the brilliance of my editor, Luisa Smith. Four books! Look at us go! I have a ball working with you every time. I love how you always push me to make everything better, and how you're always right! Thanks to my publishers, Charles Perry and Otto Penzler, my rockstar publicist Julia O'Connell, and my copy editors and proofreaders (So! Many! Commas! Haha) Nadara Merrill, Amy Medeiros, and Will Luckman. And this fire cover from Charles Brock!

As authors, we're all a sum of our parts, and our parts aren't complete without each other. I always say in interviews how lucky I am to be in the best profession, where all anyone does is lift each other up. Some of the best in the business are Vanessa Lillie, Danielle Girard, Jennifer Pashley, Mandy McHugh, Jessica Payne, and Mary Keliikoa, who always do everything to calm my anxiety and critique my work. I've met so many special and talented authors along the way: Samantha M. Bailey, Damyanti Biswas, Michele Campbell, Megan Collins (especially for helping me through my puppy trauma), Heather Chavez, Alex Finlay, Robyn

Harding, Jennifer Hillier, Bonnie Kistler, Nicole Mabry, Christina McDonald, Steph Mullin, Jeneva Rose, and Wendy Walker. I'm honored you read my work before anyone else, and I revel in your talent. You all make me strive to do better.

I moved to Florida permanently a little over a year ago, and I joined an amazing group, the St. Pete Girl Bosses, started by the incredible Sandy Bean. I've never seen so many women so apt to build each other up. When I needed support, it took one post for these amazing strangers to turn into lifelong friends. You are all amazing women who are going to change the world. Thank you for being a part of my life. Let's get that writing group going!

Where am I, or any author, without the literary support of so many trades and readers. Thank you to *Kirkus*, *The New York Times*, and *People* magazine for supporting my last book, *I Didn't Do It*. To all the librarians (Kelley Clemente I'm talking to you!) who take the time to set up book clubs and talks with authors—we appreciate you all! To the Bookstagrammers—you are your own planet and I want to live there. Too many to name personally, so I'm sorry if I forgot to mention you here, but a billion thanks for the constant support of Gare Billings, Stephanie Bolen, Tonya Cornish, Krista Crone, Katie Fulton, Briana Leigh, Dennis Michel, Kori Pontenzone, Alicia Rideout, Carrie Shields, and Nancy Wren. I know there are so many more—hundreds—that I'm lucky enough to interact with daily. I thank you and worship you!

To my readers: I don't know what to say besides thank you for investing time in my murder books :)

I will forever thank my sweet baby puppy Cosmo, who has been on my ankles every manuscript I've ever written, even the bad ones that will never see the light of day. We lost my sweet girl this year, 10/7/23. Mommy loves you, wherever you are. Play in that rainbow.

To John, just . . .thank you, my heart.